THE SIEGE

JOHN SUTHERLAND

ORION

First published in Great Britain in 2022 by Orion Fiction
an imprint of The Orion Publishing Group Ltd
Carmelite House, 50 Victoria Embankment
London EC4Y 0DZ

An Hachette UK Company

1 3 5 7 9 10 8 6 4 2

A CIP catalogue record for this book is
available from the British Library.

ISBN (Hardback) 978 1 3987 0756 6
ISBN (eBook) 978 1 3987 0758 0

Typeset at The Spartan Press Ltd,
Lymington, Hants

Printed in Great Britain by Clays Ltd,
Elcograf S.p.A.

www.orionbooks.co.uk

For the girls and boys in blue

'The worst thing in the world is to be nothing to nobody.'

John Carnochan

SKETCH PLAN OF THE CHURCH HALL

KITCHEN

FIRE DOORS

SERVICE HATCH

OPEN PLAN SPACE

MALE TOILETS

FOYER

FEMALE TOILETS

16.57 hrs

Lee James Connor

Lee James Connor was an unremarkable, instantly forgettable man, a fact he had long ago recognised and now, at last, was ready to do something about. Clean-shaven, with a pale, unmarked complexion, close-cropped light brown hair and a generally expressionless face, he might well have walked straight out of boot camp. He was twenty-two years old.

He sat silently and alone in the cramped first-floor bedsit that had been his home for the past twelve months: a single room, ten feet by eight, with a small kitchenette off to one side and an even smaller shower cubicle off to the other. Hidden away at the back of a run-down Georgian conversion in south-west London, it could only be accessed via a half-hidden side door and a rickety, narrow internal staircase that would likely have failed any kind of building safety inspection. But it suited his requirements perfectly well and it cost him just a hundred pounds a week, plus bills, always paid in cash, meticulously on time.

As far as possible, he kept himself completely to himself – sleeping for much of the day, staring at his computer screen for most of the night – remaining all but invisible, even to his immediate neighbours. If you had asked any of them about him (as the police later did), there would have been very little for them to report, aside from the rather obvious suggestion that

1

he appeared to be something of a loner. There was never any post for him among the piles of junk mail that gathered in the communal hallway and he never seemed to have any visitors. The only other detail they would likely have mentioned was the fact that he seemed to smoke a lot of weed; there was certainly no escaping the smell of it in the stairwell and on the landing outside his door. But the fact was that he had never troubled them and so they had never bothered him. None of them would have been able to tell you what he did for a living. None of them would even have been able to tell you his name. Over the course of the next twenty-four hours, that was going to change.

For Connor, the previous week, much like every other in recent memory, had been almost completely devoid of any real human contact. There were the illegal porn sites and the dark web chatrooms of course, but those were no substitute for the real thing. A half-nod to a disinterested shop assistant during a hurried early-evening trip out to buy essential supplies – a pint of semi-skimmed milk, a box of cereal, a couple of tins of baked beans and a small loaf of wholemeal bread – was as much communication as he had sought or managed. And, until now, the anonymity afforded by both his appearance and his solitary existence had suited him perfectly well.

He glanced at his watch, closed the well-thumbed pamphlet that lay open on his lap and got up from the edge of the bed to turn on the small flat-screen TV that was fixed to the wall, next to some old patches of damp that his landlord had never bothered to do anything about. The condition of the paintwork in his room was consistent with the general state of the whole building: long-neglected and much in need of the kind of investment that was never going to materialise.

Connor flicked through the channels until he found the one he wanted. Then he sat back down and stared at the fast-rotating graphic of the globe and listened to the familiar, pulsing rhythm of the audio as the on-screen clock counted down to the top of the hour.

'You're watching the early-evening news from the BBC. Our main story at five o'clock.

'Nicholas Farmer, self-proclaimed leader of the banned right-wing group Home Front, has today been convicted of conspiracy to cause arson and membership of a proscribed organisation.'

The voice of the female newsreader was accompanied initially by a head-and-shoulders picture of Farmer – evidently the one taken at the police station on the day he'd been charged with his crimes – and then by footage of a prison van being driven away from the Old Bailey, with a dozen or more photographers running alongside, lenses pressed up against its tinted windows, flashguns firing, each attempting to capture the shadowy silhouette that would occupy the following morning's front pages.

The verdict came as no surprise to Connor; he had been anticipating it for several weeks. Nonetheless, he felt a surge of silent rage as the guilty verdict was confirmed. He fought to keep his feelings in check as the television voiceover continued:

'Farmer has been remanded for pre-sentence reports, but the judge has told him to expect a substantial term of imprisonment.'

The newsreader went on to explain that large demonstrations and counter-demonstrations had been taking place in the street outside the court throughout the duration of the two-week trial. The broadcast cut to show images of ardent supporters of Farmer waving Union Jacks and chanting slogans, faced by an equally vociferous and determined number of anti-fascists. The two groups were being kept apart by a resolute combination of metal barriers and large numbers of fluorescent-jacketed police officers. The news of the jury's verdict was greeted with celebratory cheers on one side of the line and a burst of unrestrained fury on the other. The barriers rocked first one way, then the other, as a succession of missiles – bottles, coins and an assortment of street debris – flew in every direction, and officers wrestled to keep the two factions apart. In the background, a large banner held between two sturdy wooden poles flicked in the breeze.

Make Britain Great Again, it said.

There was a flash of emotion in Lee Connor's grey-green eyes and a tensing of his jawline as he switched off the TV. He had seen enough. He turned instead to his bedside cabinet and picked up the joint he'd been rolling a few minutes earlier. He lit it and inhaled deeply. The powerful, aromatic smell of weed filled the room as he breathed out slowly, allowing the billow and swirl of smoke to engulf his face. He continued to suppress his feelings about the news report as he began a slow, methodical inspection of the objects laid out on his bed:

One heavy-duty bike lock and chain
Five rolls of black gaffer tape
Three rolls of large black bin bags
Two packets of white plastic cable ties
Two large kitchen knives
One Zippo lighter
Three 125ml cans of lighter fuel

One pay-as-you-go mobile phone, fully charged, location
    services turned off
One mobile charger
One charging lead
Six bottles of water
Four cans of energy drink
Three large bags of trail mix
One wind-up camping lamp
One full change of clothes
One black-handled, silver-barrelled Baikal pistol

Satisfied that everything was in place, he picked up one of the
knives, removed its protective cover and ran his thumb along
the edge of the brand-new blade. As he did so, he could feel
the anger rising inside him again and, this time, he made no
attempt to keep it in check. He could hear the voice of Nicholas
Farmer speaking clearly to him.

'Enough is enough! In accordance with the laws of nature,
there is no cause more righteous than the preservation of
one's own race...'

Farmer's rasping, railing words trailed off in Connor's imagination, but he thought he could hear other voices too. Shouting
from a distance. Competing for his attention. Urging him on. His
demeanour changed. His expression darkened and intensified.
His eyes narrowed and his breathing became rapid and shallow.
He clenched his teeth and tightened his grasp on the handle
of the knife. Then, with a sudden, guttural cry, he lunged
forwards, driving the blade towards an invisible foe. Newly
energised, he started to bounce on his toes, like a boxer in the
gym, tilting his head from side to side, rolling his shoulders,

passing the knife rapidly from one hand to the other, daring his unseen opponent to challenge him.

After a minute or so of this, his movements slowed and he began to turn in a tight, gradual circle, with the knife held out menacingly in front of him. He was imagining a new threat, a different enemy, one approaching him from behind. His face began to twitch as he reversed his grip on the knife handle. Then, with a rush of renewed violence, he plunged the blade into the mattress on his bed.

He left the knife where it was, buried up to its hilt, and took a step back as he attempted to settle himself. He picked up his joint, relit it and took another long drag. Then he began to check and recheck each item of kit on the bed against a list, carefully handwritten in block capital letters, which was pinned to the wall on a sheet of A4 paper, next to a sprawling collection of photographs and newspaper cuttings.

He nodded and checked his watch. It was almost time.

Grace Wheatley

Grace Wheatley lived about seven miles away from Lee Connor, on the sixth floor of a residential block close to Brockwell Park in South London. The two of them had never met before. For now, neither of them even knew the other one existed.

Grace shared her small two-bedroom flat with her teenage son, Isaiah – a daughter and a grandchild of the Windrush generation. The years had been kind to her – she was in her late thirties but might have passed for ten years younger – though life itself had been far less so. At the age of twenty-one, she had fallen in love with an older man. They had moved in together and the first of their two boys had been born a little over two years later. But those days were long gone. Now she was a single parent and Isaiah was an only child. Theirs was a story of seemingly endless loss.

She worked as a teaching assistant at the local primary school. It was a tough school, with pupils drawn from some of the most deprived neighbourhoods in the country, but it was a good school, with a staff team who cared passionately about their young charges. Aside from the caretaker, who had been a feature of the place for more years than anyone could remember, Grace was the longest serving of any of them. She could have been a class teacher if she had wanted to be. She could have been a member of the school management team if she had chosen to be. She was more than bright and capable enough for either role. But she had made a decision several years before to stay where she was, doing what she was doing. She had done so for the sake of Isaiah.

Grace had a deeply held set of beliefs. She believed in God. She believed in giving her best to the staff, pupils and parents at the school. And she believed in the fundamental importance of family. She went to church and she went to work and then she came home. Because home was where Isaiah was. And he was everything to her, her first thought and her last thought at the beginning and end of every day.

'What have you got planned for this evening?' she asked him.

Isaiah was half sitting, half lying on the sofa. He glanced up from his phone.

'Not much,' he responded. 'Chris might come round and play FIFA, but not until later on.'

'Have you done all your homework?'

'Almost.'

'Almost?' She looked at him quizzically.

'Just a few maths questions to finish off and the conclusion to an essay to write,' he replied. 'Shouldn't take me more than about half an hour.'

'No FIFA and no Chris till it's done.'

Isaiah grinned and nodded his silent assent before promptly changing the subject.

'What are we having for dinner?'

She smiled back at him. Like most boys of his age, he always seemed to be hungry.

'It's the church prayer meeting this evening, so we'll eat early. Will the rest of last night's pasta bake do for you?'

That sounded just fine to him and so he turned his attention back to his phone. Grace walked through to the kitchen and switched on the small digital radio that was sitting on the windowsill, next to a pot of wilting herbs. She was just in time to catch the headlines from the Old Bailey and the latest updates on the Nicholas Farmer story that she'd been following for the past few days.

When the voice on the radio suggested that Farmer would likely be going to jail for a long time, Grace murmured her quiet approval. She had no time for hatred – hers was a view of the world based much more on compassion and co-operation – but she certainly recognised its deadly consequences. And it troubled her more than she could say. What was the world becoming? And what kind of future would Isaiah be faced with? It was always her son's prospects that exercised her more than her own.

As if in response to her thoughts, Isaiah appeared in the kitchen doorway. 'What was that all about?' he asked, nodding towards the radio, his interest evidently piqued.

She loved his enquiring nature. In many ways, he was no different to any other teenage boy in the neighbourhood, with his love of sport and music and computer games, but he also had a keen desire to know and understand more about the world around him that marked him out from many in his peer group.

'Do you remember the series of fires that were started deliberately in London last year?' she asked.

'What fires?' he replied.

'I can't remember all the details, but I think there were three or four of them – all at places that had some sort of connection with refugees and asylum seekers.'

'You mean like the one at that hotel up in Wembley?' said Isaiah, stepping through into the kitchen.

'That's right. Most of the people staying in it were young families from places like Afghanistan, Yemen and Syria. And there was one at a Refugee Advice Bureau – in Ealing, I think – and another at an Islamic Centre somewhere out in east London.'

'Yeah . . . Yeah, I remember now,' said Isaiah, his face a study in concentration as he began to recall the headlines. 'And the people who started the fires were members of some sort of Nazi group, right?'

'Right,' said Grace with a nod of acknowledgement. 'The group is called Home Front and it's been banned by the government. Even being a member of it is a crime.'

'So the man they were just talking about on the news . . . Did he start the fires?'

'Apparently not,' said Grace, 'but he's the leader of the group and the police say he was the one who planned and directed the attacks.'

'And that's what he's been found guilty of?'

'Yes.'

'What a bastard!'

'Mind your language,' Grace chided.

'I just don't understand some people,' said Isaiah with a shrug of half apology.

'Me neither,' said Grace.

With seemingly nothing more to be said on the subject, Isaiah turned round and wandered back through to the sitting room. Grace stood in reflective silence for a few moments before walking over to the fridge. She opened the door and surveyed the contents.

'Food will be ready in about fifteen minutes,' she called through to Isaiah. 'Now get on with your homework.'

'Mum?' he called back, sidestepping her instruction, his mind already on a different subject.

'Yes?'

'I need a new pair of trainers.' There was a note of hesitation in his voice. Grace suspected that he'd been weighing up for the last few days whether or not he should ask the question.

'You might need to wait a bit,' she replied with a sigh. She would gladly have bought them for him, but she wasn't going to allow them to get into any kind of debt. Which meant that he would have to make do with the old pair for now. 'I've asked to start a bit earlier at school – to help out with the breakfast club – and, if that works out, there might be a little bit more to go round,' she said, before adding, 'or you could get that Saturday job you've been talking about and then you could start saving up for them yourself!'

He responded to her gentle maternal provocation with an exaggerated groan. 'All right, Mum – you've made your point!'

She grinned. He was a good boy and they got on remarkably well. She might not have had much in the bank, but she had him. And that was enough.

Alex Lewis

Sitting in his office on the second floor at Kentish Town Police Station, Superintendent Alex Lewis leaned back slowly in his chair, closed his eyes and ran his fingers through his thinning brown hair. It had already been a long day: up just after five, in by seven for a series of prisoner detention reviews, followed by briefings at the Yard and the town hall, before a scheduled catch-up with members of Team 3 at the start of their late shift.

He was popular among the PCs, who trusted him enough to tell him the truth, and that afternoon the officers of Team 3 had told him that they were struggling. It wasn't just that crime was on the rise, it was that every other kind of demand was rising too – from teenagers missing from the local children's home, to old folk collapsed behind their own front doors, to people of all ages experiencing severe mental health crises, to every other imaginable kind of emergency. Added to that was the fact that they, along with every other team on the borough, were almost permanently short-staffed: fewer of them, with fewer resources, doing a job that was more difficult, more demanding and, frequently, more dangerous than any of them could recall. The PCs had left him under no illusions about both the scale of the challenges they were facing and the inevitable strain it was placing them under.

And he took it all personally. None of it was his doing, of course – these were the inevitable consequences of years of government cuts to policing and every other frontline public service – but he felt it deeply all the same.

He stared at the mass of paperwork piled up on his desk and told himself that it would just have to wait, that no one was going to die if he didn't get it finished that evening. He wanted to get home in time to see his two teenage sons before they disappeared off to play five-a-side. The floodlit pitch in the park closest to their home was where his boys seemed to be spending an increasing proportion of their spare time, evidently preferring the company of friends to the suffocation of home. If he stayed at work for much more than another ten minutes, he would likely miss seeing them yet again.

He winced as he felt an all-too-familiar pang of guilt. He clasped his hands together behind the back of his head and puffed his cheeks out. His mind was as exhausted as his body. His greatest fear in life was that he was failing as a father – and that he had been for years. He was incredibly proud of his boys, but, for much of the time, they seemed almost like strangers to him. Or, perhaps more truthfully, he was the stranger to them. The problem, common among far too many of his colleagues, was that he had never managed to find the right balance between work and home – between policing and parenting. When it came to a choice between those two things, the job seemed to win almost every time. How could it not, he had always insisted to himself, when there were lives to be saved, when the most vulnerable in society had to be protected, and when the most dangerous had to be confronted? The policing cause had always been just and Alex found it impossible to turn his back on it. His boys would turn out all right in the end, he kept telling himself. It was the rest of the world that needed saving.

Then there was Kathy. Alex stared at the handful of framed photographs sitting beside his computer: of his sons at various stages of their childhoods and an older one of his smiling wife, taken not long after their wedding day. But the appearance of a happy family was nothing more than an illusion, maintained subconsciously by Alex for the benefit of friends and strangers alike. The truth was that, while he remained determined to rescue his relationship with his children, he had long since given up trying to fool himself about the state of his marriage. Sooner or later, he and Kathy were going to have to face up to the inevitable.

Behind him, on the other side of the room, a muted television screen was showing pictures of the Sky News report about Nicholas Farmer's conviction. But Alex had far too much on his mind to notice, much less to pay any attention. He was in the process of taking off his tie and epaulettes when an officer several years his junior appeared at the door with an apologetic expression on his face.

'Sorry to bother you, guv,' he said, 'especially when you're getting ready to go. Have you got ten seconds?'

Not really, Alex thought to himself. But he nodded all the same. Jonesy was a hard-working PC with an excellent reputation, who was helping out in the office while he recovered from a broken arm sustained during the arrest of a violent suspect. He was one of the people Alex would always make time for.

'Go on, Jonesy, what is it?'

'The Assistant Commissioner's office have just been on the phone. They've asked for a briefing note detailing our response to the murder at the weekend.'

'But I gave the Commander a verbal update when I saw her at the Yard this morning!' Alex looked and sounded exasperated. 'She seemed more than happy that we've got it all in hand.'

Jonesy grimaced. 'Apparently, that's not good enough for the AC. He wants something in writing – by close of play this evening.'

Alex checked his watch. Just after five. He'd been going flat out for the best part of twelve hours and was unable to hide his annoyance and frustration.

'Oh for fuck's sake! Why can't they just leave us alone to get on with the job?'

The PC looked momentarily surprised. Alex rarely lost his temper and he'd certainly never sworn in front of Jonesy before. In truth, Alex had startled himself almost as much as he had his junior colleague. It was out of character for him to snap in that way. Normally, he prided himself on being a calming influence about the place, a steady hand on the wheel. But there was no denying the fact that in recent weeks he hadn't been his normal sanguine self. He'd been feeling impatient and irritable in ways that were unfamiliar to him, and he'd been troubled by a nagging sense of anxiety, which, while having no obvious source, had begun to hum almost constantly at the edge of his thoughts. None of this had been helped by the fact that he couldn't remember the last time he'd managed to get a good night's sleep. To the very limited extent that he'd wondered about the reasons for any of these things, he'd put it down to some combination of the pressures of work and the challenges of home. That, and being middle-aged. But, whatever the explanation might have been, his reaction to Jonesy bothered him and he was quick to make amends.

'I'm so sorry,' he said, his palms raised in contrition. 'I didn't mean to sound off at you.'

'No need to apologise, guv,' the PC responded with a cheery grin, 'I'm with you all the way. The woman in the AC's office was genuinely apologetic about the request; I think she must find him as difficult as the rest of us do.' He paused and studied his boss's face. 'Would it help if I drafted something and sent it to you in an email?'

Alex sighed. 'I'd really appreciate that, thank you. I'll look at it on the laptop as soon as I get home.'

'I'll get straight onto it,' said Jonesy as he turned and headed out of the room.

Alex stood up and reached for the Berghaus jacket and fleece that were hanging on the back of his chair. As he did so, he remembered the one detail he'd forgotten to mention.

'Jonesy?'

'Yes, guv?' The PC reappeared in the doorway.

'Apologies, I should have said something before. I'm back on the Hostage Negotiation rota this week and, if I get called out, I'll need you to arrange cover for whatever meetings and appointments happen to be in the diary.'

'No problem,' Jonesy replied. 'It's the first time you've done that in a while, isn't it?'

Alex nodded. It had actually been several months since he'd last been on the list.

'Haven't you got enough on your plate with the day job?' Jonesy asked.

'You're starting to sound like my wife,' said Alex with a wry smile.

Lee

Lee Connor stubbed out his joint, pulled the knife out of the mattress and stepped into his cramped shower room. He patted his pocket to confirm that he'd picked up his phone. There was just enough space between the toilet and the sink for him to stand. He tucked the knife carefully into the back of his trousers, then he took his T-shirt off and studied himself in the cheap mirror that was fixed to the wall. He had a trim, muscular frame – when he wasn't on his computer, he spent much of his time doing repeated sets of sit-ups and press-ups – and his torso was covered with a series of simple, black ink tattoos. On the left side of his chest was the number '18', inscribed above the letters 'RAHOWA'. On the right side was the number '88', above a circle overlaid with a cross. And in the middle of them all was the outline of a large clenched fist.

As he stared at his reflection, his expression changed again. And, like De Niro in *Taxi Driver*, he started talking to the figure in front of him. His voice was hostile and threatening.

'What the fuck are you looking at?' he demanded.

He pulled the knife out of his waistband and started waving it in front of the mirror.

'What the fuck are you looking at?' he repeated, more loudly this time.

His movements became more agitated, the point of the blade swishing first one way, then the other.

'What the *fuck* are you looking at?' he snarled.

The figure in the mirror backed away from any further confrontation. Connor lowered the knife, turned his head to one side and leaned on the edge of the sink. He took several deep breaths. The voices were whispering to him now, so quietly that he couldn't make out what they were actually saying. Attempting to ignore them, he swapped the knife to his left hand and pulled his phone out of his pocket with his right. Then he took a selfie and posted it on Twitter, adding the hashtag, '#HomeFrontLiberator'.

Putting the picture on social media was a significant step. Connor understood that, for the first time, he was crossing a line that separated ideas from reality, plans from action. But, far from feeling daunted by the fact, he felt pleased with himself. Confident even. He knew what he was doing. He was in control.

Back in his bedroom, he took a second photograph, this time of the items laid out on the bed. He posted it with an additional message that read, 'Almost time'. He tagged a series of media organisations into both tweets, including the BBC, ITN, Sky, CNN and Fox News, plus the London *Evening Standard* and the *Daily Mail*. None of them appeared to pay any immediate attention to his messages, but, at such an early point in the evening, he wasn't particularly bothered.

Soon enough, they would all know his name.

17.43 hrs

Alex

Alex Lewis walked the short distance from his office to Kentish Town Underground Station, pausing at the entrance to buy a copy of the *Big Issue* from a local vendor. He took the escalator down to the Northern Line and arrived on the southbound platform just as an overcrowded train was pulling in. It remained standing room only as the tube rattled and swayed through a succession of rush-hour stops. Only when a large number of passengers got off at London Bridge was Alex finally able to grab a seat.

His usual habit on the evening commute was to replay the day's events in his mind in an effort to put them in some sort of order. In the face of an apparently endless and frequently overwhelming set of demands, what had he actually managed to achieve? He thought about that afternoon's encounter with the response team and the frustrating intractability of so many of the difficulties they were faced with. He replayed his conversation with Jonesy and was annoyed with himself at his momentary and uncharacteristic loss of composure. And then there was the fact that another teenager had been fatally stabbed at the weekend. The victim was almost exactly the same age as his younger son and that alone weighed heavily on his mind. The only remotely good bit of news was that after a six-month hiatus, he was finally back on call.

Alex was one of the Met's most experienced and respected hostage negotiators. He loved the role, he was exceptionally good at it, and he had really missed it. Far from being an additional burden, the particular responsibilities associated with negotiating seemed to offer him much-needed respite from the myriad of other challenges he was facing, both at work and at home. It kept him close to operational policing and, for a number of years, it had allowed him to make a real and very obvious difference to people's lives. For him, there was nothing quite like the rush of deep satisfaction that accompanied the successful conclusion of another negotiation, of knowing that a dangerous suspect had been detained or that some poor, lost soul had been helped back from the edge.

But the last job he'd attended, in Romford, East London, had ended with the fatal police shooting of an armed man. As a consequence, he and the other members of the negotiation team had been withdrawn from operational duties while the early stages of the post-incident investigation were underway. The powers that be at Scotland Yard had been at pains to point out that this was not because they were thought to have done anything wrong. In fact, the opposite was true. The author of a draft report that a senior officer had shown Alex a few weeks earlier had gone to great lengths to praise the negotiators for the multiple lives they had saved that day, and to absolve them of any responsibility for the one that had been lost. Deep down, Alex knew that the death of the man hadn't been his fault; he knew that he and his colleagues could not have done anything more. But still.

They had been told that their break from active deployment was a welfare move, designed to give them time and space to process events and to deal with any trauma they might have experienced. But, from the first mention of it, Alex had been ambivalent about the idea. He didn't want to take any time away from the role. He and the rest of the team had been through the formal debriefing process, followed by a much longer informal one, held in a private upstairs room at a Central London pub. His memories of the latter were patchy, given the amount of alcohol consumed, but he wasn't conscious of feeling any lasting trauma and he had declined the offer of counselling on more than one occasion. Like many of his colleagues, he saw no need for that sort of thing. All he wanted was to get back to doing what he loved.

He got off the tube at Clapham North and walked the short distance home. He was reaching into his pocket for his keys when the front door flew open and two teenage boys jostled with one another to be first out. They both had sports bags looped over their shoulders.

'Oh, hi Dad!' said Luke, the eldest at sixteen. 'You're home early.'

'I wanted to get back in time to see you two . . .' Alex started to reply. But the boys were already past him and at the gate.

'See you later,' shouted fourteen-year-old Jack, glancing back over his shoulder. And, with that, they were gone.

Alex's shoulders sagged. He stared out at the street and then back at the front door. His first thought was to turn round and head straight back to the office. These days, he seemed to find a good deal more comfort and companionship there than he did at home. At work, people understood and appreciated him. At work, he had a place and a purpose. At work, he knew what he was doing.

'Is that you, Alex?' It was the voice of his wife, coming from inside the house. Evidently, she had also decided to come home earlier than normal. Reluctantly, he pushed the door open.

'How was your day?' he asked dutifully as he put his rucksack down in the hallway.

'Same old, same old,' she replied disinterestedly. She was a senior partner in a medium-sized corporate law firm and her job was never likely to match his for excitement. She had long since given up trying to compete. 'How about yours?'

Although he'd never been much of a detective, Alex had begun to suspect that she might be seeing someone else. The little signs were there: the fact that she never left her phone lying around (she even took it into the bathroom with her), the fact that she seemed to have a greater number of after-work commitments than normal – and a part of him actually hoped he was right. He certainly wouldn't have blamed her – he knew he had become more devoted to his job than he was to her – and at least it would give them a clear reason to call it a day. At some point, he would ask her about it, but, for now, he was determined that things would remain steady between them, if only for the sake of the boys.

'I've got some work to finish,' said Alex, remembering Jonesy's email, 'but do you want something to eat when I'm done?'

'If it's not too much trouble,' she replied, matching his tone. 'I've opened a bottle of wine. It's on the side in the kitchen if you want a glass.' She was already halfway upstairs.

'I'm back on call this week, remember?' he called after her. 'So no wine for me.'

She paused on the staircase and gave him a look that was more weary than it was withering. Even so, Alex could tell that she was unimpressed. She obviously hadn't remembered.

Lee

Connor finished a second helping of beans on toast and abandoned his dirty plate next to the saucepan on the grimy two-ring hob. He knew he'd have reason to be grateful for the calories later on.

Meal over, he moved back into his bedroom and started to get changed. He put on a clean black T-shirt and pair of combat trousers, a dark grey sweatshirt, a plain black baseball cap and a pair of well-worn black leather boots. Then he reached under the bed and pulled out a large, dark green army surplus kitbag. Working methodically, he started to pack it. He wrapped the Baikal pistol in a fleece, having double-checked that the safety was on, and placed it carefully at the very bottom of the bag. Next in were the two knives, followed by the lighter fuel, camping lamp, ties and tape. He laid the rolls of bin liners over those and placed the water, energy drinks and trail mix on top. Last to go in were his spare trousers, T-shirt and hoodie. Almost as an afterthought, he pulled open his bedside drawer and retrieved three deal bags of weed and a fresh pack of large green Rizlas, stuffing them deep inside the bag before zipping it shut. Then he tested the weight of it: heavy, but more than manageable.

He picked up a khaki, military-style jacket and put it on. Then he looked round his room, taking in the details one last time. He wasn't expecting to see any of it again. The newsprint and pictures remained on the walls, waiting to be found and read. The collection of booklets and leaflets on top of the chest of drawers had their place and purpose too. And his laptop. He left that open on the bed, with the password written on a scrap of paper and stuck to the screen. He was making it as easy as he possibly could for them. He wanted them to find it all.

After one final check of his bag and its contents, he walked out onto the landing and closed the door to his room behind him. He didn't bother locking up. Hoisting his pack onto his back, he made his way down the uneven stairs and stepped outside into the early-evening gloom. Morden Underground Station, the last stop on the Northern Line, was about a twenty-minute walk away.

Grace

Grace stacked the dishes in the sink.

'I'll do those, Mum,' offered Isaiah. He wandered over, put his hands on her shoulders and eased her gently to one side.

'Thank you,' she replied. 'I appreciate it.'

She left him to it and headed in the direction of her bedroom, passing her favourite framed photograph of Isaiah and his older brother hanging on the wall in the corridor. Two proud little boys, buttoned up in their smart primary-school uniforms, with all of life ahead of them. She paused for a moment and, just as she always did, touched the tips of her fingers to her lips and pressed them gently against the faces of her sons.

Life had been far from straightforward for her, but she tried to count her blessings – to focus on being grateful for what she had, rather than dwelling on what she had lost. She tried to remind herself regularly that whatever challenges she might be facing, there would always be someone, somewhere, having a worse day than her.

And, until now, that had always been true.

18.03 hrs

Lee

Connor paused to pull the hood of his coat up and the brim of his cap down, before stepping out onto the street. As he did so, he felt a flush of nervous anticipation. His senses were suddenly on edge, but he was quick to reassure himself that this was to be expected. After all, it was the first time he'd been out in the open with his full set of gear. He'd been careful to carry nothing incriminating on any of his dry runs. And so he made a conscious and deliberate effort to slow his breathing – in through his nose, out through his mouth – exactly as he had been practising for the past few weeks.

There were a handful of possible routes to the tube station and Connor had trialled them all. Timing was not a concern with the various alternatives – there was no more than three or four minutes' difference between any of them – it was the risk of discovery that had exercised him. Essentially, it came down to a choice between the likely anonymity afforded by the crowds on the high street, or the shadows and silence that were the preserve of the back-doubles. After much deliberation, he had settled on the latter, reasoning that by sticking to the quieter residential roads, he was far less likely to stumble across someone or something unexpected that might interfere with his plans. Ten minutes into his journey, his decision was almost his undoing.

Somehow, he sensed the police car before he actually saw it.

The back of his neck was already prickling when the silver Ford Focus with its blue lights and familiar blue and yellow 'Battenburg' markings emerged from a side road up ahead and turned in his direction. Instantly, his pulse started racing and he came to a momentary standstill. Fight or flight? Adrenaline surging, he knew that either of those responses could well mean the end of everything. *Easy now*, he murmured to himself, as his scrambling thoughts threatened briefly to overwhelm him. All he needed to do was remain calm and continue on his way. Maybe the lone officer in the car would have no interest in him. Perhaps he would have other, much more pressing, concerns on his mind. Connor managed to get his feet moving again and, keeping his head up and his pace steady, hoped that the small changes in his behaviour and demeanour had passed unobserved.

The patrol car eased past him and out of his immediate view. Connor waited for the engine note to fade into the distance. But it didn't. Instead, he heard the vehicle slow and come to an apparent stop. He held his breath as he fought the almost unbearable urge to look back over his shoulder. React or retreat? Hypervigilant, he scanned the road up ahead of him, looking for any potential escape routes. About thirty yards ahead, on the other side of the road, he could see an alleyway that led into a nearby housing estate. He wrestled with the frantic desire to start running. He heard the sounds of gears changing and tyres turning on tarmac. Gritting his teeth and clenching his fists, he kept walking. He was damned if it was all going to be over before it had even begun. *Easy now*, he repeated silently.

The police car rolled past him at no more than ten miles an

hour. He could feel the driver looking at him. What would an innocent man do in these circumstances? Surely they would notice the car. So he glanced briefly to his right without breaking stride.

The car pulled in at the kerb about twenty metres ahead of him and the driver's door opened. A middle-aged officer, carrying a few extra pounds around his midriff, stepped onto the pavement and looked straight at him. Instantly, Connor knew that he would be able to outrun him. And, if it came to it, he was fairly certain he would be able to outmuscle him too. As long as the officer didn't draw his Taser.

'Evening,' said the PC.

'Evening, officer,' Connor responded, somehow managing to sound much calmer than he actually felt. His clammy hands were pushed firmly into his coat pockets.

'You seemed a bit surprised to see me.'

'What do you mean?' said Connor, attempting to maintain an innocent air.

'When I came round the corner in the car, you stopped walking. It looked to me as though you were thinking about running away.'

'Not me, officer,' replied Connor, trying not to sound too defensive.

'Would you mind taking your hands out of your pockets while I'm talking to you?' said the PC.

Connor did as he was told, pulling the lining of his coat out as he did so, hoping this might reassure the officer that he wasn't trying to hide anything.

'Thank you,' said the PC. 'Can I ask where you're off to?' His voice was measured and calm. Connor tried to tell himself that this was no more than a quick check – a random stop rather than one based on particular concern. All he needed to do was hold it together for the next few minutes.

He gestured back over his shoulder. 'I've just come from home and I'm on my way to stay with my dad up in North London,' he replied, relieved that his meticulous planning had extended to the preparation of a rough script to be used in circumstances such as these. He ought to be fine as long as the officer didn't actually try to contact his father in an effort to confirm the story. He could see the PC reading his body language, looking for anything in his actions or words that might be out of place.

'It's just that, over the last week or so, we've had a few robberies in this neighbourhood. And some of them have happened at around this time of the evening.' The officer was watching Connor very closely now, evidently looking for any reaction to this statement. 'Have you got anything on you that you shouldn't have?'

'No,' Connor responded, perhaps just a little too quickly. 'Just my phone and my wallet,' he added, moving his hands towards his trouser pockets. 'You're welcome to check them.'

'I will in a moment,' said the PC. 'What about the bag? What have you got in there?'

'Just a change of clothes,' replied Connor as casually as he could, 'and some bits and pieces that I'm taking up to my dad. Do you want to have a look inside?' He was studying the police officer every bit as closely as he himself was being studied, rapidly considering the alternatives for a variety of different scenarios. He was confident that he could get to the PC before the officer got to his radio or his Taser. He was equally confident that he could be out of sight in a matter of seconds. But he wanted desperately to avoid either of those things. He just wanted to be on his way. *Easy now.*

'Why don't we start with your name and date of birth,' suggested the PC, as he pulled a notebook and pen out from one of the pockets on the front of his body armour.

There was nothing to be gained by complicating things, so Connor gave his correct details.

'Are you known to the police at all?' asked the PC, as he called up on his radio for a name check.

'Just for a bit of drugs when I was younger,' Connor responded, 'but nothing for a while now. And definitely nothing for robbery.' He was still trying to demonstrate that he had nothing to hide, though his heart rate suggested otherwise.

'So you've got your life back on track then?' said the PC, making idle conversation while he waited for the result of his check.

'I have,' replied Connor. 'You've got to learn from the mistakes you make when you're a kid.' He actually managed to succeed in sounding like a man who had genuine regrets about his past.

A crackling voice at the other end of the radio confirmed that Connor had been telling the truth about his previous criminal record. But the officer wasn't done yet.

'So let's have a look at what you've got in your trouser pockets,' he said. 'Nice and slowly,' he added as Connor reached for his wallet and phone.

The PC glanced at the phone.

'What's the first name and number stored in your contacts?'

'I don't have any names stored in my contacts,' Connor replied.

The PC seemed surprised, but a quick check of the device confirmed that Connor was telling the truth. The officer handed the phone back and turned his attention to the contents of the wallet. The details on the lone bank card were a match. The photo on the driving licence was too. Everything appeared to be in order. As the officer patted him down, Connor thought that he might be about to get away with it.

'That just leaves the bag,' said the PC. 'What did you say you had in it?'

Alex

Alex was sitting at the kitchen table, his laptop open in front of him, when Kathy appeared in the room, wearing a sweatshirt and an old pair of tracksuit bottoms. She walked in silence over to the open wine bottle and poured herself another glass, before heading straight back out of the room. Alex watched her go.

He rested his elbows on the table, leaned forwards and buried his face in his hands. He was about to start asking himself how on earth he'd managed to make such a mess of his home life, but, having asked the same question countless times before, he knew that there were no simple or straightforward answers to it. So he opted for avoidance instead, and turned his thoughts back to work. He tapped the space bar on his computer and woke up the screen. He reread the handful of changes he'd made to the briefing Jonesy had drafted for the Assistant Commissioner and, satisfied that it was up to scratch, attached it to an email and pressed send. Then he walked over to the kitchen cupboards in search of something quick and easy to cook.

Grace

'Do you have any idea how proud I am of you?'

Grace was looking at Isaiah, who was in the process of putting his schoolbooks away in his bag. He pretended not to hear her, but he did know. He was proud of her too, though, like most teenage boys, he usually found a sentiment like that too awkward to express.

'I know it can be an almighty pain sometimes,' she went on, 'but you're never going to regret any of the hard work you're putting in. It showed in your GCSE results and it's going to show in your A-Level grades too. You'll be going to university before you know it. And then who knows what adventures life has in store for you?'

'I'd rather stay here and keep an eye on you, Mum,' he responded. He was only being partly serious, but he couldn't help feeling responsible for her. After all, he was the man of the house these days.

'Oh shush!' she responded playfully. 'You know that I'm perfectly capable of looking after myself – and, anyway, I could do with some peace and quiet round here!' In truth, she was dreading the thought of him leaving.

He laughed as she picked up her coat and started towards the front door. 'I thought the meeting didn't start till seven?' he called after her, already starting to plug the games console into the TV. He planned to get some practice in before Chris arrived.

'It doesn't,' she replied, 'but I promised the vicar I'd get there early to help set things up.'

Lee

Back in South London, the lone PC was standing no more than about four feet away as Connor eased his bag off his shoulders and placed it down on the pavement.

'I'm just going to have a quick look,' said the officer. 'If you've got nothing to hide, you'll be on your way in a minute or two.'

But Connor had everything to hide. His heart was pounding furiously now. His mind was spinning. *Fight or flight*? It had almost reached the point where those were the only two options left open to him. There were conflicting voices clamouring on the edge of his thoughts urging both, with others telling him to hold his nerve. If he could draw a sliver of reassurance from anywhere, it was in the fact that he had taken great care in packing his belongings. Perhaps the PC would be satisfied with no more than a cursory look. Perhaps he would find the clothes that Connor had told him were there and begin to lose interest. Perhaps he wouldn't dig deeper. Perhaps he wouldn't notice the smell of cannabis. But each of those things was becoming less and less likely and, as the officer bent down to open the bag, Connor made a snap decision. He could no longer afford to take any chances.

Taking full advantage of the element of surprise and using both hands, he shoved the PC forcefully backwards, sending him sprawling across the pavement. Then, in a single, swift movement, he hoisted his bag onto his back, turned and started running. He was already at the entrance to the alleyway when he heard the officer shouting into his radio, 'Chasing suspect . . . Daybrook Road towards Morden Hall Park.'

He was running, quite deliberately, in the opposite direction to the tube station. And he was running fast. The increasingly breathless voice of the police officer was already fading into the background as Connor pulled his hood down, took his cap off and threw it over a nearby fence. Even the smallest change to his appearance would improve his chances of getting away. He kept going flat out, twisting and turning through a succession of walkways and cut-throughs until he was absolutely certain he was clear. He could hear a couple of sirens somewhere in the distance, but they were getting further away with every moment that passed.

He slowed to a jog, before stopping beside a low wall. He leaned over it and thought for a moment that he might be sick. Taking in gulps of air, he glanced left, right and left again. He saw nothing. He listened intently for the approach of any pursuers, but all he could hear was the sound of his own breathing.

18.15 hrs

Grace

It was a gentle ten-minute stroll from Grace's flat to the single-storey church hall, part way up Herne Hill, set a few metres back from the road on the right-hand side. The main church building stood next door. The local congregation had spent the last three years raising funds and applying for grants to refurbish the hall, and the money had been well spent. The building looked in really good shape: a modern, spacious, open-plan community facility with a large kitchen situated at the back of it.

Grace paused to scan the noticeboard outside. It displayed a whole range of information on a series of colourful, laminated A4 pages: parents and toddlers' groups on Tuesdays and Thursdays, lunch for older folk on Wednesdays and Fridays, after-school clubs, debt counselling, a marriage preparation course, a Saturday night youth club and any number of other provisions laid on for people who lived and worked in the neighbourhood. During the winter months, the hall was opened up as a night shelter for the homeless. The most recent notice had been posted by the team of volunteers who ran the local food bank, asking for additional contributions of cereal, pasta, powdered milk and tinned fruit. Grace would normally have brought along a donation of her own, but, for the time being at least, her financial situation was just a bit too tight.

As she continued up the path, Grace looked at the large wooden sign that had recently been given a permanent place above the front doors: *Refugees Welcome,* it read. A couple of months before, the church had featured prominently in an hour-long TV documentary, and in several related news reports, about families fleeing the war in Syria. The local community had been organising clothing and blanket collections for more than a year and, more recently, had been working with the council to identify appropriate accommodation for families who had been granted asylum in the UK. Now the church was stepping up its involvement even further.

'Evening, Rosie,' Grace called out as she pushed the front doors open.

'Is that you, Grace?' came the reply.

A tall, slim woman in her early thirties appeared from inside the main hall. She was wearing a clerical collar and a welcoming smile. The two women embraced warmly.

'Thanks so much for coming early. There isn't actually much to do – just the chairs to set out and the teas and coffees to get ready. But it's lovely to have the company.'

Rosie Phillips had been the curate at the church for the past two years. Grace had got to know her well in that time and had grown extremely fond of her, treating her very much like a younger sister.

'We've got the new refugee family coming this evening – Mariam and her two children. Rahel is her twelve-year-old daughter and Ittack is her fourteen-year-old son. They're Syrian Christians.'

'Mariam. Rahel. Ittack.' Grace repeated their names, trying

to fix them in her memory. 'Is it just the three of them? Has Mariam got a partner?' she asked.

'The family only had one chance to get out of the country – they had to leave her husband behind. They've not spoken to him in almost a year. They've actually got no idea whether he's even still alive.'

Grace shook her head in pained disbelief.

'And they're such lovely people,' Rosie continued. 'I've only met them a handful of times so far, but you can just tell. That said, communication is going to be a little bit tricky this evening – the interpreter called me a few minutes before you got here to say that he's gone down with the flu. We'll just have to do what we can to make them feel at home.'

'Who else is coming?' asked Grace.

'I'm not actually expecting too many,' came the reply. 'The secondary school has a parents' evening running tonight and I'm guessing that a number of our regulars will be going to that.'

'Ah well,' said Grace, 'where two or three are gathered . . .'

'. . . God is there in the midst of them,' finished the priest with a fresh smile. 'Do you mind starting on the chairs while I go and put the hot water on?'

The two of them set to work, blissful in their ignorance of what was to come.

Lee

Connor wrestled fleetingly with the idea of abandoning his plans – of giving up and retreating to his bedsit. But he dismissed the thought almost as soon as it had entered his head. It was far too late for that and, in any case, it wasn't necessary.

The encounter with the PC might have been unexpected and unsettling, but it hadn't actually changed a thing. The officer hadn't found anything incriminating and Connor didn't think he had injured him when he pushed him to the ground. Both of these facts were important, Connor reasoned, because they meant that the police were much less likely to keep searching for him once their initial burst of activity had yielded no trace of him. They would probably write him off as just another dope-head who had managed to escape with his stash. The fact that it had now been several minutes since he'd last heard any sirens reinforced this view. He retrieved one of the bottles of water from his pack. Sipping from it slowly, he took a few moments to make sure that his thoughts were back in order. When he was sure he was ready, he started moving again. Choosing his route with great care and rechecking his surroundings at each new junction, he made his way to the tube station.

The northbound train from Morden was held up for a few minutes – some unspecified problem with the signalling at Kennington – but Connor didn't let the delay bother him. He had allowed plenty of time. He sat quietly at one end of the carriage, watchful and withdrawn, replaying in his mind the events of the previous half-hour. He realised that he'd got lucky in his encounter with the PC, but wondered whether it might actually be a sign. He definitely wasn't the religious type, but maybe the gods – if they existed – were with him. Maybe they were on his side. They certainly ought to be, given the undeniable justice of his cause. Once again, he could hear the distinctive whisper of Nicholas Farmer's voice.

'We must secure the existence of our people and a future for white children,' it said.

Connor held his bag firmly between his knees, resting both hands on top of it. He knew that Caucasian boys with rucksacks riding on trains rarely attracted much attention, but, all the same, he avoided making eye contact with anyone else in the carriage. People looked past him and people looked through him, but none of them looked at him. He was nothing to them.

He was nobody.

He got off the Northern Line train at Stockwell and crossed platforms to the Victoria Line. Brixton was a single stop away and he arrived there not more than a couple of minutes later. He lifted his bag back onto his shoulders and joined the crowds heading towards the exit. As he did so, he glanced briefly but deliberately up at the CCTV cameras mounted on the ceiling, offering them a fleeting but clear view of his face. It was all part of the plan; something for the media to play and replay in the weeks and months ahead. He stood on the escalators that led from the platforms up to the ticket hall, before walking up the last set of stairs and onto Brixton High Street. The air was cool and the skies were clear. There was a dishevelled busker sitting on one side of the exit, croaking a tune that didn't match the one he was playing on his five-stringed guitar, while a tall, elegant Rastafarian in his sixties was selling bundles of richly fragranced joss sticks on the other. Connor hated the place.

'Multiculturalism is a failed experiment,' he could hear Farmer proclaiming to his rowdy audience. 'The time has come to reclaim our country from every single person who doesn't belong here. The time has come to make Britain great again.'

He scanned the area immediately around him, checking for any signs of police activity. Seeing and sensing none, he waited for the pedestrian lights to change before crossing the road. Back out in the open, he was surprised to discover that he didn't feel nervous. Instead, it seemed that the outcome of his earlier encounter with the law had left him feeling emboldened. They hadn't been able to stop him then and they definitely weren't going to be able to stop him now. He turned left and walked up the high street, past the old Morleys department store and into the McDonald's on the corner. Ignoring the lengthy fast-food queues to his right, he hurried up the set of stairs on his left and into the gents' toilet on the first floor.

Pleased to find that he was the only person in there, he locked himself inside the lone cubicle, closed the loo seat and sat down. He opened his kitbag, reached right down into the bottom of it and pulled out the rolled-up fleece. He felt the weight of the Baikal pistol in his hands and, having checked that the safety was on, placed it securely in an inside jacket pocket. Then he reached back into his pack and pulled out the second of the kitchen knives – another brand-new 8-inch butcher's blade still in its protective sheath. He rested it on his lap, ready to tuck it into the back of his trousers when he stood up. These seemed like necessary precautions to be taking – essential preparation for the possibility, however remote, that he might get stopped again before he reached his target. He checked his watch for the third time in as many minutes and then he closed his eyes. Leaning back against the cubicle wall, he deepened his breathing and then, step by meticulously planned step, he started to visualise all that was to come.

Alex

Alex pushed the remainder of his meal away from him and closed the lid of his laptop. Having chosen to eat her food alone in the TV room, Kathy appeared back in the kitchen holding her empty plate.

'Why on earth have you agreed to go back on call?' she asked him.

Her question took him by surprise. Evidently, she'd been thinking about it since he'd mentioned the fact earlier on. Her tone wasn't particularly hostile, but it was clear that she couldn't understand why he'd chosen to take on the extra responsibility. Alex chose his words carefully.

'I've got to get back to it at some point,' he ventured.

'You've got to . . . or you want to?' she responded. This time, there was a trace of accusation in her voice.

'Both,' he said after a moment's pause, not wanting to rise to any provocation. 'Besides, they're short of experienced negotiators this week and they've said that they could really do with the help.'

'But the Romford shooting was only six months ago!' she replied. She sounded more frustrated than anything else. 'The investigation seems to be taking for ever and you've still got the inquest to come.'

'That's true,' he acknowledged, 'but we know that we're in the clear. We've already been told that we aren't going to face any kind of criticism or sanction. The specialist's report found no fault in anything the negotiating team did.' He pursed his lips and offered a slight shrug. 'And the inquest isn't likely to happen until next year at the earliest. There's plenty of ground for the investigation still to cover – far beyond anything we did or didn't do that day.'

'But aren't there others with less challenging day jobs to take up the slack?' she asked.

'I'm not sure there are any of those jobs left,' he replied.

'So what about the boys?'

'Our boys?'

'Yes, our boys,' she said impatiently.

'What about them?' he said defensively. She had him at his point of greatest weakness.

'When are you actually going to spend some proper time with them? You already spend almost every waking hour at the office. And even when you do make it home, your mind is mostly still at work.' Her voice was a mixture of disappointment and defiance.

'That's why I came home early this evening.'

'What do you mean?'

'I came home early this evening to see the boys,' he said, hoping he might gain some small amount of credit for the fact.

'But they're not here, are they?' she said, not giving any ground.

'So what do you want me to do?' he responded, struggling to conceal his annoyance.

She answered with nothing more than a sigh and walked back out of the room.

Alex didn't have the energy to follow her. And he didn't have the capacity to respond to the perfectly legitimate concerns she was raising. Instead, he picked up his phone and plugged it into the charger, checking to make sure the ringtone was switched on.

Grace

The chairs were set and the hot-water urn was bubbling away in the kitchen. Rosie and Grace were able to keep an eye on it through the large serving hatch that connected the kitchen to the main hall. They took full advantage of the few moments they had spare to sit down and catch up with one another.

'I don't know how you manage to do it all,' said Rosie after Grace had been talking for a while.

'All what?' Grace responded, a puzzled expression on her face.

'All that life seems to demand of you,' Rosie replied. 'After everything you've been through. Being the only breadwinner in the family. Holding down a really demanding, full-time job. Raising a son on your own. And, somehow, still managing to find time for us here at the church.'

'Oh, I don't know,' said Grace. 'I have my moments, but things always seem to work themselves out in the end. I usually get a break in the school holidays – that certainly helps. And church is no bother. This place is like a second home to me.'

Their conversation was interrupted by the arrival in the hall of Alan and Jean Richardson, a silver-haired, salt-of-the-earth couple who devoted much of their time to their duties as elected members of the Parochial Church Council. They were both in their early seventies and, with their children and grandchildren living outside London, they always seemed to have plenty of time to give.

'Evening, you two,' said Rosie, standing up. 'Can I make you a cup of tea?'

'Oh, yes please,' said Jean.

'I never say no to a cup of tea,' said Alan, an unmistakable old smoker's rattle in his voice.

As Rosie went through to the kitchen to fetch the drinks, Grace watched as Alan removed a small plastic container from his pocket, twisted the cap off and tapped a couple of small white tablets into the palm of his hand.

'So how is that heart of yours?' she asked him cheerfully. Six months earlier, she had been cooking and delivering meals to their home while Alan was recovering from a heart bypass operation.

'Better than ever,' he responded with a chuckle. He patted

his chest with the palm of his empty hand. 'There's life in the old boy yet,' he smiled.

'He's doing really well,' affirmed Jean. 'We just have to make sure we look after his blood pressure.' She nodded at the pills he was holding as she said this.

'You worry too much,' said Alan playfully. 'I'm fitter now than I was twenty years ago.' He took up a boxer's stance and threw a couple of gentle shadow punches in support of his assertion. His wife responded to her partner of more than forty-five years with a sigh of mock exasperation.

'How about you, Jean?' Grace asked, turning to her. 'How are you doing? You've had a lot to deal with this year.'

'Oh, I'm fine,' Jean replied stoically. 'It's been nothing we couldn't manage between the two of us,' she added, patting her husband on his arm.

Before Grace could ask them anything else, Rosie reappeared with a mug of tea in each hand. And, at exactly the same moment, a woman Grace didn't recognise appeared at the front of the hall, accompanied by two teenage children. Grace realised straight away that they must be the Syrian refugee family. All three were dressed in hand-me-down clothes that had likely been donated by members of the congregation, and they seemed rather nervous. Rosie handed the cups she was carrying to Alan and Jean and hurried over to greet the new arrivals. She grasped the woman by both hands.

'It is so good to see you again, Mariam,' said Rosie, her pronunciation slow and deliberate.

Mariam smiled, but she didn't reply. Rosie turned to greet Rahel and Ittack and, through a combination of fractured phrases and clumsy hand gestures, tried to explain to the family that the interpreter wasn't going to be able to join them.

'Is OK. We pray,' said Mariam in limited, heavily accented

English. She clasped her hands together by way of confirmation, before following Rosie through to the kitchen to get drinks for the children.

Grace approached Rahel and Ittack and tried to talk to them. The girl responded with a shy smile, but the boy seemed reluctant to make any sort of eye contact with her. Grace saw very quickly that their grasp of English was even more limited than the handful of words their mother had managed to learn. So she showed them where to sit and tried her best to make them feel welcome. And, as she did so, she tried to imagine the journey that had brought them to London, and the sort of life they must have left behind. She recalled the sense of detachment and unreality she'd felt watching the harrowing news footage that had been broadcast from places like Aleppo and Homs. It had all seemed so remote and far away, and yet, here they now were, sitting in silence alongside her. She wondered about their father and felt a sense of almost overwhelming compassion for them. Though she found it impossible to grasp the full extent of all that they must have endured, she certainly understood the aching sense of grief and loss. That at least was familiar to her.

Mariam came and sat down beside them, just as two more members of the congregation arrived, holding hands with one another. Helen was a local youth worker, a young woman of Gambian descent, born and raised in Brixton, who spent much of her working week in and around the church hall. Among her many duties, she was responsible for running the youth club and after-school clubs advertised on the noticeboard out at the front of the building. Her face lit up the moment she saw Ittack and Rahel and she headed straight for them. It was obvious that this wasn't the first time they had met one another. Grace saw the children's faces brighten as Helen hugged them and she couldn't help smiling as she watched the three of them embark on a faltering, giggling attempt at some sort of sign-language conversation.

Jack sat down quietly on one of the empty chairs. He hadn't spoken to anyone else in the room yet. Grace had got to know the two of them over the course of the past twelve months and had previously noticed Jack's apparent anxiousness in group settings. He certainly seemed to be much more comfortable talking to people on a one-to-one basis. But she had also seen how good Helen was for him: drawing him out of himself, bringing out the best in him. They had been going out with one another for the past three years, having first met in their late teens at their college Christian Union. Jack had a decent, well-paid job as a computer programmer and Grace often wondered why the two of them didn't just settle down and get married. They were still young, but they were so obviously made for one another, with the whole of their lives together to look forward to.

19.18 hrs

Lee

It was dark.

Lee Connor walked out of the McDonald's, crossed the main road and headed straight to one of the few public phone boxes that remained on the high street. He dialled 999 and waited for the call to connect. As he was put through to the Met control room, he affected a breathless, panicky voice:

'I've just seen a black suspect armed with a machete, chasing another man down Stockwell Road. They were heading towards Stockwell tube station. Please come quickly, I'm afraid something terrible is going to happen.'

Then he hung up and started walking at a brisk pace up Effra Road, in the opposite direction to Stockwell Road. His intention was perfectly simple: to send every available local police unit as far away as possible from his planned route and intended destination. It seemed to him the best way of ensuring that he avoided any more unwelcome encounters with passing patrols. And his plan worked perfectly. He was able to cover the mile or so from the centre of Brixton to the bottom of Herne Hill without being interrupted or disturbed by anyone.

He stopped only when he reached the church hall. He stood on the opposite side of the road and studied the sign above the door: *Refugees Welcome*.

'Fucking immigrants,' he muttered aggressively.

Connor had given a great deal of time and thought to his selection of the right location. He had considered St Margaret's Church next to Westminster Abbey, just across the road from the Houses of Parliament. He had also wondered about All Souls, Langham Place, opposite the BBC's Central London headquarters at New Broadcasting House. Both were eye-catching choices; both were in high-profile locations. But neither was right. They were too big, with too many access points – too many windows and doors for one man to cover. Quite apart from that, aside from the occasional, non-specific encouragement from the pulpit to 'take care of the poor', they lacked any recent, obvious connection to work with refugees and asylum seekers. It was only when he saw a clip of the TV documentary about the little church hall on Herne Hill that Connor suspected he might have found the right place. A bit of further research and a couple of discreet reconnaissance visits had confirmed the fact. He had what he needed. And he reasoned that, in an online age, it was not the size of the venue that was important, but the size of the prospective internet audience. The actual geography hardly mattered at all.

He took out his phone and photographed the 'Refugees Welcome' sign. Then, stepping into a nearby alley where he knew he couldn't be seen, he pulled the Baikal out from his coat pocket. Pointing it at his phone, he took another selfie – the barrel of the gun sharply in focus, his face somewhat blurred. He attached both images to his nascent Twitter thread, with an accompanying message that read:

I hope you're watching.
It's time.
#HomeFrontLiberator

***

Across the road, the nine congregants were singing. In a news-room several miles away, a junior member of staff working the late shift on the social media desk sat up a little straighter in his chair and leaned in towards his screen.

Alex

Alex was still sitting alone at the kitchen table, caught up in the grim realisation that the house he had lived in for the best part of twenty years was feeling less and less like home with every day that passed. It was almost as if he no longer belonged there. His wife was upstairs somewhere, avoiding him. His sons would no doubt stay late at football, avoiding both of them. Not for the first time in recent weeks, he felt a tightening in his chest.

He planted the palms of both his hands firmly on the kit-chen table and tried to will himself out of the malaise. Then he stood up and walked across the room to retrieve his phone. He unplugged it from the charger and scrolled through his most recent text messages. He found nothing that required a response. He looked at WhatsApp and Facebook and LinkedIn. Nothing there either. He checked his work emails for the third time in thirty minutes, just in case anything new had come through. It hadn't. He was searching for something – anything – to distract him from the reality of his domestic situation and, finding nothing on his phone to occupy his thoughts, he wandered through to the next-door room and sat down in front of the TV, telling himself that there had to be something on one of the four hundred-plus channels that was actually worth watching. He was in for another quiet, lonely evening.

Lee

Gun concealed back in his coat pocket, Lee Connor crossed the road, checking carefully in every direction. He could hear the muffled sound of a TV set coming from a nearby open window, but, aside from the passing sight of an urban fox scavenging for scraps, the street itself was deserted. There was nothing and no one to stop him now.

He walked up the path and, as he approached the front of the hall, he could see clearly inside for the first time. 'Shit!' he muttered under his breath as he came to an abrupt stop. There were fewer people inside than he had been expecting. On the dry run a week earlier, and on the one a couple of weeks before that, there had been at least double the number, perhaps more than twenty. But, as he rapidly considered his options, he realised that nothing of substance had actually changed. In fact, this unexpected turn of events might actually work to his advantage – a smaller crowd would certainly be easier to control. Staring through the window, he counted three brown faces and two black ones. Enough to suit his purposes. He adjusted the weight of his bag on his shoulders.

It was time.

As he opened the door, they were still singing. It meant that they didn't notice him as he eased into the small foyer area at the front of the building, the men's and women's toilets on either side of him. And it bought him enough time to turn and lock the doors without being observed. As the song ended, he stepped forward into the strip-lit brightness of the main hall.

Rosie was the first of the little group of worshippers to open her eyes and she appeared delighted by the arrival of an additional person. She obviously didn't recognise him, but that didn't seem to mean she was any less pleased to see him. Murmuring to Grace to lead the opening prayers, she stood up and began to walk towards him.

'Welcome, friend,' she said.

'Sit the fuck down,' he responded, face expressionless, voice emotionless. He had rehearsed this moment repeatedly in front of the mirror, back in the privacy of his bedsit.

Rosie stopped in the middle of the room, clearly confused. Grace's prayer ended before it had really begun and everyone stared at the stranger. Mariam and her children hadn't understood the words spoken, but there was no mistaking the sudden change of atmosphere in the room.

'I told you to sit down.' His voice was a little louder this time – more insistent, though still devoid of any obvious feeling. He took the kitbag off his back and lowered it slowly to the floor, his eyes never leaving Rosie and the semicircle of people behind her. Rosie had just opened her mouth to speak again when he reached inside his jacket with his right hand, pulled the Baikal pistol out and pointed it straight at her. Rahel gasped and turned swiftly to her mother, who grabbed both her children and pulled them in close to her. Grace froze, her mouth half open. Alan started back in his seat and clutched his wife's hand. Helen and Jack reached instinctively for one another. All of them were suddenly, overwhelmingly terrified.

Rosie was every bit as scared as the rest of them but somehow managed to maintain a semblance of calm. With her palms open and arms outstretched, she began to walk slowly towards him, speaking quietly as she did so.

'I don't know who you are or what you—'

Connor took a single stride towards her, immediately closing the distance between them, and struck her fiercely across the face with fist and gun. It was a deliberately violent act, designed to shock and awe. Even so, he hit her with far greater force than he had intended. The sudden adrenaline surge of first real contact was something that no amount of rehearsal could have prepared him for. All fight, no flight.

Rosie's body shuddered and buckled and there was an immediate flow of blood from her mouth and nose. As she staggered backwards, her legs gave way beneath her and there was a sickening thud as her head hit the back of the nearest chair. She was unconscious before she hit the floor.

Alex

Alex had only been sitting on the sofa for a few minutes when his mobile rang. The nature documentary he was watching had barely got started. He picked his phone up and looked at the call display. His expression brightened for the first time since he had got home from work.

'Evening, Pip!' he said expectantly.

'Are you ready to save a life?' said the familiar female voice at the other end of the line.

Inspector Philippa Williams, known as Pip by friends and colleagues alike, was one of the Met's Hostage Negotiator Co-ordinators, and she had a habit of starting every call-out in exactly the same way. Her words had a way of focusing the mind. No time wasted with 'hello', or 'how are you', or 'I hope I'm not interrupting', just straight to the point – the only point that really mattered in moments like these. She and Alex had known one another for a long time and got on incredibly well. They'd been on the same national Hostage Negotiators' training course seven years earlier and had been deployed together on any number of occasions.

'Of course. What have you got?' Alex had already got up and walked out into the hallway. He was stooping down to his rucksack to grab a pen and something to write on when he experienced a sudden and unfamiliar jolt of apprehension. It caught him by surprise, but he brushed it off as he walked back into the sitting room, biro and notebook in hand.

'I need you up in North London. We've got a man on the roof of a block of flats, threatening to jump.' Pip spoke rapidly – accuracy, brevity and speed being three communication essentials that police officers are taught right from the earliest days of their careers. 'Locals are on scene, trying to engage with him. I've got two other negotiators on the way. I'll follow on as soon as I can.' She gave him the address and the call reference number. He tilted his head to one side, wedging his phone between his shoulder and his ear, while he wrote the details down. 'You'll need to get a fast car run,' Pip said.

'No problem,' he replied. 'I'll see you there.'

Alex hung up as Kathy appeared at the door. She looked at him with eyebrows raised.

'North London. Man on a roof, threatening to jump,' he said.

'That's you gone for the rest of the evening then,' she said without much feeling. But Alex's mind was already elsewhere, suddenly relieved of the burdens and complexities of his fracturing domestic life.

He slipped very quickly and naturally back into the old routine. Scrolling through the numbers stored in his phone, he selected the direct line for the Chief Inspector in the Met's main control room. Having got straight through, he introduced himself as one of the on-call negotiating team and requested a traffic car for the ride north.

'They'll need to pick me up at the bottom of my road – at the junction with Clapham High Street,' he said. He always tried to avoid blue lights immediately outside his own front door if at all possible.

'No problem,' the Chief Inspector replied. 'The closest car to you is probably about twenty-five minutes away though. They've been dealing with a fatal on the M3.'

Alex ended the call and texted Pip to update her before going upstairs to change into a set of warm, comfortable clothes. As he did so, his thoughts turned specifically to the stranger on the roof, and he asked himself the same set of questions that he always did in situations such as this one. Who was the man? What was his name? Why was he up there? And, perhaps most importantly of all, what was his story?

Alex understood that there is always a story – that everyone has a tale to tell. Allow a person the space to tell theirs and you might just be able to persuade them to come down from the roof. Or to relinquish the weapon they're holding. Or to step back from the window ledge. Alex knew better than most that listening to a person's story is the key to understanding who they are and how they have ended up where they are. During his many years of negotiating, it had been the key to resolving any number of difficult and dangerous situations. He also knew that these things almost always take time. Negotiation demands endless patience. You need to build empathy. You need to develop rapport. You need to establish trust. None of those things happens in a hurry, but they represent the only way. Alex Lewis understood that. He understood that listening saves lives.

He double-checked the contents of his rucksack: extra layers, waterproofs, a pencil case full of biros and marker pens, several packets of yellow Post-it notes and a small digital dictaphone with accompanying earpiece and spare batteries – the simple tools of his trade.

His phone rang again. The traffic car would be with him in fifteen minutes.

Lee

Rahel screamed as Rosie fell. The little congregation huddled frantically together.

'Shut the fuck up!' yelled Connor, pointing the gun directly at Rahel and then in a slow arc at each of his prisoners. 'Absolute fucking silence, all of you!' If he was at all unsettled by what he had done to Rosie, he didn't let it show. He made no attempt to check her condition or to offer her any kind of assistance. Rather, he stood in the middle of the carpet, staring at her crumpled form, allowing the sense of abject terror to tighten its already ferocious grip on everyone in the hall.

Most of the hostages were reacting to the horror of the situation in broadly similar ways. They were cowering in their seats, huddled close together, limbs drawn in, heads bowed, eyes screwed tight shut. Paralysed and suffocated by deadly fear.

The only exception was Jack.

Connor could sense movement at the edge of his peripheral vision. He turned his head a fraction and saw that Jack was physically shaking in his chair. His face was panic-ridden, his eyes were wild and he was hunched forwards with his gaze fixed on the front of the building.

'Nobody move,' instructed Connor, but Jack seemed oblivious to the command. He was reaching blindly behind him in an apparent attempt to take hold of Helen's hand. But her eyes were closed and she didn't respond. 'Nobody fucking move,' Connor shouted.

Jack bolted towards the main doors.

19.37 hrs

Lee

Connor didn't panic. In fact, he felt strangely calm. He felt in complete control of the situation. Taking three swift paces to his left, he had time to set himself before throwing his left arm out like a clothes line, immediately in front of Jack's face. It was the sort of move you might see in one of those hyped-up American wrestling shows, except that this one was very much for real. Jack's chin and Connor's forearm collided with such force that Jack was knocked clean off his feet. He landed heavily on his back, the wind driven out of him. It was Helen's turn to scream.

Before Jack could even think about moving, Connor was on top of him, kneeling on his chest, left hand around his throat, his fingers digging into Jack's windpipe. The Baikal pistol remained in Connor's other hand and he pressed the barrel firmly into the side of Jack's face. 'That was a very fucking stupid thing to do, wasn't it?' he hissed, as Jack struggled to breathe. Connor let go of his throat and grabbed his face instead. Jerking it to one side, he forced Jack to look directly at the still-unconscious Rosie. 'Do you want to end up like her?' Connor threatened. 'Is that what you fucking want?' Jack's only response was to gasp for air. Any shred of fight or resistance

54

had drained straight out of him the moment he had landed on the carpet and acquiescence was all that remained. Sensing Jack's full compliance, Connor looked up at the rest of the group. 'Anyone else want to try anything stupid?' he sneered. Nobody twitched a muscle. None of them said a word. The only sound in the room came from Helen, who was trying to stifle her tears.

Connor stood up, grabbing Jack by the front of his shirt and dragging him to his feet. He propelled him forcefully backwards into his chair.

'All of you, stay exactly where you are,' Connor instructed, stepping back so he could see the whole group in front of him.

Keeping his eyes and gun trained on them, he crouched down, reaching for his bag with his left hand and feeling for the zip. He managed to open it at the third or fourth attempt and, after rummaging inside it for a few moments, he pulled out one of the packets of cable ties.

'Nobody move,' he reiterated, 'except you.' He pointed the Baikal directly at Grace and threw the packet at her. It hit her in the face, causing her to jerk backwards, and fell into her lap. She stared at Connor. The expression on her face was a mixture of shock and distress. He returned her gaze with a look of undisguised hatred. *Fucking immigrants*, he thought to himself. 'Tie everyone to their chairs,' he ordered her. 'Both ankles, both wrists.'

At first, Grace didn't move. She didn't actually seem able to move.

'Now,' demanded Connor, his voice rising in volume.

A clearly terrified Grace complied with the instruction, turning first to Jean and then to each of the others, securing their ankles to the front legs of the chairs, strapping their wrists to either side of the backrests.

Connor looked down at Rosie. She was still out cold. He hadn't reckoned on that happening, but it couldn't be helped. Every conflict had its casualties. And it meant that he had one less person to worry about for the time being. He checked over his shoulder. No one at the front doors.

As soon as Grace had completed her task, he shoved her into her seat and tied her up like the others. All of them bar the priest were now secure in their chairs.

Grace

Every part of Grace's body was thudding with tension and terror. She stared in horrified disbelief at the stricken form of her friend, motionless on the carpet no more than six or seven feet away from where she was sitting. The shallow, laboured rise and fall of Rosie's chest offered the only evidence that she was still alive. Grace willed her to keep on breathing. To keep on living. *Don't die, beautiful Rosie. Please don't die.* Her prayers were silent, but they filled the whole of Grace's being. Somewhere deep inside her, she was experiencing a sense of foreboding that had started in the knots of her stomach and was now spreading upwards, through the tightening of her lungs, into the very centre of her brain. Dread experienced as physical pain. *Please, please don't die.*

But it wasn't just Rosie.

Grace looked across at Alan and Jean and could see that both were weeping. Jean was leaning towards her husband, as though she was trying to rest her head on his shoulder. He was doing his best to respond, but there was no way of getting close enough. Grace saw the pained expression on his face and remembered the two white tablets lying in the palm of his hand. *His heart*. Her own heart threatened to stop at the thought.

But it wasn't just Alan.

Grace looked at Jack and Helen. Helen was staring straight ahead, her eyes glassy, her forehead prickled with sweat. Jack was a picture of rigid desperation, teeth clenched, skin almost purple in colour. How could he have done something so utterly stupid? How could he have put everyone in the hall in even more danger by trying to escape? But the questions stalled in Grace's mind before she could even think about answering them, because her eyes had already moved on to Mariam, who had escaped from one kind of living hell, only to be plunged into another. The excruciating unfairness of it all. What on earth must she be thinking? What must her poor children be thinking?

But it wasn't just the nine prisoners in the hall.

The moment Grace thought of Rahel and Ittack, she thought inevitably of Isaiah as well. Images of her son flooded her imagination, causing her to gasp out loud. As a rapidly rising wave of pain and panic threatened to sweep her away, she reached instinctively for the only thing available to her. She started to pray.

'The Lord is my Shepherd . . .' she began, falteringly. Her lips were moving in time with the words, though there was no sound coming from them. '. . . *Even though I walk through the valley of the shadow of death, I will not be afraid* . . .' She repeated those last five words over and over again: '*I will not be afraid* . . . *I will not be afraid* . . . *I will not be afraid.*' It was both a prayer and a plea, a silent statement of determination and desperation.

Rosie moaned and stirred for a moment. Her head rolled slowly over to one side, affording Grace a clear view of her face and causing her to gasp out loud for the second time in as many minutes. Rosie's eyes were open a fraction, but only the whites were visible. Her nose was horribly misshapen and, though Grace was no expert in these things, it looked to her as though Rosie's jaw might be broken too. The blood that was smeared across her face had already begun to congeal and there was an ugly welt on the side of her forehead where she had hit the chair on the way down.

As she was still trying to take in the full horror of it all, Grace noticed Connor move towards Rosie. Tucking his gun into the front of his trousers, he crouched down behind her head, grabbed hold of her, one hand beneath each of her armpits, and began to pull her across the floor towards the rest of the group. A cry of pain gurgled from the back of her throat.

'No! Don't! Please don't!' Grace cried out, unable to stop herself.

Connor ignored her.

'Please . . . You're going to kill her!'

Connor stopped and let Rosie's body fall back onto the floor. She groaned again, a gut-deep expression of agony and distress. Several of the group looked away. It was far too much for them. Connor walked slowly towards Grace. He pushed the barrel of the gun so hard against her cheek that it formed an indentation in the surface of her skin.

'I thought I told you to be quiet, bitch.' There was particular venom in his use of the word 'bitch'.

Grace bit hard on her lip, terrified for her friend, terrified for herself, terrified for them all. *I will not be afraid. I will not be afraid . . .*

Lee

Connor turned his attention back to the priest. He hauled her up into a seated position on one of the chairs. She continued to moan with every movement. Her head lolled to one side and a fresh trickle of blood ran down her chin and began to soak into the cotton of her pale blue shirt. Connor ignored her injuries as he trussed her up in the same way as all the others.

With each of his prisoners now secure, he took a moment to survey the scene in front of him. He looked from one prisoner to the next and, as his eyes settled on Mariam, his gaze hardened. He walked forwards and stopped in front of her. He could almost smell her fear. He could certainly feel it. Without saying a word, he coughed up a large ball of phlegm and spat it in her face. He watched as it treacled down her face, then he bent forwards and leaned in close, until his mouth was right next to her ear.

'Fucking immigrant,' he whispered, just loud enough for Grace to hear him. Mariam's shoulders were heaving, as she tried to conceal her sobs from her children.

Connor straightened back up, turned round and wandered back to the centre of the room. Removing his phone from his pocket, he took a photograph of the whole petrified group. Then he took a second one of Rosie in grisly close-up. He re-opened his Twitter thread and posted both images along with a new message:

Are you paying attention yet?
This shit is getting serious.
#HomeFrontLiberator

***

In the Central London newsroom, the young reporter shouted out to his supervisor, 'Laura, you need to come and see this.' And, when she was initially slow to respond, 'Now!'

His colleagues began to gather around his desk, a succession of alarmed expressions on their faces.

19.49 hrs

'Don't respond to it. You need to call the police first.'

The reaction in the newsroom was immediate and emphatic. The young journalist picked up the phone, while several of his colleagues hurried to get the Home Front Liberator Twitter account up on their screens. Who was he? Where was he? What did he want? More urgently, who were those poor people in the picture, particularly the priest who appeared to be soaked in her own blood?

Lee

Rosie was in a dreadful state, but Connor paid her no heed. He was concentrating. He took his jacket off and hung it on the back of an empty chair. He produced the knife from the back of his trousers and placed it on the floor alongside the pistol, making sure that the hostages could see both weapons. Then, working in complete silence, he began to unpack the contents of his kitbag. He picked up the padlock and chain and walked unhurriedly towards the back of the hall. He was making a conscious effort to slow himself down – his breathing, his pulse, his actions. He was thinking through everything he'd rehearsed in the previous few weeks and recalling in detail the advice he'd picked up in various encrypted online chatrooms. He was making absolutely certain he didn't miss anything, that he didn't leave anything to chance.

He opened the door that led through to the kitchen and went straight to the double fire doors in the rear right corner of the building. Wrapping the chain several times around the two push bars, he attached the two ends to the lock. Then he walked to the front of the hall to reassure himself that the front doors were still secure. He was far too preoccupied to pay any attention to the voices that had begun to murmur again at the fringes of his mind.

He looked back at his phone. No responses yet, though he saw that he had gained a number of followers. *Good*, he nodded to himself, perhaps people were starting to pay attention. He reposted his thread, this time tagging the Metropolitan Police. 'Time for you to do exactly as you are told,' he typed.

***

The call from the newsroom went through to the police control room at Hendon in North London. The call handler immediately notified her supervisor, who in turn informed the Chief Inspector in charge. The senior officer reviewed the initial text of the call, logged onto Twitter and recognised straight away that he had something serious. But, as with the journalists, he had nothing more than the photographs to go on. No location. No identification. No confirmation of whether the pictures were current or historic. Nonetheless, he picked up the phone and dialled the number for the On-Call Commander who that week happened to be the officer in charge of SO15, the Anti-Terrorist Branch. The Commander readily agreed with the Chief

Inspector's initial assessment and told the junior man he would make some calls before driving back into town from his home in Hertfordshire.

Lee

Connor continued with the steady, meticulous execution of his plans. He unrolled and separated each of the bin bags and then walked to the front of the hall carrying a handful of them, together with a couple of rolls of gaffer tape. He covered and sealed each of the glass panels in the front doors and did the same to the windows on either side. Once that was done, he turned his attention to the series of windows that ran along each side of the hall and then to the kitchen windows and the fire doors. Even the frosted glass in the toilets was covered over. He had no problem with people knowing he was inside – in fact, he positively wanted them to know – but he didn't want them to be able to see what was happening at any given moment in time. He wanted to remain in complete control of who saw what, who knew what, and when.

Once every window and door had been blocked out, he turned his attention back to his prisoners. Without a word, he dragged each chair and its occupant to a separate part of the hall and turned them so they were facing the wall and away from one another. His intention was to deny them even the limited reassurance that close proximity and routine eye contact afforded and, in that, he succeeded. The sound of frightened sobs could be heard from several points around the room.

He retrieved his phone charger and plugged it into the wall, then he picked up a bottle of water and twisted the cap off. He walked round to each individual, feigning to offer them a sip, before smirking and tipping some of it into their laps. Asserting control. Commanding acquiescence. Then he tore off and placed a strip of gaffer tape over each of their mouths – even Rosie, whose whole body spasmed in pain as pressure was applied to her broken face.

Grace

He came to Grace last of all. As he approached her, she summoned up every ounce of her courage and spoke to him.

'My friend needs an ambulance,' she said.

He ignored her and tore off a fresh piece of gaffer.

'She needs help urgently!' Grace cried out, knowing that she was risking a beating of her own. But that was nothing compared to the very real possibility that Rosie was going to die.

Connor taped her mouth shut.

Lee

Connor stepped back into the centre of the room and addressed his prisoners. His voice was proud and defiant.

'My name is Lee James Connor and I am the Home Front Liberator. I am a freedom fighter and you are all prisoners of war.' He announced this with a broad sweep of his left arm. Then he raised his gun in the air with his right hand. 'The time has come to end, once and for all, the unchecked invasion of my country – the great replacement that has been destroying my homeland for decades. It is time to make Britain great again.'

Rosie was in no state to follow what he was saying. Five of the remaining hostages understood the words he was using, if not their full meaning. All of them were petrified.

20.07 hrs

Grace

'Where's your phone?'

Grace was straining to look over her shoulder, just able to see the back of Rosie's head. It was tilted forwards and to one side and she couldn't tell whether she was conscious or not. She certainly wasn't moving. Grace felt a surge of renewed desperation for her friend, matched in intensity only by a sense of utter helplessness. There was nothing she could do.

'Where's your phone?' Connor demanded for a second time.

This time, Grace realised he was speaking to her. She turned reluctantly away from Rosie and looked directly up at him, determined to hold his gaze. Unable to speak, she nodded her head in the direction of her tan shoulder bag lying on the carpet a few metres away from her. Connor walked over to it, bent down and emptied the contents onto the floor, scattering all that was precious and private across the carpet. Ignoring the rest of her belongings, he picked up her phone and placed it in his trouser pocket.

Crossing the room, he picked up three more bags – those belonging to Rosie, Jean and Helen – and emptied out their contents as well. He found their three phones and dropped them on the floor in the middle of the hall. Jack's mobile was in his right-hand trouser pocket. Alan's was in his jacket. Both men recoiled as Connor patted them down. Connor tossed their phones over in the direction of the first three he had recovered. He came to Mariam last. She shrank back when Connor approached her, but she made no sound. And it quickly became apparent that she didn't have a phone with her. Connor didn't bother with the children.

Satisfied that every device had been accounted for, Connor wandered over to the five that were lying on the floor. Then he stamped on them. He did so noisily and repeatedly, until he was certain that all were damaged beyond function or repair. Content with his efforts, he produced Grace's phone from his pocket and strode over towards her. Without warning, he ripped the strip of gaffer tape away from her mouth, causing her to cry out in pain.

'Code?'

Knowing she had no choice, she gave it to him. Her face was stinging. He punched the number in and stood immediately in front of her. He smelled of sweat and stale tobacco.

'Time to tell them what's going on in here,' he said.

'T-tell who?' she stammered; confused, afraid and uncertain of the part she was now supposed to play.

'The police.'

He dialled 999, touched the speaker icon and held the phone in front of her face. The call took longer to connect than either of them had anticipated, but, eventually, an operator asked which emergency service she would like.

'Police,' said Grace, her voice beginning to crack. And, as soon as she heard a second voice – that of the call handler in the Met control room – her words tumbled out in a tearful rush. 'Help us, please. We've been taken prisoner by a man with a gun. And a knife. My friend is badly hurt. I'm scared she's going to die. I—'

'Try to slow down for me.' The male voice at the other end of the line was steady and kind. 'What's your name?'

'My name is Grace.' Tears were running freely down her face. 'And I'm really frightened.'

'You sound frightened, Grace,' the voice replied calmly, 'but you're being incredibly brave. I'm going to get some help to you as quickly as I possibly can. Can you tell me where you are?'

Grace gave the name and address of the church hall.

'How many of you are there in the hall?' asked the call handler.

'There are nine of us.'

'And where's the man with the gun?' the voice enquired.

'He's standing right next to me holding the phone and he can hear everything we're saying.' Grace was speaking rapidly again, her voice rising in desperation.

At this point, Connor was content to let her do the talking. He wanted the police to know what was happening. He wanted them to hear the terrified voice of his hostage. He wanted them to understand the full horror of the situation. And he wanted them to recognise that he was in absolute control of it all.

'Is he holding the gun?' the voice asked.

'Yes, he is.'

'Are you hurt?'

'No, I'm OK,' she was trying her best to remain calm, 'but my friend is in a really bad way. She's not moving.'

'What's your friend's name, Grace?'

'Her name is Rosie,' said Grace. 'She's one of the vicars here at the church.'

'Do you know what her injuries are?' asked the voice.

'She's been hit in the face and she banged her head really hard when she fell over. She has blood coming from her mouth and her nose. I think she might have a broken jaw.' Grace looked across at Rosie. 'She's definitely unconscious. Please hurry . . . I don't want her to die!'

'We're going to get some help to her as quickly as we possibly can.' The voice continued to reassure her. 'You're doing so well, Grace. What else can you tell me?'

'We've all been tied up and he's locked all the doors and covered all the windows. I don't know who he is or what he wants.'

'Have you ever seen him before?'

'No. Never.'

Lee

Connor decided that he had heard enough. He snatched the phone away from Grace's ear and spoke directly to the police for the first time. His voice was characterised by the same lack of emotion that he had displayed earlier on.

'My name is Lee James Connor. I am the Home Front Liberator and I am in command here. Nobody does anything without my permission. If anyone so much as attempts to enter this building, I will kill every single person in here.'

With that, he cut the line dead and put Grace's phone into his pocket.

Alex

Alex heard the sirens before he saw the traffic car. As it pulled in at the kerb beside him, he produced his warrant card and held it out for inspection while simultaneously reaching for the rear nearside passenger door.

'Sorry for the wait, guv'nor.' The operator was speaking. 'It's been one of those days. Two different fatals on two different stretches of the motorway.'

'No need to apologise, I completely understand.' Alex was immediately at home in their company. 'Thanks for getting here at all.' He introduced himself properly to them and checked that they had the right location for the North London call. And with that, the driver put his foot down.

They were northbound on Vauxhall Bridge Road, approaching Victoria Station, when Alex's phone buzzed in his pocket. It was Pip again.

'Any update?' he asked, raising his voice above the noise of the sirens.

'I need you to divert, Alex. The other two have got North London covered. I need you to head back south – much closer to home.'

There was an uncharacteristic note of tension in her voice. Alex picked it up straight away. He gestured urgently to his driver to switch off the blues and twos and to pull over at the side of the road. Once they were stationary, the two traffic officers turned in their seats and looked at him in anticipation of further instructions.

'What is it?' Alex asked her.

'Only limited details at this stage, but it looks as though we might have a full-blown terrorist incident.'

Alex tensed. Pip passed on the limited details that she had and gave him the call reference number.

'Call me the moment you get there. I'm on my way, but I'm at least half an hour behind you.'

Mind racing, Alex looked up at the two PCs in the front of the car. 'Get us assigned to CAD 9787 and then get us there as fast as this car will take us.' He gave them a rapid summary of what little he knew, as the operator called up on the traffic channel and got them assigned. The driver flicked the lights and sirens back on and spun the car round. As they hurtled back across the river, the operator switched the car's radio over to the dedicated channel that had been set aside for the escalating incident.

It sounded like chaos.

Lee

Connor retrieved his mobile from its charger and walked back to the middle of the room. He turned the phone's camera on, switching it to video and selfie modes. Holding the device at arm's length, he gave the speech he had been rehearsing for several weeks:

'My name is Lee James Connor. I am the Home Front Liberator and I am here to tell you that it is time to make Britain great again! For far too long we have given power and territory to invaders – to immigrant terrorists and rapists and child abusers who have no legitimate place among us. We find ourselves on the brink of a catastrophic white genocide and it is time to take back control. We must secure the existence of our people and a future for white children.'

He held up his gun for the camera to see.

'This is now an armed struggle, and it is one I am prepared to die for.' He paused for effect, before continuing. 'I demand the immediate release from custody of Nicholas Farmer, being held unlawfully in Pentonville as a prisoner of conscience. Nicholas Farmer is a hero and a patriot, guilty of nothing more than an unwavering love for his country. If this demand is not met, every single person in this hall will be killed.'

He switched the camera lens round and walked towards the closest prisoner. Ittack was wide-eyed with terror, his cheeks flushed and smudged with tears as Connor held the gun to the side of his head and flicked the safety off.

Connor repeated the same chilling threat with each of them in turn, showing their faces in brief close-up. He saved Rosie till last. He lifted her chin using the barrel of the pistol and allowed the camera to linger on her half-closed eyes and her hideous injuries. 'It is time to make Britain great again,' he shouted.

He turned the camera off and reviewed the footage. Satisfied with his work and telling himself that Nicholas Farmer would surely approve, he posted the film to his Twitter thread. And, within minutes, it was viral. In radio and television studios the length and breadth of the country, live programmes were interrupted as the bright red 'BREAKING NEWS' ticker tape began to scroll across hundreds of thousands of screens.

20.30 hrs

Grace

Grace watched as a clearly preoccupied Connor paced back and forth on the carpet. He appeared to be listening for something, his eyes narrow and his head angled to one side as he criss-crossed the space in the middle of the room. He came to a standstill the moment he heard the sirens. Grace could hear them too. They were distant to begin with, but drawing closer all the time.

'What happens now?' Grace ventured nervously.

'We wait.' Connor glared at her, picked up the roll of gaffer tape, tore off a fresh strip and silenced her again.

Grace couldn't be certain, but she wondered whether she had picked up a faint hint of uncertainty – it might even have been anxiety – in his voice.

Alex

The traffic car hit speeds of more than ninety miles per hour as it weaved through the evening traffic, past the Oval cricket ground, down Camberwell New Road, before turning right onto Denmark Hill. Alex and his colleagues listened intently to the urgent and insistent stream of radio traffic: rendezvous points

– RVPs – being set up, cordons going in, an initial command structure being established, Trojan armed response vehicles being assigned, India 99 – the call sign for the police helicopter – lifting off from its suburban base at Lippitts Hill. None of them spoke for a while, but each of them was becoming acutely aware of the potential scale and significance of the situation they were now heading into.

In the midst of all the noise, Alex tried to focus his thoughts on the task immediately in front of him. He would be at the scene in a matter of moments. His adrenaline was surging and yet he also sensed a kind of stillness and clarity of thought that is perhaps only to be found in the very centre of a storm. In all likelihood, he would soon be talking to an armed terrorist and, in all his years as a skilled and experienced negotiator, that was something he had never done before.

He asked himself a series of practical questions: where would he set up the negotiation cell? What phone line was he going to use? What number was he going to dial? Who would pick up at the other end? What were his opening words going to be? What kind of condition were the hostages in? How were he and his colleagues going to ensure that every single one of them got out alive? Most pressingly of all, how was he – how was anyone – going to find a way to engage with an extremist?

They diverted off Denmark Hill to avoid driving straight past the front of the church hall. A rapid succession of backstreets later, as they were on the final approach to the RVP at the bottom of Herne Hill, Alex broke the silence.

'Kill the sirens, but get me as close as you can. I need to find the person in charge of all this.'

Lee

Inside the hall, Connor was pacing again. He had just posted another photo of himself, this time holding one of the knives to Helen's throat, and the text of the accompanying message had repeated his earlier warning: 'If anyone tries to get into this building, every single person in here will die.'

The number of his social media followers and interactions was growing exponentially: any number of people trying to reason with him, a small minority of anonymous far-right fanatics bellowing support for him, and a vast mass of online rubberneckers watching on in silent, morbid fascination, waiting to see what happened next. Connor tried not to be distracted by any of them, reminding himself constantly that, so far, everything was going more or less according to plan. The sound of so many sirens might have been disconcerting, but it was also precisely what he had been expecting. He was ready.

He also needed a smoke.

Grace

Grace stared nervously at Connor and found herself asking how any human being could possibly do a thing like this. Something so monstrous. But she realised straight away that it was a pointless question. Even if there had been some sort of an answer to it, it would surely be beyond any form of rational comprehension or explanation. And, in any case, the condition of her fellow hostages was a much more immediate and pressing concern. As best she could, she scanned the room, craning her neck to look left and right.

Alan and Jean were first in view. They looked utterly defeated. They appeared to have given up on their futile attempts to make physical contact with one another and their chins were resting on their chests in an act of unwitting symmetry. Perhaps that's the sort of thing that happens when you've spent more than half a lifetime with someone you love – you do the same things at the same time, without even realising you're doing them. But Grace had no time to dwell on the thought because she was far more concerned about Alan's heart. She remembered the pills again. She was fairly sure she'd seen him swallow them with a mouthful of tea, but she couldn't be absolutely certain. And she had no idea if and when he would need to take another dose. She studied him closely, searching for any sign of physical distress, but was unable to detect anything. Not yet, anyway.

Jack and Helen were similarly silent. Mariam and her children too. Which just left Rosie. Grace pictured Rosie's smiling face; she thought about her easy demeanour, her enthusiasm for life and her willingness to help absolutely anyone with absolutely anything. *'Hello, friend'* was how she had greeted the man now holding them hostage when he first entered the hall. The man who was responsible for the desperate state she was now in.

'Even though I walk through the valley of the shadow of death, I will not be afraid,' Grace repeated to herself, feeling terrified once more.

Alex

As the traffic car pulled up at the bottom of Herne Hill, Alex counted more than a dozen other police vehicles already on the scene, with more arriving all the time. Ambulances and fire appliances too. It was an undeniably impressive sight, with every pane of glass in the neighbourhood reflecting a sea of pulsing blue lights. PCs were hurrying to fix cordon tape to lamp posts, while their colleagues were redirecting traffic and attempting to herd pedestrians to relative safety. Already, a significant crowd was gathering. Everywhere Alex looked, people had their phones out, filming. First- and second-floor windows were filled with faces as people stared and took pictures. #HerneHill was one of a number of hashtags that had already started to trend on social media.

'Thanks for the ride, lads,' said Alex, 'I'd better go and find the Incident Commander.'

He grabbed his rucksack, scrambled out of the back of the car and, without a backward glance, ran the last fifty yards to the inner cordon. He produced his warrant card, ducking under the blue and white tape as he did so, and spoke to the PC standing closest to him. 'Where's the Duty Officer?' he asked.

'She's over there, guv,' responded the PC, gesturing across the road to a female officer standing beside one of the marked police vehicles, deep in conversation with two other uniformed inspectors. The man to her left was dressed in full riot gear, suggesting that he was probably from the TSG – the Met's Territorial Support Group. And the telltale Glock carried by the second officer identified him as 'Trojan 1', the officer in charge of the ARVs – Armed Response Vehicles – that were continuing to pull up at the scene.

'Alex Lewis. I'm your negotiator,' Alex said, showing his warrant card again and shaking the hands of each of them in turn. Though he didn't know any of them, he was immediately conscious of – and grateful for – the unique sense of camaraderie to be found amongst police officers in situations such as this.

'Steph Johnson,' the female inspector replied, before introducing the other two. 'The Chief Superintendent is on his way, but I'm your Incident Commander for now.'

'So what have we got?' asked Alex.

Inspector Johnson was succinct and to the point.

'Church hall, halfway up the hill on the right-hand side – it's about five hundred yards from here,' she said, pointing in the direction of the nearest junction. 'Armed suspect – he appears to have a handgun and knives – has taken multiple hostages at the location. We believe he's acting alone inside the venue, but have no definitive confirmation of that. And there's no evidence at this stage to suggest he has any accomplices on the street outside. From photos the suspect himself has posted on social media, we've counted nine hostages, one of whom appears to be seriously injured. He's demanding the release of Nicholas Farmer, the Nazi sympathiser who was remanded for sentencing at the Old Bailey earlier today.' Alex recognised Farmer's name and was able to picture his face as the inspector continued to speak. 'Our suspect is threatening to kill everyone in the hall if his demand isn't met.'

'Have you attempted to make any contact with him yet?' asked Alex.

'No, we were waiting for you,' she replied.

'Good,' Alex responded. 'So what's the plan?'

'For now, the same one as always,' she said. 'Contain and negotiate.' She nodded towards Trojan 1 as she continued, 'The ARVs have got an initial armed containment on the building. Access to the rear is tricky, but we've been able to get into two of the houses that have gardens backing onto it. I think we've now got eyes on every door and window.' She looked to Trojan 1 for confirmation and he nodded. 'And the call has already gone through for Specialist Firearms Officers to mobilise and deploy.'

The Incident Commander maintained the rapid pace of her briefing. 'Traffic and the TSG have been helping local officers put cordons in at the top of the hill and at every junction between there and here. We're currently knocking on doors, telling people to stay inside and away from their windows. There are too many of them and not enough of us for a full evacuation at this stage.' She paused, before adding as an afterthought, 'The press have started to gather too. I've got a couple of officers keeping them in check at one of the cordons, but we're not taking any questions. To be honest, I think they know as much as we do.'

The three inspectors looked at Alex. He was senior to them in rank but, in his specialist role as a negotiator, was there to take instructions from them. They all understood this, but, in that moment, they were deferring to a man who, in almost any other situation, would have been their boss. Alex was quick to offer his reassurance.

'It sounds to me as though you've got everything under control,' he said.

'I've never dealt with anything like this before,' Steph Johnson confessed to him.

'I don't think any of us has,' Alex replied, a grim expression on his face. 'But it's going to work out just fine. There's only one of him and there will soon be hundreds of us.' He managed to sound more optimistic than he was actually feeling. 'Now, I need to put in a call to one of my colleagues – there should be a whole team of negotiators on the way by now. As soon as I've done that, I'll find the right place to base the negotiation cell.'

20.53 hrs

Lee

Lee Connor was waiting for the police to make contact. He reached into his bag and retrieved some of the skunk and the packet of Rizlas. He started to roll a joint. Though he wasn't letting it show, he was feeling nervous and edgy and having a smoke would help to calm him down.

He had noticed that there was a sprinkler system fitted to the ceiling and he didn't want to risk setting it off, so he walked through to the kitchen. The open serving hatch between the kitchen and hall allowed him to keep everyone in view. He wandered over to the oven and turned on the extractor hood that was fixed to the wall immediately above it. Then he took out the Zippo and lit the joint. As he exhaled, he blew the smoke up into the whirring fan.

Alex

Pip Williams picked up the moment Alex's call connected. He was standing in the middle of the junction at the bottom of Herne Hill, a maelstrom of activity all around him. Local uniformed officers were running in every direction, shouting instructions to one another and at any members of the public venturing out of their front doors or otherwise straying into places they shouldn't have been. Armed officers were unloading kit from the backs of their liveried BMW X5s. All the while, the crowds of fascinated onlookers were swelling.

'I'm still about ten minutes away,' she said, 'what's the latest?' In the background, Alex could hear the sirens of the vehicle she was travelling in.

He filled her in on the details of his briefing with the three inspectors. 'They're doing a good job, Pip,' he began, 'as good as they possibly could be, given the circumstances. But this is big and it's going to get much, much bigger.' More emergency services vehicles were pulling up even as he spoke.

'What's the plan?' she asked, though she already knew what the answer would be.

'Contain and negotiate,' he confirmed.

'OK,' she said. 'I've got other negotiators on the way, though it will just be you and me for the next little while. Can you get the cell up and running by the time I arrive?'

'I hope so,' he responded. 'I just need to find a friendly local resident who doesn't mind lending us their front room.'

Grace

Grace had her back to the kitchen and, for the time being, she couldn't see Connor. But she could see Rosie, and she noticed that her friend seemed to be moving slightly: small twitches in her shoulders and torso; tiny movements in the fingers of her left hand. But she had no idea whether these were signs that Rosie was rallying, or evidence that her condition was worsening. She wanted to reach out to her, to hold her hand, to talk to her, to dress her wounds, but there was nothing she could do. She remained utterly powerless. And she lurched between prayer and fear, fear and prayer.

Alex

Alex hurried up the lower part of Herne Hill and knocked on the door of the first house on the left. There was no answer. As he stepped back onto the street, he glanced up the road and could see the steeple of a church, about two hundred yards ahead of him. He assumed it must be close to the hall. What the hell was happening in there?

The second door he knocked on was opened by a man about the same age as him, dressed in suit trousers and a tie-less shirt, the leftovers of that day's work attire. Alex produced his warrant card and introduced himself.

'Your colleagues have already been round,' the man said. 'They told us to stay inside.'

'Yes, that's the right thing to do,' said Alex. 'Is it just you here?'

'Me and my partner,' the man replied.

'I need to ask you a large favour,' said Alex. 'Could I use your front room?'

The man looked confused for a moment. 'What for?' he asked.

'I need a base for me and a small handful of my colleagues. I promise you we won't make a mess and that we'll keep out of your way.'

The man still didn't understand, but he didn't hesitate. 'Of course, officer, of course,' he said, 'whatever you need.'

He led Alex into the hallway and showed him through the first door on the left.

'Will this do?'

Alex looked round the room. There was a sizeable three-seater sofa occupying most of one wall, together with two large armchairs. The coffee table in the middle of the room matched the sofa in length and the broad bay window offered a direct view out onto the street.

'It's perfect,' Alex responded. 'I'll take it.'

'Can I get you something to drink?' the man asked, fumbling awkwardly for the right thing to say, given the circumstances.

'I'm all right at the moment,' Alex replied, 'but I suspect that a cuppa for me and my colleagues later on would be very welcome.'

'OK.' The man hesitated, before venturing to ask the question that everyone else in the neighbourhood wanted an answer to. 'Er, are you able to tell me what's actually going on out there?'

'That's just what I'm in the process of finding out,' Alex said as he opened his rucksack. 'The next person to knock on the door will probably be a female colleague of mine. Her name is Philippa Williams. Would you mind showing her straight in?'

The man nodded and recognised the none-too-subtle hint to leave a preoccupied police officer in peace. His partner – a slightly older man, dressed more casually – had appeared in the doorway and the two of them retreated to the kitchen, doubtless to wonder at this latest extraordinary turn of events.

Lee

Connor finished his joint, stubbed it out against the tiled wall behind the oven, switched off the extractor fan and walked back into the main hall. The police still hadn't made contact with him and the longer the delay went on, the more anxious he was feeling. It was one of those parts of the plan that he didn't have complete control over – he recognised that they would call when they were ready and not before – and, consequently, one of the parts he felt least comfortable with. It was a situation made worse by the fact that the voices were whispering to him again. He couldn't tell where they were coming from, or what they were saying, but the fact they were there was enough to keep him on edge. Even as he was telling himself to be patient, he was restless to get on. He pulled his mobile out and addressed his next tweet directly to the main Met account. 'Ready when you are,' he typed.

As he put his phone back in his trouser pocket, he noticed that the priest was stirring in her chair. At first sight, her movements were slow and awkward, but, as he looked more closely, they morphed into something else. The change, when it came, was sudden and swift. Within seconds, she appeared to be having some sort of fit. Instinctively, he strode across the room towards her. As he rounded the front of her chair, he could see that her eyes were bulging and that she seemed to be on the verge of choking. Without pausing to think about what he was doing, he reached forwards and tore the strip of tape away from her mouth. Rosie screamed in agony and promptly vomited over herself and onto the floor in front of her. A grim, multicoloured mixture of blood and vomit speckled the toecaps of Connor's boots as Rosie's head slumped to one side. Connor had stepped away rapidly as soon as he had realised she was being sick and the expression now on his face was one of both revulsion and confusion.

'What the fuck?' he exclaimed. He made no attempt to offer Rosie any help.

He could feel everyone in the room turning and staring at Rosie and him. Out of the corner of his eye, he could see Grace straining against the cable ties that were holding her in place, apparently desperate to get to her friend. But he ignored them all. Grumbling wordlessly to himself, he picked up a jumper that Jack had left on the floor and used it to wipe his boots clean.

Rosie was gasping for breath between howls of pain and distress, while Connor was feeling momentarily uncertain about what he should do next. He looked around the room, his eyes flicking constantly from one person to the next, as he tried to focus his thoughts. It wasn't the plight of the priest that was bothering him – he couldn't have cared less about her – it was the possible impact of her immediate condition on the next stages of his plan.

Because the plan was everything to him. He had been preparing it for weeks. He had imagined it and rehearsed it and sticking to it now was the only thing that mattered to him. Except that none of the scenarios he had been preparing for involved a hostage being so seriously injured at this very early stage in proceedings. The real violence was supposed to come later, and only then if his demands weren't met. Nobody was supposed to die this early in proceedings. And there was no avoiding the fact that Rosie was in a very bad way – certainly a whole lot worse than he had intended. And the sudden deterioration in her condition had tipped him momentarily off balance. He tried to concentrate, working silently and rapidly through his options.

He expected the police to call him at any moment, at which point he would renew his demand for the release of Nicholas Farmer. And he wanted to be playing his strongest possible hand when he did so. He didn't need the condition of the priest to be a distraction. He didn't want to give the police the opportunity to focus on her as a reason to delay or avoid other, much more pressing, topics of conversation.

And so he was forced to make a rapid decision. He wasn't entirely happy with it, but it was the best he could come up with on the spur of the moment. If he got one of the women – none of whom would be any match for him if things got physical – to look after the priest, he would be able to use the fact to shut down any police concerns as soon as they were raised.

He walked over to his bag, tucking the Baikal back into his belt as he did so. He bent down and picked up one of the butcher's knives before returning to Rosie and slicing through the cable ties that were holding her in place. Her strength had completely deserted her and, with a half-strangled cry, her body crumpled sideways. There was nothing and no one to break her fall and she landed on the carpet with a dull thud. Her head rolled over to one side and she lay there, silent and motionless. He thought about checking on her, but decided to leave her where she was, lying a few feet away from the puddle of foul-smelling blood and vomit that was soaking into the carpet.

Still holding the knife, he crossed the room and approached Grace, who hadn't taken her eyes off Rosie. He stood in front of her and waved the blade to and fro.

'The priest needs someone to look after her and I've got more important things to be doing.' He jabbed the knife in Rosie's direction. 'Think you can do that without causing any trouble?' Grace nodded, though it was apparent that she didn't fully understand what was being asked of her. 'But if you even think about playing up,' he added with renewed hostility, 'I will not hesitate to kill you.'

He made sure that last threat was loud enough for everyone in the room to hear. Grace nodded again.

For the second time, Connor ripped the strip of tape away from her mouth. For the second time, Grace cried out in pain. And, this time, several small trickles of blood ran into her mouth as a series of small lesions opened up along her top lip. Then he cut the cable ties holding her wrists and ankles. Her limbs were now free, but she stayed in her chair, clearly still unsure of what exactly he was asking of her and evidently terrified of making the wrong move.

'Get on with it,' he hissed, pointing towards Rosie.

She lurched across the room towards her friend.

Alex

Standing alone in the unfamiliar surroundings of a stranger's sitting room, Alex opened the BBC News app on his phone. He was looking for anything – names, faces, emerging details that hadn't filtered through to him yet – that might assist him in preparing for whatever lay ahead. He scanned the initial couple of paragraphs under the 'BREAKING NEWS' banner, but there was nothing helpful there, just the inevitable first flush of ill-informed speculation and ignorant armchair opinion. He turned his attention to Twitter and, for the first time, read the full series of messages posted on the Home Front Liberator account. When he saw the photograph of Rosie, he flinched and instantly looked away from the screen, both surprised and unsettled by his reaction. After all, he'd seen far, far worse in his time. In the preceding twenty years and more, he'd attended hundreds of crime scenes and seen more than enough blood and carnage to last a dozen lifetimes. But there was something about the picture of the wounded priest that got to him.

The film footage was even worse. He knew he needed to watch it, but, as he did so, he experienced an unfamiliar, crawling sense of unease. Uninvited questions started to nag at him: how was this one going to play out? How was he going to get the hostages out? How was this particular day going to end? In an instant, his mind had taken him back to another place. Back to East London. Back to Romford. And he recoiled at the remembered sound of gunshots.

He tried to compose himself. 'Get a grip, man,' he muttered out loud; not so loud that the owners of the house would have heard him, but loud enough for him to hear the sound of his own voice. He told himself that there was a job to be done, that there were lives to be saved and that he needed to step up and do his bit. He reminded himself that hostage negotiators are optimists by nature, and insisted that everything was going to be fine – that it almost always was and that there was no reason to think that it would be any different this time round.

The brief flurry of self-talk seemed to have the desired effect and he found that he was able once again to focus on the immediate task in hand. He reached into his bag for a pen and a fresh pad of yellow Post-it notes.

Grace

'I'm here, Rosie. It's me . . . Grace.'

Grace was kneeling on the carpet next to her friend, speaking quietly as she tried to work out what she should do. She felt horribly afraid; her lips and hands were quivering in unison. *Don't die, beautiful Rosie. Please don't die.* She had done some first-aid training at the school where she worked, but that had been a while ago and she had only ever been called upon to treat the occasional nosebleed or grazed knee. Nothing remotely like this.

She reached gingerly for Rosie's left wrist and tried to find her pulse. At first, she couldn't feel anything and this caused a surge of panic to flood through her. She adjusted her grip and, this time, she thought she could just detect the rhythm of Rosie's heart. She checked again and she was sure of it. It was faint, but it was there. She almost wept with relief as she offered a hurried prayer of thanks. She reached over and grabbed Helen's navy blue puffa jacket from the back of a nearby chair. She folded it and eased it gently under Rosie's head, catching her breath as Rosie groaned in response. She was unconscious and clearly in unimaginable pain. The right side of her face was swollen and disfigured, her top lip was split wide open and Grace could see she was missing a couple of teeth. The remainder of her face and much of the top half of her body was soaked in drying blood and vomit, the smell of which was overpowering.

But she's still alive, Grace told herself.

She looked in Connor's direction. He was studying his phone, with no apparent interest in anyone or anything else. His spare hand rested on the handle of the pistol, still tucked into his waistband.

'I need to go to the kitchen and get the first-aid box.'

Grace was speaking to him. She didn't feel as brave as she was being, but the urgent and almost overwhelming sense of concern she felt for her friend seemed, for the moment at least, to override her fear. She was determined to do everything she possibly could for Rosie.

With a wave of his arm, Connor indicated that Grace could make her way to the back of the hall. She paused and picked up a coffee cup from the floor.

'What are you doing?' he growled, drawing the gun and pointing it at her.

'I need some water to clean her face with.'

He allowed her to keep the cup, but walked closely behind her, jabbing the barrel of the pistol into the small of her back as she moved towards the kitchen.

The first-aid box was in a cupboard next to the sink. Grace retrieved it, filled the cup with tap water and walked back into the hall.

All the while, the other hostages listened and waited, each of them alone with their terror.

Rosie lay still on the floor.

Alex

In the house a couple of hundred yards down the hill, Alex had started making notes. His mind was clear now and he was completely focused on what was in front of him. The surface of the coffee table was filling up with a succession of large yellow Post-it notes, each with a limited number of details written on it:

Hostage Taker:
Lee James Connor

Leader of Home Front:
Nicholas Farmer

Number of Hostages:
9

Hostage 1:
Believed to be Rosie Phillips – Vicar
Needs urgent medical attention

Hostage 2:
Grace?

Alongside this, there were seven other numbered Post-it notes, each awaiting a name.

Demands:
8.20 p.m. – Release of Nicholas Farmer

Alex paused when he heard the doorbell and the sound of footsteps hastening along the corridor. He heard Pip introducing herself to their host and, moments later, she appeared in the living-room doorway, accompanied by Steph Johnson, the Incident Commander whom Alex had spoken to earlier on.

Pip walked over to Alex and hugged him, all the while continuing a conversation with Steph. 'I think you've met Alex Lewis already,' she said, interrupting herself to make the introduction. The inspector nodded at Alex as Pip continued. 'The negotiation cell will be based in here and I'll be your point of contact for everything. I'll keep you updated with what's happening and, if you want anything from us, it will need to come through me. Once we get started, no one is to come into this room apart from me and the other members of the negotiating team.'

The inspector nodded. 'My boss will be arriving to take over any minute now,' she said. 'I'll make sure he's briefed.'

'Thank you,' said Pip. 'Now, are you happy for us to put the first call in?'

'I am,' the inspector replied.

21.04 hrs

Alex

Inspector Johnson headed back out onto the street and Pip sat down next to Alex.

'Hey, friend,' she said as she nudged him with her shoulder. 'How are you doing?' She was already leaning forward and absorbing the limited details on the Post-it notes.

'I'm good,' he replied. 'How about you?'

'I'm fine,' she replied distractedly. She finished reading and looked up from the coffee table. She turned in her seat to face him. 'Are you ready for this?' she asked.

'Ready as I'll ever be,' he replied. And he believed that he was. The latest kick of nerves and adrenaline was propelling him rapidly forwards. 'What else do we know about this Lee James Connor?' he asked.

'They've run a PNC check and found an old custody photo that looks to be a good match. He's got previous for drugs, but nothing for violence,' she replied.

'Have you seen his tattoos?' Alex asked, showing his colleague the half-naked selfie that Connor had posted. 'They obviously have some sort of specific meaning.'

Pip studied the image.

'I've worked some of them out, but not all of them,' Alex said.

93

'The numbers refer to letters of the alphabet,' said Pip.

'Those were the ones I recognised,' said Alex. '1 and 8. The first and eighth letters. A and H. "18" is Adolf Hitler and "88" is Heil Hitler. But what about the others?'

'I think I read somewhere that RAHOWA is shorthand for Racial Holy War,' Pip replied. 'I'm not a hundred per cent sure about the circle and cross or the fist, but I imagine they're both White Power symbols of some sort.' She looked more closely at the photograph.

'A proper Nazi fanatic then,' said Alex.

'Uh-huh . . .' agreed Pip.

'Anything else?' Alex asked.

'We think we might have an address for him – somewhere in Morden. Local CID down there are in the process of applying for an out-of-hours warrant. Who knows what we might find once we get inside.'

'So what now?' asked Alex.

'I think the priority has to be to get him talking. The rest of the team are on their way, but we can't afford to wait for them. I think we need to make a start.'

Alex nodded in agreement.

There was a sudden commotion outside, the sound of screeching tyres, followed by slamming doors and a succession of raised voices. Pip walked over to the bay window.

'Looks like the SFO teams are here.'

'Blimey, they were quick,' said Alex, crossing the room to join her.

They watched as the last in a succession of high-powered saloon cars pulled up at the bottom of the hill, joined moments later by a nondescript white Transit van. More than a dozen men and women dressed in unremarkable T-shirts and sweat-shirts jumped out of the vehicles. As they assembled in the middle of the road, they untied the overalls that were knotted round their waists and started to kit up. Several of them already had handguns strapped to their thighs.

'Come on,' said Pip, 'let them get on with what they've got to do, while we get on with what we've got to do.' Her voice and manner were calm – a conscious and very deliberate counterpoint to the rapidly evolving chaos all around them. Out there, everything was moving at a thousand miles an hour – the armed net tightening around the church hall, snipers taking up positions in upstairs windows and on rooftops, urgent briefings being conducted on street corners, a team of investigators racing to an address in South London, the clamour from a hundred or more journalists for the latest update, a large proportion of the nation now glued to a screen, watching to see how it all played out, everyone knowing something, no one knowing everything. Inside the living room, Pip's job was to slow everything down, to shut out every possible form of distraction and give Alex the space and support he needed to do his job. 'Are you ready to put the call in?' she asked.

'I am.'

'So what's your first line?'

'Same one as always: "My name is Alex. I'm with the police and I'm here to help".'

'Sounds good to me,' she responded. 'Here's the number that was used to make the 999 call. It's registered in the name of Grace Wheatley – I'm guessing she's the hostage who spoke to the 999 operator. It's the only one we have at the moment and it seems to be our best chance of getting hold of him.' She copied a mobile phone number onto a fresh Post-it note and placed it alongside the one that had Connor's name on it. 'All right,' she said, 'time for you to do what you do best.' She reached over and squeezed his arm.

Grace

Grace was kneeling on the floor. Rosie appeared to have rallied ever so slightly. Her pulse was still faint and her breathing still pained and shallow, but she hadn't given up. Grace was willing her to keep fighting as she whispered a stream of prayers and gentle exhortations.

Grace removed Rosie's clerical collar and carefully undid the top button on her shirt, hoping to aid her breathing. She wanted to clean away the blood and vomit from Rosie's face, but her features were so swollen and the damage so extensive that it seemed almost impossible. Grace attempted to dab gently at her chin, but Rosie recoiled in agony. So, instead, Grace unravelled one of the larger bandages from the first-aid kit, soaked it in the cup of water and laid it carefully across Rosie's forehead.

Rosie drifted in and out of consciousness. Grace watched her intently, searching for even the smallest change in her condition, keeping hold of her hand. And whenever terrible thoughts threatened her, Grace fought back against them with a fury. There was no way she was going to lose her friend. Not today. Not any day soon. 'The Lord is your Shepherd,' she whispered defiantly. 'The Lord is *your* Shepherd . . .'

Her words were interrupted by the sound of her phone ringing in Connor's pocket. She recognised the ringtone straight away and her first thought was that it must be Isaiah. She had completely lost track of time, but perhaps he was wondering where she was. For a split second, she stopped worrying about Rosie and began instead to fret about her son. Did he know what was happening? Did he know she was involved? What was he thinking? What was he doing? She felt a fresh wave of despair, before forcing her thoughts back into the room and to the immediate task in hand. She felt again for Rosie's pulse.

'Stay with me, Rosie,' she begged.

Lee

Everyone else in the hall heard the mobile ring too. But Connor didn't answer it straight away. He was determined to take his time, to let everyone know that this was going to play out on his terms and according to his plans. On the fourth or fifth ring, he pulled the phone out of his pocket and pressed the green button.

'Who's this?' he demanded, his voice cold and empty.

'My name is Alex,' the voice replied. 'I'm with the police and I'm here to help.'

'Here to help who?' Connor retorted.

There was the briefest of pauses at the other end of the line.

'I'm here to help you and everyone else in there with you,' the voice said, 'here to make sure that nobody gets hurt.'

'It's a bit late for that.' There was no obvious change to the tone or tempo of Connor's voice. He'd practised this first part of the conversation plenty of times. 'People are already hurt. And it's going to get a whole lot worse if you don't do what I say.' With that, he terminated the call.

That would show them.

Alex

Inside the negotiating cell, Alex looked up at Pip, a flicker of concern on his face. His mobile phone was lying on the coffee table, loudspeaker activated, with the dictaphone running alongside it. Pip had heard the whole brief exchange.

'No problem,' she said. 'He's obviously just trying to gain some sort of psychological advantage. Call him straight back. You've got this.'

Alex redialled the number.

'What?' The voice was a little more aggressive this time.

'It's Alex here. Can we start again?'

'Well, that depends entirely on whether or not you're actually going to help me.'

Alex had seen the picture of Connor and tried to imagine him now. He guessed that he was probably in his early- to mid-twenties.

'I am going to help you,' said Alex. 'I want to help you and everyone else get safely out of there tonight. And I need you to help me understand what's happening here . . . Perhaps I could start with your name? What should I call you?'

'You know my name. You must have seen my film on Twitter.' Connor sounded quietly defiant, apparently unwilling to concede any sort of initiative.

'Yes, I have seen it,' Alex said.

Alex had always held to the rule that negotiators never lie – a rule established as much for operational reasons as ethical ones. Lies invariably get found out in the end and for a negotiator it can have devastating, even fatal, consequences when that happens. If you have proven yourself to be a liar, then you have shown yourself to be undeserving of trust. And, in the midst of a negotiation, trust is everything. Alex chose his next words carefully.

'But this is the first opportunity I've had to speak to you. I don't know you or anything about you. Is Lee Connor your real name?'

'Of course it's my real fucking name. Why would I need to pretend to be someone else?'

Alex maintained his own measured tone. 'People change their names for all sorts of reasons. I just wanted to check. What would you like me to call you?'

'Well, why don't you call me Mr Connor?' A sneer this time. Connor clearly wasn't about to allow any kind of familiarity. Evidently, he believed he was holding all the cards and he wanted the police to know it.

'No problem, Mr Connor,' Alex replied. 'Like I said, it's always good to check.' Then, as carefully as he could, he changed tack. 'Are you injured in any way?'

'Of course I'm not injured, you fucking idiot.'

'What about the people who are in there with you?' asked Alex, brushing aside the rebuke. He glanced up and saw that Pip was nodding at him in encouragement. 'Can you tell me how many other people there are in the hall?'

'There are nine of them.'

Alex placed a large tick next to the number '9' on the relevant Post-it note.

'And how many of them are injured? I could see on your film that one of them appears to be very badly hurt.'

'She's the only one . . . so far.' There was a dismissive tone to his voice. 'And she'll be fine. You don't need to worry about her.'

'But I am worried about her,' Alex insisted. 'She looks as though she urgently needs medical help.'

'She's got someone looking after her,' came the reply.

Alex hadn't been expecting that. 'Someone looking after her?' he queried.

'Are you hard of hearing? Yes, there is someone looking after her.'

'I don't understand?'

'Are you stupid as well as deaf? One of the others is looking after her. Because I am not some kind of savage. Because I have a conscience as well as a cause.' He was scoring a point, attempting to gain credit. Alex allowed it.

'Thank you for doing that,' he said. 'Do you have any medical equipment in there with you – bandages and that sort of thing?'

'She's got everything she needs. I'm telling you, the priest will be fine.'

Alex was acutely conscious of not pushing the point too far, but neither was he willing to concede it. At that particular moment in time, the welfare of the nine hostages was his singular and overriding concern.

'What's the name of the person looking after the priest? Can I talk to them?'

'No, you can't.'

'I just want to ask them about the priest – I think her name's Rosie. I need to know what the full extent of Rosie's injuries are.'

Alex glanced at Pip, who, once again, was nodding vigorously. Yes, she was indicating, give the hostage a name. Don't allow her to remain an object to be discussed and discarded. Identify her as a human being, someone deserving of concern and care.

'Why should I do anything for you, when you've done nothing for me?'

Alex took a risk. 'I need to know that I can trust you. That works both ways, of course. You need to be able to trust me too. That's the only way we're going to get anything done tonight. And I just want to make sure that Rosie is going to be OK.'

There was silence at the other end of the line. Had he pushed it too far? He and Pip stared at one another, waiting.

'You can talk to her.'

'Can you repeat that? I couldn't quite hear you,' said Alex, stalling for time as he got his thoughts together.

'I said you can talk to her. But I'm putting the phone on loudspeaker, so don't even think about trying or saying anything stupid.'

'I won't,' said Alex. 'You have my word.'

There was a muffled, unidentifiable noise at the other end of the line and then the sound of a hesitant, obviously terrified female voice.

'Hello?'

'Hello.' Alex's voice was gentle and reassuring. 'My name is Alex and I'm with the police. Who's this?'

'My name is Grace . . . Grace Wheatley.'

'It's good to hear your voice, Grace. You must be very frightened.'

'Get on with it.' It was Connor, growling in the background.

Alex continued, not missing a beat. 'Are you hurt at all, Grace?'

'No, I'm OK,' she replied, 'but Rosie is in a really bad way.'

'I'm so glad you're there to help Rosie,' he said, in gentle, measured tones. 'Are you able to tell me what her injuries are?'

'She's been hit in the face with a gun,' Grace responded, 'and she hit her head on a chair as she fell. She looks like she's got a broken nose and maybe a broken jaw as well. There's a lot of blood.'

'Where's Rosie now?' Alex asked calmly.

'She's lying on the floor next to me. I've been trying to make her as comfortable as I can.'

'You're an amazing person and you're doing an amazing job,' said Alex. 'How's she looking right now?'

'Not good. She's drifting in and out of consciousness. Her pulse is weak and her breathing seems laboured to me. We need to get her to a hospital as soon as possible.' Grace burst into tears. 'I don't want her to die,' she sobbed.

21.28 hrs

Alex

'Rosie's not going to die.' Alex spoke to Grace gently but firmly. 'We're going to get her to hospital as soon as we possibly can. And, in the meantime, she's got you right there with her . . . You're doing amazingly well, Grace.'

'I'm doing my best,' she replied, her voice quivering as she spoke.

'I know you are,' Alex replied, 'and that's all that anyone could ever ask of you.' He paused for a beat, conscious of the need to check on the other hostages, acutely aware of the fact that he didn't know a single thing about any of them. 'Can you tell me about the others who are in there with you?' he asked.

'No, she fucking can't!' It was Connor again. His voice was clear on the line. Evidently he had retaken possession of the phone. 'Don't push it. You've got what you asked for, now it's your turn. "Quid pro quo," as they say. What are you going to do for me?'

'I'm going to listen to you,' said Alex.

'You're going to have to do a whole lot more than that,' Connor responded.

'OK,' said Alex, 'but all of this is new to me. I need you to help me understand what's actually happening – how we got here.'

'You've seen the video,' Connor retorted. 'You know exactly how we got here and you know exactly what I want: the release from prison of the patriot Nicholas Farmer. So why don't you call me back when you're ready to get down to actual business.'

With that, the line went dead again.

Alex stared at his phone. 'Shit!' he mumbled.

'Good job,' said Pip, deliberately ignoring his expletive. 'You're doing just fine.'

She meant it too. She had listened to every word and, given the extremes of the situation, she couldn't think of any way in which he might have handled it any better. The fact was that, for all their combined experience, neither of them had ever negotiated with a terrorist before.

'Do you think I should call him straight back?' Alex was reassured by Pip's encouragement, but he didn't want to lose any momentum he might have started to build.

'I think we can afford to let him sit and wait for a few minutes,' she replied. 'Let's let him wonder what our next move is going to be. The most important thing at this stage is that Rosie is alive and she's got someone with her.'

'She's alive,' Alex acknowledged, 'but I don't like the sound of her condition. We need to get her out of there, and fast.'

At that moment, the doorbell rang again, signalling the arrival of the other members of the negotiation team.

Lee

Inside the church hall, despite feeling a bit jumpy, Connor was pleased with himself. He'd stuck to the plan. He'd called the shots. He'd let them know who was in charge. He checked his phone and saw that he now had hundreds of new Twitter followers and an ever-growing stream of notifications. People were paying attention. People were learning his name.

But, tempting though it might have been to bask in the newfound attention, he knew he could not allow himself to get distracted by the outside world. He wondered when the police would get his Twitter account shut down – he certainly expected them to. And when they did, he knew it would not make the slightest bit of difference. The photos and the footage were already out there, being posted and reposted on dark web sites and encrypted apps like Telegram and Discord and 8Chan, and who knew where else besides. The message had been sent and the damage had been done. In that sense, he told himself, an important part of his mission had already been accomplished.

He opened a fresh bottle of water and drank deeply from it. Then he opened a bag of trail mix and grabbed a generous handful of the contents, knowing how important it was to remain fuelled and alert. He walked round the room – gun in one hand, helping of trail mix in the other – inspecting his hostages. He placed the barrel of the pistol under Ittack's chin, lifted his head and forced the terrorised boy to look him in the eye. He did the same with each of them in turn, reinforcing their sense of helplessness, of abject fear, and his sense of absolute control. He came to Rosie and Grace last.

'I need to take a piss. You need to sit back down.'

He waved Grace towards the nearest chair and she had no choice but to obey him. She touched Rosie's arm and insisted again that everything was going to be all right. 'I promise I'm not going anywhere, Rosie. I'll be just over there.'

Connor finished the last mouthful of trail mix, shoved Grace onto the chair and grabbed a fresh handful of cable ties. He secured her in place and, as an apparent afterthought, bound Rosie's ankles and wrists where she lay prone on the floor.

As he walked towards the gents' toilet, he thought for a moment about unsticking the edge of one of the bin liners and taking a quick look outside. But he dismissed the idea immediately. There was no need to be taking even the slightest risk. Everything was exactly as he wanted and needed it to be. He just needed to remain patient.

Alex

Alex looked up as DCI Richard Wells walked into the living room.

'Evening, Rich,' he said, getting up from his seat on the sofa.

The two men shook hands. Richard was a member of the small permanent Hostage Negotiation team based at New Scotland Yard. He and four of his colleagues were based in an office on the fourth floor of the Met's headquarters and, unlike Alex and every other volunteer on the call-out rota, negotiation was their full-time job. Rich was highly experienced – he had been doing the job for years and had been one of the instructors when Alex and Pip had first trained for the role.

Richard turned to introduce the officer who had arrived with him. 'Alex, meet Angie. She's relatively new to all of this – she was on the course we ran four months ago – but she's good.'

A bright-eyed, freckle-faced redhead, Angie was obviously determined to make a positive first impression. 'Just tell me what you need me to do,' she said.

It was Pip who responded. 'Alex will continue as Number One negotiator. He's made an excellent start and I want us to build on that. Rich, you'll be Two. Angie, you'll be Three. I've got to go and update the Incident Commander, but Alex will bring you up to speed with everything. And, as soon as I'm back, I want us to get Connor back on the line.' With that, she headed for the front door.

Alex followed her as far as the corridor, before turning left towards the kitchen. He tapped on the door before opening it. The concerned, expectant faces of the two occupants of the house were turned towards him.

'Excuse me,' Alex said, 'I don't suppose I could trouble you for that cup of tea now? In fact, is there any chance we could have a pot and some mugs?' His hosts were only too happy to oblige – pleased to have been given a useful job to do, however small and insignificant.

Drinks order placed, Alex returned to the living room to find the other two hunched over the coffee table, taking in the information on the Post-it notes. Alex filled them in on all the remaining details.

'Connor certainly sounds like he knows what he's doing,' Rich observed as Alex reached the end of his short briefing. 'I imagine he's been preparing for this for some time.'

21.48 hrs

Alex

Pip reappeared in the cell.

'The local Chief Superintendent has taken over command – for now at least – and I don't envy him the task. It's absolute madness out there. The whole world seems to be turning up at the main RVP, and every senior officer in London appears to want their own personal briefing. The poor man's phone rang five times just in the short period I was with him.

'No change for us though – the plan stays exactly the same. SO15 have got the search warrant from the local CID and they should be at the South London address by now. They seem to think it's where Connor has been holed up for the last few months. If they find anything there that might be helpful to us, they'll let us know straight away.'

She looked at Alex.

'Have the three of you settled on what you think the next move should be?'

Lee

With all his prisoners secure, Connor had returned to the kitchen to smoke a second joint. He'd been using cannabis since his early teens, but, during the previous couple of years, he had turned increasingly to skunk. It helped him to stay calm, but it also rendered him vulnerable to intermittent bouts of acute paranoia. It was also the reason why he frequently heard the voices of people who weren't really there. In short, it messed with his mind. One moment he would feel like the king of the world, and the next he would be certain that they were all out to get him. Whoever 'they' might be. It came and it went, good days and bad days, and bad moments in otherwise good days. For the moment, though, his mind felt relatively settled. He knew what he was doing. He felt in control. When Grace's phone rang in his pocket, he once again took his time answering.

'Has Nicholas Farmer been released yet?'

Alex

Alex was caught somewhat off guard by the blunt immediacy of Connor's question. He had known that it would come, of course; he just hadn't anticipated it first up.

'What's that noise in the background?' he responded, buying himself a few additional seconds. 'It's difficult to hear what you're saying.'

'I forgot you were hard of hearing,' Connor mocked as he turned off the kitchen fan. 'Is that any better for you?'

'Much better,' Alex said. 'Thank you.'

Connor repeated his enquiry. 'Has Nicholas Farmer been released from prison yet?'

'No, he hasn't.'

'Why not?'

'I suspect you already know the answer to that question,

Mr Connor.' Subtle flattery, playing to his ego. 'It's almost ten o'clock and the prison is already in lockdown for the night.'

'I don't care what time it is,' Connor fired back. 'There are nine people in this church whose lives depend on his release.'

Alex took the chance he had been presented with. He asked about the hostages.

'How are the nine of them doing? How's Rosie doing?'

'She's fine.'

'What about Grace?'

Alex made sure to keep placing particular emphasis on their names.

'Stop wasting my time. You don't need to be worrying about any of them.'

Alex took a chance and pushed back. 'But I am worried about them, Mr Connor. Rosie urgently needs to go to hospital. That's not just my opinion – that's what Grace thinks too and she's there in the room.'

Keep using those names. *Keep* using those names.

'No one is going anywhere until I get what I want.' There was a rising note of defiance in his voice. 'I think I've made my position very clear.'

The other members of the negotiation team were listening intently. As the Number One negotiator, Alex's job was to engage with Connor. Rich was sitting alongside him, Bic biro in hand, ready to write prompts and suggestions on blank Post-it notes – anything that might assist his colleague. It was hardly a hi-tech system, but it was the tried and proven way of doing things.

In the meantime, Angie had been putting up large sheets of flipchart paper in every available space on the living-room walls. Initially, the details written on them in marker pen had simply duplicated those set out in smaller form on the coffee-table notes, but new information was being added all the time.

On the sheet headed 'Hostage Taker', Lee Connor's name had been joined by his age (his date of birth having been confirmed by a check on the Police National Computer), his believed address and a two-line summary of his criminal convictions. And there was plenty of space for additional details to be added as they became available.

There was a separate page for each of the hostages – still almost entirely blank – and individual sheets with titles such as 'Demands', 'Deadlines' and 'Positive Police Actions', but so far with minimal information on them beyond the headings themselves. The idea was for Alex to be able to glance up at any moment in time and know that the details would be immediately and clearly visible to him.

Alex responded to Connor's last remark.

'You've been very clear about what you want. But you also know that these things always take time . . .'

'So speed things up,' Connor interrupted him.

'That's not something I can just click my fingers and do,' Alex said, glancing at a handwritten note that Rich had just placed in front of him. 'There are all sorts of people involved here, and any big decisions about what happens, and when, will be taken by the people in charge.'

'What do you mean, "the people in charge?"' Connor asked with undisguised contempt. 'I thought you were in charge?'

'No, I'm not,' said Alex. 'My job is to talk to you – to listen. It's the job of other people – people much more senior than me – to make the big decisions.'

'Then I'm wasting my time here. Get me the man in charge.'

For the third time in less than an hour, Connor cut the line dead.

21.57 hrs

Alex

'It's all good.'

Rich was looking directly at Alex. He'd taken over from Pip – who had left the cell to attend the latest command team meeting – as the primary source of encouragement in the room and he had started to offer his reassurance the moment the call had ended.

'It's all good,' he insisted.

The problem for Alex was that he wasn't at all sure that this was true. They hadn't been going for long, but, already, everything seemed to be running out of control; at least, out of his control. Connor was dictating everything. He seemed to have them right where he wanted them. And the jarring way in which the calls kept ending was unsettling. Alex had been negotiating for years, but never quite like this.

Rich could see the doubt and concern in Alex's face. But he was insistent.

'You're doing a cracking job and we're in a good place.'

Alex frowned in response. The full weight of nine lives – plus Connor – was beginning to settle more heavily on his shoulders. The same sense of unease that had earlier caught him unawares was beginning to whisper to him again. *They don't all end well*, said the voice that only he could hear.

'The hostages are all alive and we're buying some much-needed time,' Rich continued. He nodded towards the bay window and the street beyond. 'We're giving everyone out there a chance to draw up their plans and get into position.'

Alex glanced across at Angie, who nodded her head in agreement with Rich. Two against one. Alex once again told himself to get a grip. His rattled train of thought was interrupted by Pip's reappearance in the cell.

'They've found Connor's address,' she said.

'And?' enquired Rich.

Pip opened her notebook and began to relay to them the details that had been given to her a few minutes earlier. An SO15 investigation team, accompanied by three carloads of Trojan officers and members of the Bomb Squad, had been able to identify the building containing Connor's bedsit.

There had been no time to mount any kind of surveillance operation at the location – the situation was far too urgent for that. Instead, they had surrounded the premises and broken the communal door down. They had rapidly evacuated the building's occupants – a bewildered bunch of twenty-somethings, full of questions but given no answers – and local officers had set up cordons in the street outside. Then they had made a cautious approach to Connor's front door, using up several precious minutes in ensuring that he hadn't wired up any unpleasant surprises. They needn't have worried.

Once inside, they had found everything apparently as Connor had intended. The wall behind his bed was covered with a grotesque gallery of dozens of newspaper cuttings, all telling stories of past terror attacks, interspersed with enlarged pictures of the people who had carried them out. Some of those perpetrators were dead, some were serving multiple life sentences, one was still on the run, but all were far-right extremists who had carried out targeted attacks on individuals and minority groups in countries all around the world. Someone, presumably Connor, had filled any remaining spaces on the wall with a series of names and slogans, written in large print using a thick red felt tip pen. Pip read them out in turn:

White Power

David

Home Front

Anders

Make Britain Great Again

Thomas

End the White Genocide

Brenton

Execute the Will of the People

Dylann

White Lives Matter

Lee

Take Back Control

There were also repeated images of swastikas and multiple renderings of the double lightning flash of the *Schutzstaffel* – the Nazi SS. The whole scene had the unmistakeable appearance of a twisted shrine.

An initial search of the room had revealed a vast quantity of printed literature bearing titles such as, *'Le Grand Remplacement'*, *'Identitariansim'*, *'Eurabia'* and *'The Battle of Vienna'*. A brief initial scan of the recent search history on the unlocked laptop had yielded more of the same. A Word document stored on the hard drive – with a link to it displayed prominently on the home screen – carried the filename *'Manifesto'*.

The full forensic search of the bedsit would take many hours, possibly a couple of days, but a rapid series of initial, urgent phone calls had been made to colleagues at Scotland Yard, at the Security Services and at the scene of the siege itself. Digital photographs taken of the initial evidential trove were being sent to the same recipients.

It was abundantly clear to everyone in the cell that Connor was exceptionally well prepared and deadly serious about what he was doing. Recognising the fact did nothing to ease Alex's state of mind.

'When do we get to see the pictures?' asked Rich, focusing on immediate and practical considerations. 'There might be something in them we can use.'

'As soon as I have them,' answered Pip. She put her notebook down on the coffee table and looked at each member of her team in turn. She wanted to move the conversation on. 'What's the latest on the negotiation?' she asked them.

'He hung up again,' said Alex grimly.

'Connor is just trying to assert himself,' said Rich firmly. 'Alex is doing fine.'

Except that Alex didn't look – or feel – at all convinced that this was the case.

Pip couldn't help noticing his expression. She knew him much better than the other two did and it was obvious to her that he was feeling the pressure of the situation. But she retained absolute confidence in his abilities. 'So what should our next move be?' she asked the team.

'Get him back on and keep him on,' said Rich. 'We need to get the priest out of there.'

Lee

Once again, Grace's phone rang in Connor's pocket. Once again, Connor delayed before answering it. He didn't know whether or not the search of his bedsit was already underway, but he reasoned that it wouldn't be long.

'I'd better be speaking to the person in charge.' His voice was clear and controlled.

'No, you're still speaking to Alex. Can I—'

Connor interrupted him. 'I thought I made it perfectly clear that I wanted to speak to the person in charge. Do you fuckers actually want me to start hurting people in here?'

'People are already hurt in there,' the negotiator ventured carefully, but firmly. 'Rosie is seriously injured and she needs urgent medical help. And no, of course I don't want you to hurt anyone else.' Connor tried to interrupt him a second time, but Alex kept going. 'We need to get Rosie to a hospital straight away. And we need to get Grace and everybody else in there home safely tonight.'

'We'. Not 'I'. Not 'you', Alex had said. He was apparently trying to suggest that there were things they could achieve by working together. Connor wasn't buying it.

'But you're not the one calling the shots here, are you.' It was a statement, not a question. Connor's voice sounded ice-cold now. 'I hold all the cards – every last one of them – and unless you do what I tell you to do, no one is going to leave this building alive.'

Alex

Sitting in the cell, Alex found that he was able to focus again, pushing any lingering sense of anxiety beyond the periphery of his thoughts. Connor had his complete attention.

'Yes, you hold all the cards, Mr Connor,' Alex affirmed, 'but Rosie could die if we don't get her to a hospital very soon.'

'Why should I care whether she lives or dies?' His voice sounded hollow, devoid of feeling.

'Because if she dies, it will damage whatever it is that you're trying to achieve here. It will certainly make it a whole lot less likely that you'll get what you want.'

'No, it won't,' he insisted petulantly. 'All it will do is prove how serious I am. It will confirm the fact that I am perfectly willing to kill for my cause...' He paused for a beat, before adding, '...A cause that I am equally prepared to die for.'

'That isn't going to happen.' The challenge from Alex was immediate and emphatic, though he was still taking enormous care to measure the pitch and tone of his voice. He wasn't trying to pick a fight, but he was trying to send a clear and unequivocal message. Nobody needed to die. Connor himself didn't need to die. Alex continued without pause. 'What would killing people achieve? What would your death achieve?'

'It would send a message,' came the reply.

'What message would it send?'

Connor's voice rose a notch in both volume and pace. 'That we are serious. That our cause is just. That the existential threat we are facing is real. That this white genocide must come to an end.'

'Slow down a bit for me,' Alex ventured. 'I don't understand. White genocide?' He echoed Connor's specific use of the term.

117

'We must secure the existence of our people and a future for white children.' That phrase again. Connor had used exactly the same form of words in the video clip he had earlier posted online.

'What do you mean?' asked Alex. Rich was nodding encouragement at him, making a rapid circling motion with his right index finger. Keep going. Keep him talking.

'The Fourteen Words: We must secure the existence of our people and a future for white children.' Connor appeared to have assumed that Alex would know exactly what he was talking about.

'I'm sorry,' Alex offered, 'I still don't understand. The fourteen words?'

'Have you never heard of David Lane?' Connor sounded genuinely surprised.

'I haven't, no . . . Tell me about him.' Alex was telling the truth. And he was willing Connor to keep talking, to give a little more of himself away. And, on this subject at least, Connor seemed perfectly willing to oblige.

'David Lane was a great American patriot. He was a prophet too – a man who saw and understood the nature and extent of the coming storm. He was the one who wrote the Fourteen Words. But he wasn't just a man who wrote things down, he was a man of action too. Same as me. He gave his life for the cause and I am prepared to do exactly the same.' There was an added note of defiance in his voice.

Rich scribbled on a Post-it note, 'David Lane?????' and handed it to Angie. They needed to know more about him.

'I want you to tell me more about him,' said Alex, torn between upsetting the genuine sense of momentum that seemed to be building in their conversation, and not wanting to lose sight of the most urgent and immediate of all his tasks, 'but I also need to keep talking to you about Rosie. We desperately need to get her to a hospital. I'm asking you to let her go. As a gesture of goodwill. Of humanity.' He paused, before adding, 'Quid pro quo.'

'What's with the talk of "quid pro quo" when you've done precisely nothing for me?' Connor sounded as though he was digging in, refusing to budge.

Rich tapped Alex on the arm and jabbed his finger across the sitting room, to the piece of flipchart paper headed 'Positive Police Actions'. PPAs. Alex nodded and continued.

'But there are a number of things that we've done for you — that we *are* doing for you.'

'Like what exactly?' Connor spluttered.

'Like the fact that I'm talking to you now, listening to everything you have to say. Like the fact that the police haven't come bursting through the doors of the hall, trying to rescue the people in there by force—'

'Big fucking deal,' Connor interrupted him. 'You know full well that if you made any attempt to come in here, everyone would die. And then whose fault would that be?'

It would be Connor's fault, Alex was certain of that, but he chose not to say so. Instead, he continued to read from the list on the wall.

'The police have left the electricity on. You've still got heat and light in there.'

'Again, big fucking deal,' Connor came back. 'I've got everything I need in here to see us through the night, whether the power is on or not.'

Alex, encouraged by Rich alongside him, kept going. 'And we are doing everything we can to make sure that Rosie gets the help she needs and that no one else gets hurt — including you, Mr Connor.'

'But I couldn't care less about any of those things. I couldn't give a shit about them,' said Connor confrontationally. 'And I don't care what happens to me. All I actually care about is the cause – and about Nicholas Farmer's release from prison. Which is the one thing you appear to have done precisely fuck all about.'

Lee

In Connor's mind, Nicholas Farmer had assumed some sort of messianic status. He was the British David Lane, a man called for at just such a time as this. He was a speaker of truth in an age of fake news. He was a lone voice of reason in a world gone mad. He was the embodiment of a cause that Connor was ready to lay down his life for.

Connor had read and reread everything that Farmer had ever written. He could recite much of it from memory. He had watched and rewatched every recorded speech the man had ever made, and every news clip and piece of interview footage that had ever been posted online. The Fourteen Words, the Eighty-Eight Precepts, and all the rest. Farmer alone seemed to have understood the overwhelming urgency of the situation: the immediacy of the existential threat facing the white race. He was able to articulate, in language that ordinary people could understand, the dangers posed by ineffective immigration policies and the damage being done by the thousands of black and brown people flooding in through Britain's porous borders. It was time to take back control – and to do so by any means necessary. Nicholas Farmer was the real thing.

But what had been his reward for all of his achievements? A sham of a trial and the four walls of a prison cell. Well, fuck that. Connor was going to get Nicholas Farmer out. And if that didn't happen, people were going to die.

Alex

'I've passed your request about Nicholas Farmer up to the people in charge,' insisted Alex, 'so I have done something.'

Connor responded with what sounded like a snort of derision and lapsed into silence.

Alex scrambled to think of what to say next.

'What would Nicholas Farmer say about Rosie?' he asked, doing his best to conceal the hint of uncertainty in his voice. It was not a question the team had discussed using, and there was no predicting how Connor might react to it, but Alex's instincts told him that there might be an opportunity to be seized and that now was the moment to try. His rationale was that Farmer's opinion on any given subject might be something that would matter to Connor – something he might pay attention to. His instincts were right.

'What do you mean?' replied Connor, seemingly caught off guard by the question.

Alex picked up instantly on the subtle change in Connor's tone. He rephrased the question. 'If Nicholas Farmer was here now, what would he tell you to do about Rosie?' He glanced to his right. Rich gave him a thumbs-up sign and a firm nod of encouragement.

'What kind of a fucking stupid question is that?' Connor growled after a pause that felt much longer than it actually was.

'I don't think it's a stupid question,' Alex replied. 'I think I'm right in saying that Nicholas Farmer is someone you admire. And I thought it would be reasonable to consider what he might say in this situation.'

'So you don't think I'm capable of thinking for myself?' said Connor, moving back onto the front foot.

'No,' responded Alex, shooting a concerned glance sideways at Rich, 'that's not what I said.'

'It's what you meant.'

'I promise you it's not, Mr Connor.' It was Alex's turn to try to find the right thing to say. 'I was simply trying to find a way through this situation – and to get Rosie the help she so obviously needs. No one needs to die in there.'

'Well, if you're so fucking keen for me to know what Nicholas Farmer thinks, why don't you bring him here and I can fucking ask him myself.'

The line went dead yet again.

22.25 hrs

Lee

Inside the hall, Connor was once more feeling rather pleased with himself, so much so that he actually smiled for the first time in as long as he could remember. That would fucking show them. The simple act of cutting off the conversations with the negotiator made him feel powerful. He was in complete control of the situation and he wasn't going to be pushed around by anyone, least of all the fucking police. He was the Home Front Liberator and soon the whole world would know his name.

He plugged Grace's phone into the charger and took another long swig of water as he continued to congratulate himself. But the stream of self-affirming thoughts was disrupted by the unexpected sound of someone speaking.

'Please, sir, will you let Rosie go?'

Connor wheeled round, his smile gone. He had clearly forgotten to put any tape back on Grace's mouth and the sound of her voice caught him completely unawares.

Seeming to sense his hesitation, she spoke again, ignoring the fact that she was placing herself directly in harm's way as a consequence.

'Please let Rosie go,' she pleaded. She was looking across the hall at the priest, whose condition once more appeared to be deteriorating. Connor followed her gaze, trying to assemble his thoughts.

'What the fuck has it got to do with you?' he demanded, as he started to walk towards her. He was feeling a strange mixture of anger and confusion. He wasn't at all sure how he was supposed to respond to her.

She shrank back in her chair as he approached.

'Because she's my friend,' Grace whispered, 'and because I'm scared she's going to die if she doesn't get the help she needs.'

Connor looked closely at her. She was without guile and there was no doubting her courage. He might almost have been tempted to admire her, had it not seemed so clear to him who and what she was.

'And why the hell should I pay the slightest bit of attention to what someone like you has got to say?'

'Because you're not a savage.'

He stared at her, wrong-footed by her words for the second time in as many minutes.

'I heard you talking on the phone earlier,' she said, filling the silence. 'You said that you weren't a savage, and I agree with you. I don't think you're a savage either . . . You also said that you had a conscience and I agree with that too.'

Connor had lost his voice, just as Grace seemed to be finding hers.

'You proved it by letting me look after her before,' she said simply, 'and I'm asking you to prove it again by letting her go.'

'Fuck off,' said Connor, more in frustration than anger, as much at himself as at Grace. He didn't like the uncertain and unsettled way the black woman was making him feel, but, for some unfathomable reason, he couldn't bring himself to shut her up. He turned his back on her and headed towards the front of the building, intending to check the doors.

Rosie groaned loudly as a fresh wave of pain poured through her.

'She's going to die if you don't help her,' cried Grace.

Connor put his hands to his ears, trying to block out the sound of her voice.

Alex

In the negotiation cell, Alex was furiously replaying the events of the previous twenty minutes, trying to work out how and why he had failed, terrified that the priest might die as a consequence of his mistakes. In his imagination, he could see her lifeless body, covered by a white sheet, being carried away on a stretcher. *Get a bloody grip, man.*

Pip watched him from across the room, trying to strike a balance between offering reassurance and giving him some time and space to work it through. She knew he was struggling and she wanted to make it right for him, but, at the same time, she was acutely aware of her wider responsibilities for the whole team and for making the right decisions about what they should do next.

Should they call Connor back again, or should they leave it for a few more minutes? What should their approach be when they did make the call? There were no right answers to those questions. All she had to rely on were her instincts, her experience and the skill of the people around her.

Lee

Connor took his time checking the doors, trying to give himself some space to think. He was acutely aware of the fact that the black woman was watching him, but, for the time being, she had at least stopped calling out to him.

He thought about what she had said and, in spite of himself, he also thought about what the police negotiator had said. What would Nicholas Farmer say? He turned his distracted attention to the security of the windows running along both sides of the main hall. What *would* Nicholas Farmer tell him to do?

22.40 hrs

Alex

Alex was still sinking under the weight of his own thoughts when his phone lit up and started to ring. The sight and sound acted as an instant antidote to his malaise and he snapped himself to attention, once again alert and focused. Before any other member of the team could say anything, Alex had already grabbed the handset and connected the call.

'This is Alex speaking,' he said. Initially, there was no response at the other end of the line. 'Can you hear me, Mr Connor?' he asked anxiously.

'The priest can leave,' said Connor after an imagined eternity. He sounded reluctant, begrudging and hostile.

Alex stared at the phone, stunned. The rest of the team stared at Alex, every bit as shocked as he was.

'Can you say that again? I couldn't quite hear you.' Alex's mind was racing at a furious speed and he was trying to absorb what he'd just heard.

'I said the fucking priest can leave,' repeated Connor irritably.

'Thank you,' was the only thing that Alex could think to say. 'Thank you, Mr Connor.'

Had the phone signal been a fraction stronger, Connor might have detected the near-silent sigh at the other end of the line

127

– a long, slow exhale of relief. Had he been able to see inside the cell, he would have seen Rich place his left hand on Alex's shoulder while punching the air with his right.

Lee

But Connor didn't hear and he couldn't see. And, in any case, just at that moment in time, he was far too preoccupied with his own thoughts to pay much attention to anything that might have been happening at the other end of the phone line. He was feeling deeply conflicted, not remotely convinced that he was doing the right thing. The Nicholas Farmer question from the negotiator and the subsequent intervention of the black woman had caught him very much by surprise and he feared that any early release of a hostage would be a display of weakness, as well as an unwanted and unnecessary departure from his carefully laid plans. From the beginning, he had been unwilling to concede any ground and now he was feeling as though he had somehow been cornered into making a bad decision, one that he would later come to regret.

But, even as he had tried to face this rising tide of concerns, a completely contrary succession of thoughts had clattered into his head, vying for his attention. Perhaps it was actually the right decision to make. Maybe it would do more good than harm. Was it possible that Nicholas Farmer might actually approve of the decision? He knew that Farmer claimed to be a Christian. Perhaps that was important. Might he say that the death – even the unnecessary suffering – of a priest would damage the cause? Because the cause was the only thing that really, truly mattered. Connor didn't know the answer to his questions, but he had been forced to at least acknowledge their existence. He had never met Farmer, much less spoken to him, but he revered the man. And he wanted desperately to please him, to earn his approval. What would he say?

The arguments pinged back and forth in Connor's head. One moment he was fighting the thought that he was making a dreadful mistake, the next he was telling himself that it was all for the greater good. And he tried to remind himself that the unexpected was always to be expected and that he still possessed every possible advantage. These thoughts and fragments of thoughts continued to pursue one another around his brain. He raised his free hand to the side of his head in a futile attempt to slow them down.

'Thank you, Mr Connor,' the voice was repeating at the other end of the line, 'you're doing the right thing.' After a moment's silence, the negotiator continued, 'We're going to need a few minutes to put together the plan for getting her out safely—'

Connor interrupted him. 'You will call me back in ten minutes.' There was emphasis on the word 'ten'. 'And you'd better have a plan in place by then, or I might just change my mind.' Before Alex had the chance to say anything else, Connor ended the call. He was done talking for the time being. And he definitely needed another smoke.

Grace

Grace didn't take her eyes off him, mostly through fear, though partly through fascination. Had she heard him right? Was he seriously going to let Rosie go? She was watching his body language and noticed a slight sag in his shoulders as he put her phone back in his pocket. He was moving a fraction more slowly and deliberately than he had been only a few minutes earlier, apparently lost inside his own head. There even seemed to be a faint tremor in his hands as he began to roll a fresh joint. There was certainly a hitherto unseen vulnerability in him. But there was also unpredictability and violence and rage broiling not far below the surface, and it was the threat of those things that made her shudder as he brushed past her on his way to the kitchen.

Alex

'What the hell just happened?' Alex looked in astonishment at his colleagues as he put the phone back down.

'I haven't got a bloody clue,' responded Rich, 'but we haven't got time to think about that now. We need to get cracking.'

As ever, it was Pip who took control. 'My request for separate Delivery and Surrender plans went in to the firearms teams a while ago. They ought to be ready by now. Give me five of those ten minutes and I'll get them to adapt what they already have to cover Rosie's release.' And with that, she was gone.

Rich took over, gesturing to the flipcharts on the walls. 'Angie, you need to make sure the boards are bang up to date – and you'll need to prepare a new one for the hostage release plan.' He turned to Alex. 'How about standing up and stretching your legs while we have a chance?' He wanted to make best use of the limited time they had available, not least in getting the blood circulating in Alex's limbs.

The two of them walked out of the living room and down the corridor towards the open front door. Outside, they could see Pip deep in conversation with the Firearms Commander and a number of his colleagues. They were all gathered in a tight group in front of one of the marked BMW X5s, poring over paperwork – including an enlarged map of the street – that had been laid out on the bonnet. The steady rise and fall of their voices was the only sound that could be heard in what was, for the time being, an otherwise eerily silent street.

At the top of the hill, on the far side of the outer cordon and far beyond earshot, Alex imagined the news crews gathering en masse. Satellite trucks would likely have been parked wherever space could be found and reporters would be broadcasting live from the scene, while their colleagues knocked on doors, searching for soundbites.

Grace

For the time being, Connor was once again out of Grace's direct line of sight. She could hear the fan running in the kitchen and she could imagine him drawing on his joint, but she couldn't see him. Instead, she looked back round the room. The only person moving was Rosie. Her hands and feet were bound, but she was squirming uncomfortably as she lay on the floor, occasionally moaning quietly. Grace wanted to call out to her, but she didn't dare risk the wrath of their captor and the possibility that he might suddenly change his mind. Still, she wanted to tell Rosie that she would soon be out of there, though she remained uncertain whether or not that could possibly be true. Her heart was lurching between hope and despair, her mind between terror and numbness, one minute believing that all of this was somehow going to be resolved peacefully, the next facing up to the horribly real and immediate prospect that they were all going to die.

Her thoughts drifted out of the room. Isaiah would almost certainly be wondering where she was by now. She wasn't sure of the exact time, but she imagined it must be past when he would have expected her to be home. And just as she was thinking these things, she heard her phone. It rang three times and then stopped. There was no sound from Connor, just the continued whirr of the kitchen fan. Her phone rang again and the same thing happened. It had to be Isaiah, she was sure of it. And it appeared that Connor was cutting him off. All of a sudden, she felt frantic. Perhaps her son had turned the TV on. Perhaps he had heard something from one of his friends. He would be frightened. She wanted to hold him, to talk to him, to be home with him. Her body tensed. Her hands strained so hard against the cable ties that they began to cut into her skin. She felt rage. And then a fresh wave of helplessness broke over her and the tears began to flow.

She looked across at Rahel and Ittack – children younger than Isaiah. What must they be thinking? What must they be feeling? She looked at each of the adults, heads bowed and silent. She worried about Alan's heart all over again. And her gaze lingered for a moment on Jack. He was making no sound, but she could sense his desperate, twitchy anxiety from across the room. Then she looked back at Rosie. Whatever energy Grace had left seemed to drain right out of her body and she let the tears flow.

Alex

Pip hurried back into the house, collecting Rich and Alex from the front path as she did so. They had four minutes left on Connor's deadline.

'Right, listen up,' she said. She looked down at her clipboard and checked through her notes. 'There will be a Trojan officer coming to join us in here any minute – to provide the teams on the ground with a live feed from the cell. In the meantime, here's the detail for the agreed rescue plan.' She looked straight at Angie, 'Make sure you get all this on the flipchart,' then across at Alex, 'and you need to make sure that you're happy with every single word of it.' Her words were clipped, purposeful, conveyed with an inevitable sense of urgency.

The doorbell rang. Moments later, a firearms officer in full kit – dark blue overalls, body armour, ballistic helmet, carrying a small arsenal of equipment – appeared in the doorway, accompanied by the owner of the house, who was continuing to play his faithful supporting role in the night's unfolding events. He retreated to the kitchen to brew a fresh pot of tea and Pip closed the sitting-room door. After a very rapid set of personal introductions had been completed, she got on with the detail.

'A team of twelve armed officers will approach the main doors at the front of the building. They will be visible from inside the hall at all times. The four officers at the front will be carrying ballistic shields. They will be followed by two medics and two stretcher-bearers, backed up by four more armed officers providing additional cover. At no stage will the officers make any attempt to enter the building. When the front door to the hall opens, the two medics will step forward to receive the casualty. If the casualty is unable to walk, they will place the stretcher in the open doorway and allow those inside the building to lay her down on it. Once she is secure on the stretcher, the two stretcher-bearers will pick her up and carry her directly out onto the street, down the hill and into a waiting ambulance. The officers providing armed cover will then retreat from the front of the building and the front door will be closed.' She looked up from her notes and around the room. 'There is a critically injured casualty in that hall and we need to get her out before it's too late.' There was a look of fierce determination on her face. 'Is everybody clear about the plan?'

They were.

'Then let's run through it again,' she said.

Grace

Connor walked back into the main hall. He approached each of the seated hostages in turn and checked that their bonds were secure. He came to Grace last of all. Inside, she cowered back. Outside, she determined to be strong.

'I'm letting her go,' he said, jerking his head in Rosie's direction.

Grace's heart jolted. So she hadn't misheard or misunderstood his end of the earlier phone conversation. She felt an extraordinary sense of relief for Rosie, though it only served to intensify her fears for the rest of them.

'But you'll be doing the hard work.' Connor continued issuing instructions as he used one of his knives to cut away Grace's cable ties. 'You will get her ready to leave. When I tell you to, you will help her to the front door. And you will do exactly as you are told. If you even think about doing anything stupid, it will be the end of both of you.'

He spat the last words out as he cut the final tie. Grace rose shakily to her feet, then crossed the floor and knelt down once again beside her friend. Up close, Rosie looked even worse than before. The swelling had increased and the extensive bruising on her face had become much more obvious. Her eyes were bloodshot, puffy and half closed. Her pupils were different sizes. But she at least appeared to be conscious.

'Can you hear me, Rosie? It's Grace.'

Rosie's lips moved, but the only sound she made was a gurgle, a mingling of blood and mucus in the back of her throat. Grace was quick to soothe her.

'Sssh . . . !' she whispered. 'You don't need to say a word; I just need to know you can hear me.'

Rosie offered a slow blink by way of confirmation.

'You're going to hospital.' Grace hesitated. 'He's letting you go.'

Grace stared at her as the news slowly registered. A single tear formed in the corner of Rosie's left eye. She reached out with her bound hands and tried to take hold of Grace's arm. Grace responded by placing her own hands on top of Rosie's.

Before Grace could say or do anything else, Connor appeared next to them, knife in hand. Silently, he cut the ties from Rosie's ankles and wrists.

'Stay right there,' he hissed at the two women. Grace ignored him. For the moment at least, Rosie occupied all of her thoughts.

'Do you think you're going to be able to move?' Grace asked, forgetting once again that Rosie was unable to speak.

Rosie responded by rolling slowly to one side and trying to raise herself up on her elbow. She moaned in pain and distress and Grace was quick to catch her before she sank back down.

'It's all right. I've got you. You're going to be out of here in the next few minutes. The doctors will be waiting for you at the hospital.' Grace was murmuring in quick sentences, trying to offer Rosie as much reassurance as possible. She was also trying to reassure herself. She curled her right arm around Rosie's back and allowed her injured friend's weight to rest against her body. Rosie was slight in stature, but tall, and Grace was going to need all her strength to move her across the room. For now, the two remained still, finding some limited degree of comfort in their closeness.

Grace looked across the room and saw Jack stealing a glance in their direction. His face was stained with tears, his eyes wide with alarm. Grace nodded gently at him. *We're going to be all right*, she was trying to say.

22.53 hrs

Alex

In the negotiating cell, the armed officer – a highly experienced member of the SCO19 team – was speaking on the radio to his colleagues on the ground. He was wearing an earpiece, meaning that Alex could only hear his end of the conversation.

'The negotiators are good to go,' the officer said. 'What's it looking like out there?'

The negotiation team waited while he listened to the response.

'Understood. Standing by.' The armed officer looked across at Alex. 'They just need another ninety seconds to get everyone and everything set. I'll give you the go-ahead as soon as I have it.'

Alex straightened up and stretched his arms above his head, then bent down and touched his toes. He rolled his head around his shoulders and felt a pressure-releasing click in the back of his neck.

'You've got this,' Pip repeated to him for the fourth or fifth time. It was becoming something of a mantra, an expression as much of faith as it was of fact.

In the street beyond the bay window, an ambulance moved into position and a pair of paramedics jumped out and opened the rear doors.

Lee

Grace's phone rang. Connor checked the display for a moment before answering. The screen showed a series of unopened texts from someone called Isaiah. But Connor had no interest in them. At least, not for now.

'You took your time.' His tone was surly.

'We went as quickly as we could,' Alex replied. 'The most important thing is to make sure we can get this done safely,' he said, before adding, almost as an afterthought, 'for everyone.'

Connor grunted.

'You're setting the pace here, Mr Connor,' Alex continued, 'but would it be all right if I explained how we would like to do this?'

'Be quick.' Connor's response was terse. Grumpy. He sounded like a teenager being compelled to act against his will, largely because he remained unsure that he was doing the right thing. It was only the thought of Nicholas Farmer and what he might say – the reluctant acknowledgement that the cause might indeed be harmed by the death of the priest – that persuaded him, begrudgingly, to listen to the plan as it was explained to him in painstaking detail. Alex went through it twice, line by line, checking that Connor understood it.

'We're ready when you are,' the negotiator said.

'Well, I'm not ready,' Connor replied, in a renewed attempt to reassert himself. 'I'll call you back when I am.' He ended the call and plugged the phone back into the charger.

'You two,' he gestured at Rosie and Grace, 'stay exactly where you are and do not move.' His instruction was firm, but his voice was laced with anxiety.

He stalked across the room and grabbed the back of Rahel's

chair. She screamed in shock, the sound muffled by the tape covering her mouth. Twenty feet away, Mariam struggled with her bonds, a mother's instinct compelling her to respond to a daughter's cry. But she was as helpless as Grace had been before her and she let out a consequent low howl of despair.

Tilting Rahel's chair backwards, Connor dragged it – and her – towards the front of the hall and into the foyer. He moved her into a position immediately in front of the main doors, about six feet back from them. Then he repeated the same move with Ittack, who had determined that he would remain silent – that he would not betray his terror. And so Connor lined up the two children like human sandbags in his planned defence of the building.

Alex

In the negotiation cell, among the armed teams outside, and in a whole host of locations around London, where senior officers and officials were anxiously awaiting updates, the seconds passed like minutes and the minutes passed like hours.

Outside in the street, in gardens and on rooftops, the fingers of snipers rested alongside trigger guards as eyes peered through telescopic sights. Everyone was watching; everyone was waiting. Those who were in the habit of saying prayers did just that; those who weren't considered the possibility of doing so for the first time in a long time.

Inside the cell, Alex paced the room, desperate to get on with it, afraid that something was about to go horribly wrong. He was once again feeling the full weight of it all and it was threatening to overwhelm him completely.

He only hoped it didn't show.

Grace

Connor gave Grace a sharp kick in the thigh as she sat beside Rosie. 'Time to get moving,' he said. Grace would not give him the satisfaction of crying out or reacting in any other way. She kept looking at Rosie.

'I don't know if I'm going to be able to lift her,' Grace said.

'Just fucking get on with it,' growled Connor impatiently.

Grace realised that there was no sense in pushing the point. She was acutely conscious of the precarious nature of the situation and the volatility of Connor's mood. There was nothing else for it — it was up to her to get Rosie out of there, and the depth of the concern she felt for her friend was greater than the sum of all her fears.

'Time to go,' she whispered quietly, as she took a firmer grip around Rosie's back. 'You can lean your weight on me,' she said. Grace then manoeuvred herself gingerly onto her haunches. 'Here we go,' she said and, with one almighty effort, stood up, pulling Rosie with her.

Grace was doing her best to be as careful and gentle as possible, but she shuddered as she felt Rosie's body spasm.

The sudden change of position had set a storm of pain and nausea raging all the way through Rosie's body. She retched and, had there been anything left in her system, she would have been sick again. She lapsed momentarily back into unconsciousness, another trickle of blood and fluid emerging from the corner of her mouth.

Grace was now bearing the full weight of her friend and she stumbled under the load, only just managing to remain on her feet.

Connor made no attempt to help either of them. He remained

standing a few feet away, a distant look in his eyes, the Baikal pistol in his right hand.

Grace braced herself like a weightlifter between clean and jerk, knees bent a little, leg muscles trembling. Her mind was suddenly empty of all other thoughts, save an absolute determination to get the job done. Rosie rallied slightly and managed to take some of her own weight.

'Let's get you to the door,' Grace said and the two of them began a painfully slow shuffle-drag from the hall to the foyer. It seemed to take for ever, Grace needing to pause every two or three paces to catch her breath, Rosie juddering with each new rush of pain. But, eventually, they made it to the place where the two children were sitting.

Right arm still wrapped around Rosie, Grace reached out with her left hand for a lone chair that sat beside the front doors, a pile of Bibles stacked on it. She managed to tip the Bibles off, pull the chair towards her and lower Rosie onto the seat. Then she sank to her knees, utterly exhausted, her forehead resting on Rosie's lap, her arms wrapped around her to make sure she didn't fall to the floor. Ittack and Rahel stared at the two of them, unblinking and desperately afraid. As she tried to gather herself, Grace could sense Connor close by. Then she felt the barrel of the gun pressed once more against the side of her head.

'Listen to me very carefully,' he hissed. 'You need to do exactly as I tell you – when I tell you – or this is going to get very ugly. Do you understand?'

Grace nodded but didn't turn her head to look at him. He responded by grabbing her hair with his spare hand and yanking her round so that she was facing him. She gritted her teeth and, slowly, raised her eyes to meet his.

'When I give you the instruction, you are going to unlock

the front door. You are going to open it halfway and you are going to hand the priest over to whoever the fuck is waiting out there. You are not going to mess around; you are going to get it done as quickly as possible. Then you are going to close the door and lock it again.' He was still holding a fistful of Grace's hair and he pulled it hard again for emphasis, jerking her head backwards. 'If you even think about doing anything stupid, these two kids will both get a bullet in the back of the head. Do you understand?' His voice rose towards a sort of crescendo as he asked the last question.

Again Grace nodded. She was holding Rosie's hand now and both women tightened their grip on one another.

Lee

Connor went back into the hall to collect Grace's phone. There had been more texts from Isaiah, the last of which could be read in full in a preview bubble on the screen. *I really love you mum. I'm scared. Please come home soon x.* Connor ignored it, opening up the call log and selecting the number at the top as he moved back into the foyer.

There was obvious relief in the police negotiator's voice as the call connected. 'There you are!' he said. 'I was getting worried.'

'I'm ready now,' Connor muttered. 'You can come and get the priest.'

Except that Connor wasn't at all sure that he was actually ready. He was still arguing furiously with himself about whether he was doing the right thing. Yes, he was. No, he wasn't. The debate continued to fly backwards and forwards in his head. He was unsettled and confused.

'Thank you, Mr Connor,' said Alex, oblivious to Connor's

state of mind. 'If you stay on the line with me, I will talk you through everything that is now going to happen – as it happens. I promise you that there will be no surprises and I promise you that no one will make any attempt to enter the building. You have my word.'

'There are two children tied to chairs immediately inside the door, with a gun pointed directly at the back of their heads,' Connor responded icily. 'If anyone does try to come in, the kids will be dead before your officers have even crossed the threshold.' There was a pause at the other end of the line while this news was digested.

'I understand,' said Alex, 'but I have given you my word: no one is coming in. I don't want anyone else to get hurt tonight. I want everyone to get out of there safely . . . Everyone.'

'Get on with it.' Connor sounded frustrated. Though he would never have admitted it and was scarcely even conscious of it, he was actually afraid. Afraid that he was doing the wrong thing. Afraid that he was losing his grip on the situation. Afraid of the unknown.

'Everything is going to happen exactly as I explain it to you,' said the negotiator. 'There will be no sudden moves, I promise. The armed officers are going to approach the front of the building now and I will tell you when they are in position.'

Connor was holding the gun in his right hand and the phone in his left. The two children were positioned between him and the door. He pointed the Baikal at Grace. 'Get ready,' he hissed.

Grace braced herself to lift Rosie up from the chair. 'Nearly there,' she whispered. Rosie nodded slowly, perhaps not fully aware of what was about to happen. The atmosphere in the hall was increasingly tense. Connor sank to a coward's crouch behind Ittack and Rahel.

'They're moving up the path towards the hall now.'

Alex was maintaining a steady commentary. Connor was feeling ever more on edge, a succession of quick-fire thoughts clattering through his mind: what if the door to the hall burst inwards and the police came flooding through? How would he react? What if the damned black woman tried to escape once the door was opened? What would he do if that happened? What if everything he had been so carefully preparing for so many weeks was all about to come crashing down around him? He could feel the paranoia starting to settle in and take root. He hated it. He tried to regulate his breathing. Every muscle in his body seemed to be twitching. His index finger moved to the trigger of the gun.

'They're outside the door now. They're ready when you are.'

Grace

Grace couldn't hear Alex's voice. She hadn't heard the plan being explained. She could only guess at what was happening outside and at what the next few moments would demand of her. But she felt a renewed sense of gritty determination – she was going to get her friend out of there.

'Now,' demanded Connor, 'open the door and fucking get rid of her.' Then, just as Grace was starting to move, he shouted at her, his voice renewed in its intensity: 'Look at me,' he demanded. He was nervy. On edge.

Grace stiffened, before turning and looking at him. He was half hidden behind the gaunt, haunted children, pointing the gun at her.

'Don't even think about doing anything stupid.'

Checking carefully that Rosie was able to hold herself upright in the chair, Grace reached out towards the door. Her hand was shaking and, at first, she struggled to grip the lock. She willed the shaking to stop and tried again. This time, she managed to turn it. She heard a click and felt the weight of the door easing back against its hinges. Then she opened it slowly – no more than halfway, as instructed – and found herself face to face with an armed police officer, illuminated from behind by nearby house lights and street lamps. The barrel of the gun that was pointed directly at her was lowered a fraction. Grace couldn't tell initially whether the officer was male or female: their ballistic helmet was pulled low, their eyes were covered with protective goggles and their mouth and chin were hidden by a balaclava. For a split second, the two of them stared at one another, before the officer gave her a nod of recognition and reassurance.

'You must be Grace.'

The officer was female. Her voice was strong and reassuring. And there was nothing that Grace could do to hold back the tears. She was feeling a mixture of relief and fear and uncertainty and exhaustion and hope and fear all over again.

'It's all right,' said the voice from behind the balaclava, 'you're doing an incredible job, Grace. Let's get Rosie out of there, shall we?' The officer reached out a hand and touched Grace gently on the arm.

There were more tears as Grace tried to steady herself. Then she turned back to Rosie. She crouched down next to her and placed her right arm behind her back. She heaved Rosie up onto her feet as Rosie spluttered and groaned in discomfort and distress. Slowly, she began to ease her towards the door and the officers who were waiting to receive her.

'Wait!' bellowed Connor.

23.06 hrs

Alex

Inside the negotiating cell, the firearms officer was relaying a live commentary from one of his colleagues who was positioned out at the front of the hall. Alex and his colleagues had been listening intently to his description of the main door opening and the reported sighting of Grace just inside the building. They were almost there.

'Hold on,' the firearms officer said, 'something's not right.'

Alex stared at him in alarm.

'Apparently, the front door has just been closed again,' the firearms officer reported. 'There's no sign of the hostages.'

Grace

Grace was physically and psychologically shattered. She had been so close to getting Rosie out. But when Connor had yelled at her to wait, she'd had no choice. His gun had been pointing straight at her.

'Shut the fucking door!' he had shouted at her.

And she had complied, struggling to support Rosie with one arm, while reaching out with the other to close it.

'Lock it!' he had demanded. And she had done so. She had

managed to lower Rosie back onto the chair and was now kneeling next to her, staring in frightened dismay at Connor, who was pacing rapidly backwards and forwards behind Rahel and Ittack. Both children were crying.

Lee

Connor was feeling furious with himself. Furious at the situation. Furious at his reaction to it. Furious that he felt so unprepared for it. For all his meticulous planning, he had failed to envisage any scenario involving the release of a single hostage. That had never even been a consideration. Either Nicholas Farmer was going to be released, in which case he would let them all go, or Nicholas Farmer wasn't going to be released, in which case none of them would be leaving. In his mind, it had been either one or the other and he had made no allowances for anything in between.

The moment Grace had opened the door, he had experienced a sudden, dizzying sense that he was losing his grip on what was happening. He had felt as though he was starting to slide towards the edge of a precipice. And he had panicked. Yelling at Grace to shut the door had been his way of trying to regain control of the situation.

But it hadn't worked. Even as he tried to convince himself that he was still in charge, all he could actually feel was a renewed sense of uncertainty and confusion. His thoughts crowded in on him. Shouldn't he just have let her go? He was a fucking idiot. No, he wasn't. What should he do now? His mind offered him no respite. Other voices started to crowd in on him. He should have let her go. No, he shouldn't. He was still in control of what was happening. No, he wasn't. Yes, he fucking was.

Alex

'What the hell is happening?' Pip was shouting at the firearms officer.

'Nothing,' came the uncertain reply. 'No movement. No sound. Nothing.' He pressed his finger to his earpiece and listened for any news.

Pip looked at Alex. 'Get him back on the phone,' she instructed him. 'We need to know what's going on in there.'

Alex responded instantly, relieved to have been given something of substance to do. It would help to keep his anxieties in check. He grabbed his mobile and connected the call. It rang once. Twice. Three times.

'What?' demanded Connor when the call finally connected. His voice curt, his temper was short.

'Mr Connor, it's Alex.'

'I know who it fucking is!' Connor snapped.

Alex winced and breathed in sharply. 'Is everyone all right in there?' he asked as calmly as he could, wanting to draw the sting from Connor's mood, but afraid of what might happen if he didn't succeed.

'We're fine,' came the blunt reply.

'What about Rosie? Is she all right?' Alex asked. The image of the wounded priest – the one he had seen on Twitter earlier in the night – flashed back into his mind. He didn't dare imagine what state she might be in now.

'I told you, we're fine,' said Connor, his voice dropping in volume. He was beginning to sound surly again.

'That's a relief,' said Alex, wanting to take Connor at his word but unwilling to allow his hopes to get ahead of him. 'Can I ask what just happened?'

'Nothing,' came the unhelpful response.

'I'm sorry, I don't understand what you mean,' said Alex. 'I thought we were going to get Rosie to the hospital.'

'We are,' came the monosyllabic reply.

'Er ... OK,' Alex responded, trying to interpret Connor's intentions; edging his way towards finding the right thing to say; desperate to avoid triggering an adverse response at the other end of the line. 'That's ... that's very good news,' he said, his words stumbling a little. 'Does that mean you're going to let her go now?'

'Just be ready,' Connor said.

The line was cut before anything more could be said.

Alex looked straight at the firearms officer, uncertain of Connor's exact intentions, desperate for any report of renewed movement at the front of the hall.

Lee

'Get her out of here,' Connor said to Grace.

After a further, chaotic barrage of conflicting thoughts, and with immense reluctance and frustration, he had reverted back to his original decision. Letting the priest go remained the lesser evil.

Grace

Grace was feeling so exhausted that it required a huge effort on her part just to get back on her feet. She said a rapid prayer, asking for strength, then she lifted Rosie up and walked her slowly back towards the door. She managed to turn the lock first time and she pulled on the handle. The same female fire-arms officer was waiting just outside, with two of her colleagues standing next to her.

'Let's get this done, shall we, Grace?' the officer said.

As Grace was in the process of handing the fragile burden of her friend over to them, she was faced with a moment of sudden clarity, of stark realisation. She had been so preoccupied with Rosie that she hadn't properly considered it before: the possibility of making a break for it. The very real and imme-diate prospect of escape was now presenting itself to her. And she realised that it wouldn't even be difficult. The officers were no more than three feet away from her. The path from the front door of the hall to the street outside was right there in front of her. Connor was too far back to make any kind of grab for her. She would be safe in seconds.

Alex

In the cell, everyone was silent. They had been told that the door to the hall was open again. There was a collective holding of their breath as they listened fearfully for the staccato sound of gunfire.

But there was none.

'She's out!' It was the voice of the firearms officer breaking the silence. All eyes in the cell were on him.

Grace

Grace stared out into the street as Rosie was being lowered carefully onto the waiting stretcher. It would be so easy to run.

And yet, it was also impossible. She knew exactly what would happen to the children if she abandoned them. And so there were no second thoughts. She knew that she would never, ever leave them behind; that she would sooner die with them in the hall than live with their deaths on her conscience.

She closed and locked the door. Then she crumpled to the floor and sobbed.

Alex

'She's out of the building,' the firearms officer confirmed. 'She's on the stretcher and they're bringing her down to the ambulance now.'

'Get in there!' exclaimed Rich, clapping Alex on the back. Alex joined the others as they crowded into the bay window. They watched as Rosie was hurried down the hill towards the back of the ambulance, a team of armed officers and paramedics jogging alongside her. They loaded her in and one of the armed officers climbed in with her. Moments later, the ambulance was on the move.

'How is she?' Alex asked urgently.

'Difficult to be sure at this stage,' replied the firearms officer, 'but they think she's going to make it.'

Pip enveloped Alex in a hug. 'Thank God for that,' she said as she released him and fixed her eyes on his. But after the elation of the moment came the bitterness of the realisation.

'There are eight more of them in there,' said Alex.

Lee

Connor had watched it all from his hiding place behind the two children. He had been entirely preoccupied by the possibility that armed officers were about to force their way into the hall, or that the black woman was going to make a run for it. He relaxed a fraction when Grace finally relocked the doors, but the passage of events had left him weary and unsettled. He had experienced it as a kind of defeat, though he tried to insist to himself that the reality was otherwise.

He still had eight hostages after all.

He grabbed Grace by the arm, pulled her to her feet and shoved her back into the hall. Then he pushed her down onto her chair, resecured her hands and feet. Feeling a sudden thirst, he reached for a bottle of water, leaving her mouth untaped.

23.14 hrs

Alex

Alex stared up at the ceiling from the armchair he had slumped into. Pip appeared from the direction of the kitchen carrying a large tin that she'd managed to requisition. It contained biscuits and bars of chocolate, willingly donated by the owners of the house. She was also holding a bunch of bananas.

'Get some food inside you,' she said to him.

Alex didn't much feel like eating, but he knew that he ought to. Who knew how many more hours they had ahead of them? One hostage was safely out, but there were eight more still inside.

The flipchart pages in the cell had all been updated. They displayed the names and approximate ages of the remaining eight prisoners, all supplied by a fortunate member of the congregation who would have been at the prayer meeting himself had it not been for the school parents' evening. Someone, from somewhere, had also managed to produce screenshot photographs from Connor's Twitter film, so they had pictures too. Names and faces, all lined up on the wall in front of them. Eight lives in their hands.

Alex studied each picture in turn. He tried to commit their names to memory. Mariam. Rahel. Ittack. The two children looked similar in age to his own two boys. Grace. So that's what she looked like. Helen. Jack. Alan. Jean.

'We can't sit back now,' he said. 'We need to get straight back into him. He's let one person go, maybe he'd be willing to do the same with some of the others.'

'I agree,' said Pip. 'We should start with the children.'

Lee

'Thank you for doing the right thing – for letting Rosie go,' said the voice of the negotiator at the other end of the line. 'She's on her way to hospital and she's going to get the help she needs.'

Connor had spent the previous few minutes alone with his thoughts, trying to slow himself down again, reminding himself repeatedly that he still had a plan – that he needed to play the long game. He had rechecked for the fifth or sixth time that each of the remaining hostages was still tied securely. He had been to the back of the hall to confirm that the fire doors remained locked. He had drunk a full bottle of water and had been part way through another large handful of trail mix when Alex called.

'Quid pro quo,' he responded sourly, 'I've done what you wanted. Now it's time for you to do what I want. When is Farmer going to be released?'

'I don't know the answer to that,' Alex responded, anticipating the question this time. 'You know that's not a decision I can make – it's way above my pay grade. But I have passed your request on to the people in charge – as I said I would – and I promise to let you know as soon as I have any kind of update.'

'How long is that going to take?' said Connor impatiently.

'I honestly don't know.' Alex sounded sincere. 'It's after

eleven o'clock now and I suspect the people we need to speak to from the prison service – and wherever else – are all tucked up at home in bed.'

Connor came straight back at him. 'They'll all be watching this live on TV,' he said somewhat grandiosely. 'Just like everyone else.' He was talking on Grace's phone while scrolling through his own and he had already seen that he had hundreds of fresh Twitter notifications. Thousands probably. And that felt good. He knew for certain that people were watching and he was beginning to feel more positive about the potential size of his audience. He was still in control.

'I honestly don't know what's happening out there,' said Alex. 'You have my full attention.'

Connor didn't respond. He had become momentarily distracted by some of the responses on his Twitter feed: the voices of those urging him on, countered by those who were pleading with him to stop what he was doing. And when they weren't all shouting at him, they were yelling at one another.

'How are Ittack and Rahel?' asked Alex.

'Who?' said Connor.

'Ittack and Rahel,' Alex continued, 'the two children you have in there with you.'

'Ah, so you've found out who they are, have you?'

'Those are their names, yes. And their mother is called Mariam. They're just children, Mr Connor – innocent refugees, who have only just managed to escape from the war in Syria.'

'And your point is?' said Connor, sullen again.

'Your argument isn't with them,' suggested Alex. 'They don't belong in there.'

'They are prisoners of war,' replied Connor, rediscovering his defiance. 'Prisoners of war, just like their mother. Just like everyone else in here.'

'But they're children,' persisted Alex, his voice measured and clear. 'You've already done the right thing once. You let Rosie go and I'm incredibly grateful to you. And I want to ask you to consider doing the right thing again by letting the children go.'

'Fuck off!' exploded Connor, instantly furious. 'What kind of a fucking fool do you take me for?' He cut the call off before Alex had any chance to respond.

'What kind of a fool do they take me for?' He was talking to himself now. 'What kind of a fucking fool?' he said. He started striding round the room in his angst. Then, in a surge of rage, driven by nerves and adrenaline and a fresh sense of confusion about whether or not Rosie's release had been a good idea, he picked up the chair that was closest to him and smashed it repeatedly against one of the walls. Bits of wood and fabric and fragments of plaster from the wall scattered in every direction. Each of the hostages held their breath and tried to make themselves smaller. All of them closed their eyes. None of them dared look in his direction. The air in the hall had been consumed by fear.

Alex

In the negotiating cell, Alex had gasped as the line went dead again. Though Connor had ended calls several times already, each time it had happened, Alex had experienced it as a fresh blow, but this one had hit him especially hard. Instantly, he had started questioning and second-guessing himself again. What had gone wrong? What had he just said? He tried to remember the exact words he had used. Why had Connor blown up so suddenly? And what the hell was now happening inside the hall? Were the hostages being harmed? If they were, it was surely all his fault.

Shit.

Shit, shit, shit.

Pip was reliably swift to offer her reassurance.

'You didn't do anything wrong, Alex . . . What you said was spot on, exactly as we'd all agreed. We know he's volatile, but none of us could have predicted that he'd go off like that. Let's just give him a few minutes to cool down and then we'll call him back.'

Alex didn't respond to her. He was on a runaway roller-coaster of concealed emotions and, once again, his mind was drifting back to another part of London. Once again, he was remembering the sound of gunfire. Pip was the only one in the room who noticed the look of distress in his eyes.

'Let's all take a breather for a minute or two,' she suggested. She seemed to know exactly what was required. 'All of you, clear your heads, get some food inside you. We've got a long night ahead of us.'

She nodded at Rich and then towards the door. He understood immediately. He nudged Angie and the armed officer out into the corridor and towards the kitchen. It meant that Pip and Alex were alone in the sitting room. She walked slowly over to where he was sitting. She crouched down in front of him and placed her hands on his knees. Alex sighed and leaned towards her, suddenly in desperate need of the comfort of a friend.

'Come on,' she said to him, 'let's get some fresh air.' Without waiting for a reply, she took him by the hands, pulled him up to his feet and ushered him out towards the front of the house.

'Have you got a cigarette?' he asked her as they emerged through the front door.

'You don't smoke,' she replied, a look of surprise on her face.

'Maybe not, but you do.' He attempted some sort of grin as he said this but managed only a grimace. 'And the occasional one is hardly going to do me any harm. To be honest, I reckon I've earned it.'

'Your wife will kill me if she finds out! You're always telling me how much she hates the habit.'

'To be honest, I don't think she'll care,' Alex replied. 'She's got other, much more pressing, concerns on her mind at the moment,' he added, without elaborating.

Pip shrugged her shoulders and chose not to press the issue. She produced a pack of Marlboro Lights from her jacket pocket, flipped the top open and held it out to him. He took a cigarette and, hands cupped round the tip of it, stepped closer to her as she offered him a light. He inhaled, turned his head to one side and blew a plume of smoke out towards the street.

'How are you doing?' she asked him, as she lit one of her own.

'I'm fine,' he said.

'What does that mean?' she asked. Her tone was kind but firm. She knew he wasn't fine at all.

He tried to look her in the eye, but found it difficult to hold her gaze.

'None of us has ever been involved in anything like this before,' she said, 'anything remotely as big as this. You must be feeling it . . . I know I am.' Her honesty was disarming and this time he managed to look at her.

'How's this one going to end, Pip?'

'I don't know,' she acknowledged simply, 'but negotiators are optimists, remember?'

'They are until a job ends badly.' He blew another cloud of cigarette smoke in the direction of the street.

The look of concern on Pip's face was replaced with one of sudden realisation. 'Is this about Romford?' she asked.

Alex didn't answer her straight away, but he was unable to hide his body language. He felt his head drop and his shoulders follow. There was a faint tremor in his hand as he took another drag on his cigarette. He coughed as he exhaled.

'Probably,' came his eventual, reluctant reply.

'I wouldn't be the least bit surprised if it was,' she said. 'In fact, I'd be more surprised if Romford *wasn't* somewhere in your thoughts.' She allowed the silence to linger for a while before she continued. 'Why don't you tell me what happened there?'

'Don't you know?' He looked confused. 'I thought everyone knew.'

'I know the headlines, of course,' she said, 'but not the details.'

'And you want to hear them now?'

'Why not?' she said. 'We've got a little bit of time. And it might actually do you some good to talk about it.'

'Maybe,' he said. He wasn't convinced by her suggestion. If it had been anyone else asking, he would have tried to change the subject straight away, but Pip seemed to have a way of opening him up. And she was one of the few people he trusted completely.

'It was the middle of the afternoon,' he began, 'I think it was a Wednesday.' He frowned as, once again, he found himself transported back in time. 'I was in the office catching up on paperwork when the phone rang. Rich was the co-ordinator that week and he filled me in on the basic details. The locals had been on scene in East London for a good hour before we were even called. The address in question was well known to them for domestic violence – they got calls there pretty much every week – and the children were all on the Social Services "At Risk" register.'

Alex hesitated as he remembered the faces of the terrified children.

'The first officers to arrive on scene had expected things to play out in the same way they always did: with him being carted off for a night in the cells, with her refusing to supply any kind of statement, and with a whole pile of seemingly pointless paperwork for them all to complete. But it rapidly became apparent that things were different this time round. The suspect had always been a drinker, but on this occasion, it turned out he'd been taking cocaine as well. He'd barricaded himself into the house with his wife and the three kids – all of them under the age of ten – and he yelled to the officers outside that he had a gun. That's when they called us.'

Pip nodded at him, encouraging him to keep going. It occurred to Alex that he had already told her more about the incident than he had ever told his wife.

He kept talking. He told Pip about their eventual arrival on scene; about the long, tense hours that followed; about the eventual release of the children and their mother. The kids had been incredibly shaken up, but they were physically unharmed. Their mother had multiple cuts and bruises, but no broken bones. The only person left in the building was the suspect.

'Initially, things looked promising,' Alex continued. 'He was engaging with us intermittently, appearing at the front door before disappearing back inside. But then it all changed. He must have taken some more gear because he went completely berserk and started wrecking the place. He smashed all the windows and started throwing furniture and clothing and children's toys out into the little yard at the front of the house. Then, after several minutes of sustained carnage, he appeared back at the front door.'

Alex could see it all as he spoke: the mad-eyed, bare-chested man standing on the steps, holding a large kitchen knife in each hand; the line of armed-response officers crouched behind ballistic shields, carbines raised. He and the other negotiators were crouching immediately behind the armed team and he was trying absolutely everything to reason with a man unhinged. It was quickly becoming a losing struggle.

'The threats to us rapidly started to escalate – he was making repeated stabbing and slashing movements with the knives. And then, without any kind of warning, he charged. He ran directly at the officers in front of me and, if they hadn't shot him, there's absolutely no doubt in my mind that he would have stabbed one or more of them. Three of them fired simultaneously and he died instantly.'

'Suicide by cop,' Pip said quietly.

'Suicide by cop,' repeated Alex, barely louder than a whisper.

'And it all happened right in front of you.'

Alex nodded. He could recall every last detail with forensic accuracy. The weather had been changeable that day: he could feel the breeze on his face, and the light smattering of rain. He could hear the instant, shocking volley of gunshots. And he could see the man fall, just a few feet away from where he was standing. He could see the body sprawled on the ground, blood beginning to pool around it. He turned away from Pip as if he was turning away from the scene.

She moved a step closer to him and placed her hand on his arm. 'There was nothing else you could have done,' she said softly.

Alex stared up into the night sky. He knew she was right. In addition to the debriefing process and dozens of private conversations with Rich and the others, he had mentally relived and replayed the Romford negotiation a hundred times and more. And it always ended the same way: with the suspect lying dead in front of him. He was as certain as he ever would be that there was nothing else he – or any of them – could have done. But it haunted him all the same.

'You saved four lives that day,' Pip continued, 'four precious human lives. The only person who died was the one who chose to die.'

'I know all that, Pip,' said Alex, turning slowly to face her again, 'but it doesn't seem to make it any easier.'

'Of course it doesn't,' she acknowledged. 'It's going to take time. These things always do.'

'I suppose you're right,' he said.

'I know I am,' she replied.

It was Alex's turn to reach out and put a hand on her arm. Somewhere in the wild swirl of his emotions, there was at least some sense of relief at having begun to share the burden with her.

'Thanks, Pip,' he said.

23.21 hrs

Grace

Connor was looking agitated. Sitting a few feet away from where he was standing, Grace was feeling desperately alone. While she was incredibly relieved that Rosie was safely out, it was as though a large part of her own hope had left the hall alongside her friend. She worried about Isaiah, who must surely know what was happening by now. He was mature for his age, but he was still just a boy. Who would he turn to? Who would think to check up on him? Perhaps the police would go round to the flat. Perhaps that would make things worse. She thought about the reaction from her elderly mother who, if she didn't know already, would find out sooner or later. And what would that do to her brittle health? She thought agitatedly about the friends and family members she hadn't spoken to in a while and about the colleague at work with whom she had exchanged angry words the day before. It had been about nothing really – a simple misunderstanding and an unfounded accusation that had upset her. She had been blameless in all of it, but she had been planning to say sorry all the same.

And then there were the others trapped in the hall with her. Alan and Jean were in their seventies and Alan had a dodgy heart. What must all of this be doing to the two of them? Jack was alarmingly unpredictable and Helen, bound and gagged,

163

was in no position to calm him down. And then there was Mariam and her children – strangers in a country where they'd sought refuge from chaos and war; guests in a little church hall where they ought to have been completely safe. Grace was beginning to lapse into despair.

The comforting words of the twenty-third Psalm eluded her.

Lee

Eventually, Connor stopped prowling. He had made up his mind about what to do next. He grabbed hold of Grace's chair and dragged it into the middle of the room, almost tipping her over in the process. Grace managed not to scream. He did the same with Mariam, placing her next to Grace, leaving enough space for him to be able to walk freely between the two of them. Then he went out to the foyer and, one after the other, dragged the children and their chairs back into the main hall, placing them on either side of Grace and Mariam: one black Briton and three Syrian refugees, arranged like the four points of a compass. Connor stood and stared at them, holding the gun in his right hand and one of the knives in his left.

'Look at me,' he ordered.

Grace was the only one who responded.

'Look at me!' he demanded, irritated by the apparent non-compliance of the other three.

'They don't speak English,' Grace said quietly. 'They don't understand what you're saying.'

'Fucking immigrants,' he muttered with contempt.

He walked up to Mariam. He planted the barrel on the gun in the centre of her forehead and pushed her head backwards, forcing her to look up at him. Then he drew the blade of the knife across the front of her throat. He wasn't trying to cut her, merely to reaffirm his sense of power and her sense of helplessness. Mariam set her jaw and fixed her gaze somewhere beyond him.

'Fucking immigrant.' Connor spat the words in her face, working himself up some more as he did so.

Then he moved round to Ittack. He pressed the gun into his forehead and, finally, it was all too much for the boy, who wet himself. He was wearing light grey tracksuit bottoms and Connor watched the damp patch spread inevitably outwards. Ittack wept with fear and shame.

'Filthy fucking immigrant.'

Connor put the knife down on the floor and pulled his own mobile phone out of his pocket. He pressed on the Twitter icon and discovered that the Home Front Liberator account had been suspended. It came as no surprise. It had actually taken them longer to do it than he had anticipated, but it was always going to happen at some point and he had a plan ready for when it did. He switched the camera on and began filming.

He started circling the four hostages seated in the middle of the room and he spoke as he walked.

'First there were nine hostages. Now there are eight. This is because I have chosen to show my humanity – and the justice of my cause – by letting the priest go. I am the Home Front Liberator and my fight is not with Christian men and women of pure white blood.' His tone was superior, pompous even. 'My battle is with those who would seek to steal what is ours: the illegal immigrants, the so-called-refugees, the cockroaches who are invading our country like some kind of medieval plague. You've read the articles in the *Mail* and the *Sun* and the *Telegraph*. You've seen the pictures on a thousand websites: endless boatloads of people who don't belong here, bearing down on the *White* Cliffs of Dover, wanting to take what belongs to us. And I, for one, am not prepared to stand by silently and let it all happen. Every single decent, law-abiding, English man and woman has had enough . . .' He stopped walking and fixed the camera on Ittack's soaking-wet lap. 'It's time for them to go back to the shithole countries they came from. Either they go home in their boats, or they go home in a bag.'

He switched the camera off and reviewed the footage. Content with it, he posted it on an alternative Twitter account, confident in the belief that it would swiftly go viral. Then he scrolled through his photographs to find one he had taken the day before. It was an image of a single page of typed script headed 'The Manifesto', a carefully worded companion piece to his earlier speech. It was the same text that the SO15 team had found on his computer during the search of his bedsit. He had always planned to post it at some point during the night and now seemed to be the right time. The page ended with the words, 'It is Time to Make Britain Great Again'.

He nodded approvingly to himself as he reread it. Then he posted it online.

Alex

'Listen,' Pip said to Alex, 'do you want me to put Rich in as Number One for a while?'

The two of them were still standing outside the front of the house. They had been talking for a while and she was offering him the chance to take a break from his role. It was a perfectly reasonable consideration, an option she had turned to in several previous negotiations, on occasions when someone had needed a break. She had seen and heard enough in the past hour or two to feel a sense of legitimate concern, not just for Alex on a personal level, but for the ability of the whole team to move the negotiation forwards. But, at the same time, she understood that all of them were feeling the extreme pressure of the situation. The greater surprise would have been if Alex hadn't been showing some signs of strain, particularly given events in East London six months earlier.

'No, you don't need to do that,' he responded. 'I'm fine. I'm ready to go back in.'

'And Romford?' she asked him.

'Romford's in the past,' he replied. 'We're here now. And we've got a job to do.' He was feeling more positive than he had done for a while. 'Don't forget, Rich was at Romford too and you're not worried about him.'

Talking had helped, the cigarettes too. But it was actually spending a bit of time with Pip that seemed to have helped most of all. Alex looked at her and it occurred to him that she probably understood him better than his wife ever had. She seemed to appreciate him a good deal more too. It was a moment of realisation he hadn't anticipated, but there was no time to dwell on it.

'I'm good,' he reiterated. 'Just give me a moment to get myself set for the next call.'

23.50 hrs

Alex

A minute or two later, Alex followed Pip back into the sitting room and found the team gathered round a laptop. They had Connor's latest video up on the screen and had been waiting for Alex before pressing play. The five of them – four negotiators and the firearms officer – watched it in silence. Then they watched it through a second time to make sure they hadn't missed anything. Next came the image of Connor's 'manifesto' and they all took their time studying the wording.

'We've also had these come through from SO15,' Rich said once they had finished reading. He opened another tab on the computer to show them a series of photographs that had been sent through from the investigators who were on scene at the search of the bedsit. They showed the newspaper cuttings, the names and phrases scrawled on the walls, the front covers of a succession of leaflets and books.

'Bloody hell!' said Alex.

'Hmm,' responded Pip. 'I suppose that all this really gives us is confirmation of what we already know: that we're dealing with a far-right extremist; that we're negotiating with a terrorist.' She paused and looked round at her team. 'We know he's serious. We know he's well prepared. We know he's capable of violence. But – and here's the most important thing – we also know that it's possible to talk to him.'

'So what should our next move be?' asked Angie.

The team talked at length about whether or not Alex should renew his appeal for the children to be released. They were clear about the dangers involved in doing so, particularly given the nature of Connor's response the first time the question had been raised. But, equally, there were obvious risks in not doing so. There were two young lives at stake, alongside those of the remaining six adults. The whole team agreed that their immediate priority had to be to try to get the children out and, for that reason, they decided they had to take the risk.

Lee

Connor was back in the kitchen smoking when he heard Grace's phone ring. He had left it on charge in the main hall and he chose to ignore it. He would finish his joint and he would take the call only when he was good and ready. Though his mood was erratic, he retained a clear sense of what he was trying to achieve.

Alex

In the cell, Alex glanced up at his colleagues. The call had gone through to Grace's voicemail – something that hadn't happened before. He thought about leaving a message for her – one of simple encouragement and reassurance – but he reasoned that she would be highly unlikely to hear it any time soon. So he hung up.

'Give it a few minutes and then try again,' suggested Rich. 'If that doesn't work, we'll start to go through our other options.'

Pip nodded her agreement.

Alex

The next time Grace's phone rang, five minutes later, Connor was ready to take the call.

'Have you seen my new film?' His voice was curt.

'Yes, I have,' Alex replied calmly. 'I've seen Grace and Mariam and Rahel and Ittack.' As before, the use of the hostages' names was conscious and very deliberate. 'And they all look absolutely terrified. Especially the children.'

'Of course they look terrified,' came the retort.

'Have you given any more thought to the possibility of letting the children go?' Alex put the question carefully, bracing himself for the response as he did so.

Lee

'No I haven't and no I won't.'

Connor's response to the negotiator was blunt and unequivocal. The difference on this occasion was that he remained calm. He had anticipated the question. But he had no intention of being drawn any further on the subject. He had determined that he was going to be in complete control from this point onwards – and he certainly wasn't about to offer them what they wanted.

Before Alex could come back at him, he changed the subject. 'It's about time we got back to the real business. When exactly is Nicholas Farmer going to be released?'

'I don't have that information,' responded Alex.

'Why not?'

'Because, as we've said before, these things take time. I know you understand that.'

'Well, it's taking too much time — far too much time. What I'm telling you to do isn't fucking complicated. Even a four-year-old would be able to understand the instruction.'

'It isn't complicated, but it is difficult,' came Alex's reply.

'What the hell is that supposed to mean?' Connor demanded.

'It means that Nicholas Farmer has been convicted of some very serious crimes — so serious, in fact, that he's likely to be spending a number of years in prison.'

'Fuck that! His trial was a sham,' insisted Connor, retreating once more to the familiarity of his pre-prepared script. 'The only thing he's guilty of is an unwavering love for his country.'

'But the lives of dozens of people were put at risk when those fires were started at the hotel, at the Islamic Centre and at the Refugee Bureau.' Alex was firm in his challenge. 'It's an absolute miracle no one was killed.'

'Nicholas Farmer didn't start those fires,' Connor protested. Firmness met with defiance.

'Maybe not,' replied Alex, 'but he directed and supported and encouraged the people who did.'

'That's fake news.'

'That's not what the jury thought,' Alex insisted, 'and they heard all the evidence. Nicholas Farmer was part of a plot to target a group of completely innocent people and he now has to face the consequences of his actions.'

'The jury were wrong. The judge was wrong,' Connor retorted. 'Nicholas Farmer is a patriot.'

Alex

In the cell, prompted by a fresh note from Rich, who was still sitting to his right, Alex changed the subject.

'I've read your manifesto,' he said.

'And?'

'I wanted to ask you about it.'

When they weren't pushing directly for the release of the hostages, Alex and the team were still trying to buy as much time as they could.

Inside the cell, the atmosphere was one of relative stillness, but, outside the house, the activity remained relentless. There were more than two hundred police officers on scene by now – armed and unarmed; uniformed and detective; visible and hidden from sight – and the entire local neighbourhood was in lockdown. The Specialist Firearms Officers had moved into their forward positions and the military were on their way. Plans and contingencies that had been drawn up were being rehearsed and redrawn. Command structures were being renewed and enhanced. Frantic conversations were continuing to take place in the corridors of power – at Scotland Yard, at the Home Office, at the headquarters of MI5 and at any number of other locations in between. And an arsenal of surveillance equipment was now being deployed alongside the more conventional forms of weaponry. It meant that Alex needed to buy all the time he could.

He and the team had discussed the potential benefits – as well as the significant risks – of beginning to challenge Connor's ideological motivations. Connor had stated very clearly that he was prepared to die for his cause. But what if it were possible to somehow challenge the justice or the validity of that cause – to question whether he might be mistaken in his beliefs and that none of it was in fact worth dying for? It would have to be done incredibly carefully, but perhaps it was worth cautious investigation, particularly while Connor remained unwilling to countenance even the possibility of releasing the children.

'It makes a whole lot of sense, doesn't it?' There was pride in Connor's voice.

Alex avoided the question; avoided the suggestion that, no, it made absolutely no sense at all. He changed tack. 'Tell me about this idea of white genocide,' he said. 'It's not a phrase I've come across before.' Once more, he was telling the truth.

Connor was on solid ground now, confident of his subject matter. 'White people are facing an immediate existential threat, a fight for their very survival – the threat of a genocide far greater than any other in all of human history.' It sounded as though he was reciting lines learned from one of the pamphlets he had left in his bedroom.

'I don't understand,' Alex responded, again quite genuinely.

'Of course you don't. Your ignorance and blindness are part of the fucking problem.'

'How so?' Alex asked, continuing to use open questions. He understood that closed questions – those requiring only a 'yes' or 'no' answer – do little to open up or progress a negotiation. Closed questions rarely encourage a person to talk.

'Because you are part of the left-wing, hand-wringing, liberal elite who line up to excuse and defend these people who are tearing our country apart. Of course you don't fucking understand – because if you did, you'd be standing in here alongside me.'

'So help me to understand,' said Alex. He wasn't being provocative, he was simply encouraging Connor to keep talking.

'For the last seventy years – longer in fact – immigrant terrorists have been invading this country, intent on destroying our very way of life. They refuse to learn our language. They refuse to embrace our culture, choosing instead to impose their own on us. They hide away in backstreet mosques and plan for our destruction. They don't fucking belong here. Britain is ours; the rest must go.' Connor's voice pitched up and down as he spoke. One moment he was sounding almost considered and clear, the next he was starting to rant and rage.

'But I don't understand why you refer to them all as "immigrant *terrorists*",' Alex responded. 'When I think of immigrants, I think of people working as doctors and nurses and teachers and scientists and care workers and all the rest – individuals who are adding incredible richness to our society.' He didn't pause long enough to allow Connor to interrupt. 'And then I think of the Windrush generation – citizens of the Caribbean invited over here by the British government at the end of the Second World War because *we* needed *their* help to rebuild our country.'

'You just don't get it, do you?' Connor said with unveiled contempt. 'Who is it carrying rucksacks filled with homemade explosives? Who is it blowing up our buses and trains and concert halls? Who is it driving vans into crowds and attacking innocent citizens on London bridges? Someone has got to take a stand against this relentless evil.' Connor seemed to have no interest in what Alex was saying, nor any apparent awareness of the obvious hypocrisy in his actions and words. He had his own narrative, his own set of facts – and he wasn't going to deviate from it.

'But the men who carried out those attacks weren't immigrants,' Alex replied. 'They were British citizens, just like you and me.'

'Oh, for fuck's sake! Are you being deliberately stupid? They were either immigrants or they were the sons and grandsons of immigrants. What fucking difference does it make?' Connor made no attempt to disguise his anger.

'But what about the white men who carry out terrorist attacks, not just in this country, but in other places all round the world?' Alex was wondering how far he could – or should – push the debate. But Connor wasn't going to be drawn.

'Who was it who carried out the attacks on 7/7? Who was it who murdered that police officer outside the Houses of Parliament – your colleague, for fuck's sake? And, come to think of it, who was it who raped all those kids in Rotherham and in a dozen other towns? The perpetrators are immigrants and the victims are the white working class. Every. Single. Time.' His words were starting to flow now. 'Who the fuck is standing up for the white working class in this country?'

'The crimes you're describing are horrendous,' Alex readily agreed, 'but the point I'm trying to make is that people don't commit those crimes because of where they come from. They commit them because of who they are.'

'That's bollocks, and you know it.' Connor clearly wasn't about to change his mind.

'But what about the tens of thousands of immigrants – the overwhelming majority I was referring to before – who have brought only positive benefits to this country?'

'Well, first of all, there aren't tens of thousands of them – that's another piece of fake news. And, second of all, they are part of the fucking problem.'

'How so?'

'By raising children who blow up underground trains. By refusing to condemn the procession of hate preachers calling for jihad. By isolating themselves in their own communities. By stealing our benefits and placing strain on the National Health Service and the rest of our country's infrastructure.

Every single one of them needs to go back where they came from. And, when they're gone, we won't need a wall like the Americans to keep them out . . .'

Lee

The line had gone suddenly quiet.

Just as Connor had been building up a full head of steam, he had heard a sound coming from the roof above him. At least, he thought he had. He stopped pacing and was looking intently up at the ceiling. He drew the pistol out from his waistband.

'What the fuck was that?' he asked.

'What was what?' Alex sounded confused.

'That noise on the roof above me.'

'What noise?'

'That scraping sound. It came from the roof above me.'

'Are you sure?'

'Of course I'm fucking sure.' In fact, Connor wasn't sure at all, but his mind was running away with the idea. He was in the grip of his paranoia. 'There's somebody up on the roof. What the hell are they doing up there?' His words started to tumble out, 'I swear, if anyone tries to come in here, all hell is going to break loose.'

'Whoa, steady on. Slow down.' Alex was firm and reassuring. 'I'm sure there's nobody up on the roof.'

'If anyone tries to get in here . . .' Connor was becoming increasingly agitated.

Alex interrupted him, no doubt afraid that Connor might be about to do something dreadful. 'Nobody is trying to get in there,' he insisted passionately. 'I gave you my word before and you have my word now.'

Grace

Meanwhile, Grace had stumbled into a very dark place. She had fallen deep into her thoughts and had, for the time being, almost completely forgotten about the rest of the hostages. She was thinking instead about Isaiah and the various members of her family, both those who had long since passed away and those who were still alive. She was thinking about her elderly mother. She was thinking about mistakes, large and small, that she had made down the years and about things she had left undone that she believed she ought to have done. She was thinking about regret and loss and grief and sorrow, and her last remaining hopes were ebbing as her fears continued to flow. She was walking through the valley of the shadow of death.

00.14 hrs

Lee

Connor began to wonder whether he had indeed imagined the noise up on the roof. The hall was completely still. Though he strained his ears, he could hear no sound coming from above him. The hostages were all silent, heads down, eyes closed. There seemed to be nothing untoward or out of place.

'Are you still there?' It was Alex again.

'Yes.'

'I told you that you have my word no one is coming in.'

'And why should I believe you?' Connor was cautious and sceptical.

'Because I have kept my word at every other point along the way.'

Reluctantly, Connor had to accept that this was true, though he could still think of no material benefit he had gained as a consequence. He offered nothing more than a grunt by way of a response.

'Can I ask you something about your manifesto?' The negotiator was being nothing if not persistent.

'If you must.'

'My colleagues have been doing some research on David Lane while we've been talking,' said Alex. 'And they tell me that he was sent to jail for a whole series of terrible crimes.'

'He was a great man – a patriot,' Connor insisted.

'But he was sentenced to 190 years in jail for racketeering, conspiracy and murder,' said Alex.

'You have your facts and I have mine,' replied Connor.

Alex

Though Alex was feeling frustrated by Connor's intransigence, he had no option but to keep going. 'So you believe that the future of white children is important?' he suggested, adjusting his point of approach while simultaneously renewing his resolve.

'Of course it's important. What a fucking stupid question. Their future is everything.'

'I've got children.'

Alex said it almost without thinking. And, in doing so, he gave away something of himself – something personal, beyond his profession; something beyond his reason for being there that day. It was an instinctive decision, not something that anyone else on the team would have asked or expected of him. But he was trying to find a breakthrough.

Initially, Connor offered him nothing by way of a response.

'I've got two teenage boys,' Alex continued, 'and they mean absolutely everything to me.'

'Then you must understand exactly what I mean,' Connor replied.

'Sort of,' Alex said. 'I understand that there's nothing I wouldn't do for my children.'

'And that is precisely my point,' crowed Connor, thinking perhaps that Alex was at last coming round to his point of view. But he had somehow failed to see the obvious question that was coming next.

Pip was out of the room, so Alex glanced sideways at Rich for reassurance. Rich nodded and Alex took a breath.

'But why only white children?' he asked.

Connor let out a groan of exasperated frustration. 'Because whites are the superior race, and we need to take back – by force if necessary – all that we are in danger of losing.'

'But don't you think that a black parent feels exactly the same way about their children as I do about mine?'

'Why should I care?'

'Because, obvious as it sounds, skin colour is only skin deep. Beneath that, we're all the same.'

'No we fucking aren't.' Connor sounded outraged by the suggestion. He was once again agitated and volatile.

'Have you ever seen the Mauritian flag?' Alex interjected. He was thinking quickly, improvising, attempting to defuse Connor before he blew up again. And his unexpected question had the desired effect. Connor was thrown by the sudden change of direction. His immediate response was one of bafflement rather than rage.

'What the hell's that got to do with anything?'

'Mauritius is one of the most beautiful places on earth. I know because I've been there. Actually, I lived there with a friend for a few months before I joined the police.' Alex was offering up a little more of himself, searching to find any possible point of resonance or connection with the man on the other end of the line. 'Mauritian people are beautiful too,' he added. 'It's an island nation, inhabited by people of almost every colour, faith and language. Over the centuries, people from Africa, India and Europe have all settled there. The Mauritian flag is made up of four coloured, horizontal stripes – red, blue, yellow and green – and the Mauritian people are incredibly proud of it.'

'And?' Connor was immediately tired of the subject, unable to work out where Alex was going with it. 'What's your point?'

'Blue is the colour of the Pacific Ocean that surrounds them. Yellow is the colour of the sun that gives life to them. Green is the colour of their farmland and forests. And red is the colour of the blood that they all bleed, regardless of who they are, or where they and their families come from. Mauritian people understand that just below the surface of their skin, they are all the same – that they all share the same DNA.'

'They're wrong.'

'I don't think they are,' said Alex carefully. 'And they have both science and history on their side.'

'I disagree.' Connor was digging in, sounding increasingly obstinate.

'The point I suppose I am trying to make,' continued Alex, 'is that I care about the future of every child. I care about my own children, but I also care about Ittack and Rahel. I care about their future too.'

Connor didn't respond.

'Have you got children, Mr Connor?'

'No.'

'But you care about children.'

'I care about white children.'

'I'm asking you to care about Ittack and Rahel too.'

'Well I don't. I don't give a fuck about them. All I care about is the release of Nicholas Farmer and you're wasting my time.' His voice started to rise again. Alex heard the change in his tone, and once again tried to alter his approach.

'What would your family say about what you're doing here today?'

The negotiation team had earlier reasoned that Connor's strength of feeling about children – albeit only white ones – might extend to a belief in the importance of family. They could not have been more wrong.

'I have no family,' came the reply, his voice rising in intensity.

'What about your parents?' asked Alex, relying on one of a list of planned questions. But asking it was a serious mistake, one that made things immeasurably worse.

'My mother is dead and my father is dead to me.' Connor's voice accelerated to a roar.

And the line went dead again.

Grace

In his sudden fury, Connor had hurled Grace's phone against the wall, smashing it into dozens of pieces. One after the other, he picked up three chairs and launched them across the room. He stormed back and forth like a man possessed, kicking out at walls and furniture, raging at no one and nothing in particular. Eight terrified human beings cowered in their chairs. The storm was only just beginning to subside when Grace spoke.

'I'm so sorry for your loss,' she said. Her voice was soft and sad.

'What did you say?' Connor was completely and utterly blindsided by her. He came to a sudden standstill and spun round.

'I said that I'm sorry for your loss,' she repeated gently, venturing once more to make eye contact with him.

'What loss?' He seemed deeply confused, and in his confusion, his anger continued to ebb.

'The loss of your mother,' she responded. 'I heard you say on the phone that she had died.' Grace was now looking directly

at him. She had no real idea why she had said it to him, only
that it had come from a place deeper than her fears. And it
rendered Connor speechless.

Alex

In the negotiating cell, Alex had made several rapid attempts
to get Connor back on the line. But the phone wasn't even
ringing, much less connecting. He was experiencing a growing
sense of dread and desperation. His colleagues were reassuring
him. He had stuck to the plan, they said. He had followed the
script, they told him. None of them would have said or done
anything differently, they insisted. But, once again, he wasn't
hearing them. He was hearing gunshots. And he was falling.

Lee

'Why the fuck would you care?'

Connor had found his voice, but there was no menace in it.
He seemed lost.

Grace continued to hold his gaze.

'Because I know what it's like to lose someone you love.'

Connor offered no reply. What was it about this fucking black
woman? There was something about her that confounded him.
He had felt it earlier in the night when he saw her caring for
the priest. He felt it even more strongly now. And his feelings
made no sense to him whatsoever.

'I lost my husband,' Grace continued, 'and I lost my eldest
son.'

'Why would I give a shit about any of that?' Connor replied.

Grace

Connor seemed to be trying to reassert himself, but without much success. For the moment at least, much of the earlier aggression and antagonism was missing from his voice. Without intending it, Grace had him on the ropes.

'I'm not asking you to care about me or my life,' she said. 'I just want you to know that I understand how it feels. And I want you to know that I am sorry for your loss.'

In her own way, Grace was feeling no less confused than her captor. She could still sense the darkness all around her – darkness that Connor alone was responsible for. And she still felt deeply afraid. But something had begun to stir in her that she couldn't fully explain. It was almost as though she was starting to feel sorry for the violent, troubled man standing in front of her.

For his part, Connor didn't appear to have the slightest idea of what to say or what to do.

'I lost my husband to cancer,' Grace continued. 'He was thirty-seven years old when he died. He was the only man I ever truly loved and he was the father of my two sons. His name was Joel.'

Connor remained mute. Grace could sense his uncertainty. She could feel his confusion. And, as she studied his face, she saw something she thought she recognised. She had seen that look before, or certainly something very like it. She had seen it in the eyes and expressions of a handful of the boys she had taught in school. Boys who had been neglected and abused; boys who were known to Social Services; boys who were struggling in any one of a thousand different ways. Boys she

184

loved. They were a lot younger than Connor, of course. They were innocent too. None of them had ever committed the sorts of terrible crimes that Connor was now responsible for. But Connor had once been their age and it occurred to Grace that there might still be some things he had in common with them. Over the years, she had come to understand that people who hurt others are almost always people who have, at some point in their lives, been hurt *by* others. And she suspected that this must be true of the man now holding her hostage. Not that it offered any kind of excuse for what he was doing, of course, but she wondered whether it provided at least the beginnings of an explanation for his actions.

These were thoughts that left Grace feeling a strange and wholly unexpected sense of something that almost resembled calm. She carried on talking about her husband.

'He was a bit older than me – six years older actually. I was only nineteen when we first met at church. But I fell hopelessly in love with him almost straight away. He was the kindest man you could ever have hoped to meet. We got married a couple of years later, we managed to get a little flat on the estate and we settled down to start a family.' Grace actually smiled at the memory of her husband and the early years of their life together. 'We were truly happy for the next few years. The boys arrived, he was getting on well at work and we thought we were the most fortunate people on earth.' But the smile vanished from her face just as swiftly as it had appeared. 'And then the cancer came,' she said. 'They didn't catch it until it was too late.' She closed her eyes.

For a while, there was complete silence in the hall. Eventually though, Connor couldn't help himself.

'What about your son? What happened to him?' He obviously lacked the sensitivity or even the basic emotional intelligence to say anything about her husband, to offer even a half-hearted expression of regret for her loss, but that hadn't stopped him asking about her son.

Grace's head dropped, her voice fading to little more than a whisper. 'He was murdered,' she said.

00.23 hrs

Alex

Pip reappeared in the cell. Alex was slumped back on the sofa, his face grey with anxiety. He looked to Pip like a man awaiting the gallows.

'How are you doing?' she asked him, concerned by his appearance.

Alex didn't respond.

Rich offered a swift update on the state of the negotiation. He was affirming of all that Alex had done and clearly meant it when he said that there was nothing he would have done any differently.

As always, Pip was quick to offer her own reassurance and, this time, she had some hard evidence to supply in support of her words.

'I've got some positive news for you,' she said. 'The tech guys and girls have worked their miracles and managed to get a visual on the inside of the hall. No audio at the moment, but we can at least see what's happening in there.'

'How the hell have they managed to do that?' asked Rich.

'By climbing up onto the roof of the hall. I think that must have been the noise Connor heard earlier on. He wasn't imagining it; there were people up there. They weren't trying to get into the hall themselves, but they were trying to find a way to get cameras in.'

'And?' asked Rich.

'It would appear that Connor inadvertently left a small gap at the top of one of the windows. It was all they needed.'

'What can they see?' Alex had pushed himself into an upright position, his voice a mix of hope and anxiety.

'Everything seems to be remarkably calm in there,' Pip replied. 'There's some broken furniture lying around the hall, but the remaining hostages appear to be unharmed. They're all tied up, but none of them has any visible injuries. At least, that's the case as far as we can see.'

Alex leaned back again, the crippling burden of the preceding few minutes eased a fraction by the news. In his imagination, he had been playing out a dozen different scenarios, none of which had turned out remotely as well as the one now being described to them.

'Thank God for that,' he sighed.

Pip looked at him, more concerned about his state than at any previous point in the night. 'You look awful,' she said.

'Thanks very much,' he said wryly, in a half-hearted attempt to lighten the mood. 'Actually, I feel a whole lot better after hearing what you've just told us.' He continued after a pause, 'I had definitely been starting to the fear the worst.' The constant see-sawing of his emotions had been taking as much out of him as the demands of the negotiation itself and he saw no sense in hiding the fact. He told himself that everybody must be feeling the same and that there was no alternative other than to get on with it.

Pip eyed him carefully, before moving to the middle of the room. She decided she would have another private conversation with him when she'd finished updating them.

'I've got a handful of other details from the command team meeting, but, first, tell me where you think we're at?'

'Before we get to that, what about Rosie?' interjected Rich. 'Is there any news on her?'

'Shit, I'm so sorry,' said Pip, raising her hand by way of an apology. 'Too much going on. That should have been one of the first things I mentioned. The good news is that it looks like she's going to make it. She's been taken to King's College Hospital. They've confirmed a broken jaw and severe concussion; the rest they're still checking on, but she's still with us.'

'That is very, very good news,' murmured Alex, half to himself.

'So where are we?' Pip returned to her question.

Alex looked up at Rich, who responded on behalf of them all.

'Right, well let's begin with the positives, starting with the updates you've just given us,' he said. And he began to list them: 'One, Rosie is out and we know she's safe. Two, thanks to the ingenuity of the surveillance people, we've got some reassurance about the condition of the rest of the hostages. Three, we now have constant visual on the hall and Connor knows nothing about it. Four, Alex has managed to buy us a significant amount of time.' He looked across the room. Angie was nodding. 'Five, we've started to challenge his beliefs and have at least sown in his mind the thought of releasing the children.'

'Which didn't go well,' Alex interjected.

'I wouldn't necessarily say that,' interrupted Pip. 'I watched a bit of the live feed once the command meeting was over. Connor seemed remarkably calm.'

'Can't we get the live feed in here?' asked Angie.

'I'm not sure that's the best idea,' responded Pip, who had clearly been thinking it through. 'As Rich has already mentioned, he doesn't know we can see him and, for all the reasons you can probably imagine, it would be better to keep it that way. If we're watching the feed while we're talking to him, it's possible that we'll let slip the fact without intending to. Rest assured though, we'll know the moment anything changes in there.'

'In the meantime, we're not talking to him,' said Alex, still engaged in his own silent struggle. 'How are we going to get him back on?'

'Good question,' said Pip, once again noting Alex's demeanour. She remained upbeat. 'It looks as though the phone line we've been using is gone. The picture quality on the feed is pretty good and you can see a whole pile of broken phones lying on the floor. I suspect the one we've been calling him on is somewhere among them. But I'm hoping he still has his own mobile. And I'm hoping we have the number.'

'How have we managed to get that?' asked Rich.

'Twitter,' she replied. 'It's the number he seems to have been using for his online posts. They've already blocked his main account and have now identified another – the one he used for his manifesto and latest film.'

'Do you want me to call it straight away?' Alex was reaching for the chance to do something positive and proactive.

'Not just yet,' Pip said. 'I don't think there's any immediate sense of urgency given his current behaviour and I've got a handful of other updates that might be useful.'

'Such as?' It was Angie this time.

'Well, according to the security services, he's not on any kind of watch list. As we know, he's got previous for drugs – both possession and supply – but that's it. There's nothing in his criminal history or on any available intelligence database that offers even the slightest indication that he might have been building up to this.' Pip gestured towards the window, in the general direction of the church hall. 'He's got nothing for violence. Nothing for hate crime. He's not known to have attended any of the recent far-right marches and demos in London or elsewhere. He doesn't have any known associates. It would appear that his radicalisation has happened entirely online and over a relatively short period of time. It's still early days with the laptop they found at his address, but, so far, they haven't discovered anything of real concern that's more than a year old.'

'The only other information of potential use at this stage,' Pip continued, 'is the fact that he is obviously a heavy skunk user. They found a couple of dozen empty deal bags during the search of the bedsit. Which might help to explain some of his behaviour, not least his sudden mood swings.'

'And his paranoia,' added Angie, who was busily updating the flipcharts with the new information as Pip was supplying it.

Alex remained silent.

Grace

'He was called Reuben.'

As soon as she said his name, Grace was standing back in her kitchen. She heard herself calling out to her oldest son, telling him to be back in time for his tea. And she heard his cheerful response. He was heading out to the park with his friends, ball tucked under his arm, the same as always. She followed him as far as the front door and watched as he disappeared down the communal stairs. Isaiah, three years Reuben's junior, was watching TV.

'He was a good boy,' Grace murmured, 'a really good boy. Never in trouble at school. Never in trouble with the police. Then, one day, he went out to play football and he never came home.'

Lee

Connor didn't respond. He didn't actually know how to respond. The black woman was confusing him and her story was upsetting him. And he didn't like either of those feelings.

Grace

In the silence that followed, Grace sank deeper into her memories. She remembered the unexpected knock at her front door and the immediate sense that something was terribly wrong. She had just known. She remembered the awkward, nervous expression on the face of the PC as he asked to come in. She felt the irreversible movement in her heart, like a shifting of the earth's plates. She remembered hurrying Isaiah into the boys' bedroom and closing the door behind him. She remembered her world disintegrating.

The police officer told her that Reuben had done nothing wrong. There were a number of witnesses who could confirm that. He and his friends had been minding their own business; playing their game of football. A gang of boys had appeared and started calling them names, shouting 'coon' and 'wog' and that sort of thing. One of Reuben's friends had shouted something back, and that had seemed to be the trigger for what followed. One of the gang had a knife and Reuben hadn't been fast enough. He was stabbed just once, but the blade went directly into his heart. The first officers on the scene, and the paramedics who arrived shortly after them, had done absolutely everything they could, but it was too late. He died at the side of the pitch.

'He was a good boy,' she said again. 'He hadn't done anything wrong.' Tears were streaming down her face as she looked directly at Connor.

Clearly unsettled, he turned away from her.

'That's what hatred can do,' she murmured, so overwhelmed by the memories of her son that she'd given no thought to the possibility of provoking Connor by saying so. But he didn't react – he was already walking back towards the kitchen.

Alex

'You look like you could do with another cigarette,' said Pip, as she offered the packet to Alex. At her insistence, he had followed her back out to the front of the house. He took one and Pip offered him a light, before lighting one of her own. 'I'm taking you out and putting Rich in,' she said.

'No!' The reaction from him was immediate and emphatic. His facial expression was one of alarm. 'Please don't do that, Pip.'

'You're in a bad way,' she responded, 'and I'm genuinely worried about you. And it's not just about you. There are eight people in that hall who are depending on us and I can't have you falling apart on me.'

'That's not going to happen,' he said, with a look of fierce determination. 'I know I've had my moments in the last few hours,' he admitted, 'but I'm sure we all have.'

'Of course we have,' Pip replied. 'But don't forget that I know you pretty well. I've been watching you, and your face gives you away every time.'

'I'll be all right, I promise,' he said, as much in an attempt to persuade himself as her.

193

They both paused and looked skywards in response to a fast-approaching noise. Two military helicopters swept overhead, no more than a couple of hundred feet above them, and began to descend somewhere over Brockwell Park.

'Reinforcements?' Alex suggested.

'That would be my guess,' came Pip's reply. But she wasn't going to allow herself to be distracted. 'We both know that Rich is more than capable of taking over. Give me one good reason why I shouldn't put him in the chair.'

'Because a change of negotiator at this stage might well undermine whatever rapport I've been able to establish with Connor,' he said as he tried to straighten out his thoughts. 'And because I'm good at this, Pip – I want to see it through. Taking me out would be far worse than leaving me in. Being involved is a whole lot better than being on the sidelines. And it's not as if I'm on my own, is it?'

'Hmm,' said Pip, clearly uncertain whether she would be making a mistake by agreeing. 'Perhaps. But if I do put you back in, I reserve the right to pull you out at any time, if I believe it's the right thing to do.'

'That's fair enough.' He didn't like it, but he had to concede it.

She threw her cigarette butt over the front wall and onto the pavement and was just about to walk back inside when she stopped herself.

'How many jobs have we been out to together?' she asked him.

'Goodness knows,' he replied. 'At least twenty, I should think.'

'And how many of those ended badly?'

'None of them,' he conceded.

'How many other jobs have you been to?'

'Another twenty plus?'

'How many of those ended badly?'

'Only one – only Romford.'

'And, in that one and only case, an independent review has already absolved you of any blame. In fact, my sources tell me that you've actually come in for a huge amount of praise. As I told you earlier on, there's absolutely no doubt in my mind that you saved people's lives that day. And I suspect that, if the suspect hadn't died, you'd have ended up with all sorts of commendations.' She was almost certainly right. 'Sometimes shit happens, Alex, and there's nothing any of us can do about it.'

'But that doesn't change the fact that it did happen,' Alex replied. 'It doesn't change the fact that a man died – and that it happened on my watch.'

'I know and I'm sorry . . . I'm genuinely sorry.' Pip put her arm round him. 'But here's the thing . . . You're telling me that you have been deployed as a negotiator on something like fifty occasions. And that, on forty-nine of those fifty occasions, things turned out all right – at least, as all right as these things ever do. That is, by any measure, a bloody good set of numbers.' She took a step back and faced him, this time placing a firm hand on each of his arms. '*That's* why negotiators are optimists. Because the numbers allow them to be.'

He nodded. Part of him was convinced – the better part – but part of him was still wrestling with a nagging sense of malaise. There were faces and places he knew he would never forget.

'So are you ready to save some more lives?' she asked. It was her way of telling him that she still believed in him.

Alex followed her back in through the front door.

00.31 hrs

Grace

Grace sat in silence and found the words of the Psalms returning at last to comfort her. *The Lord is my Shepherd, I shall not want* ... She repeated the phrase slowly and silently. Her tears for Reuben had fallen as a kind of balm and had left her feeling almost peaceful. The fear was still very much present – in her and all around her – but, for a few precious moments at least, it no longer seemed to be the dominant force in the room. She said prayers for Isaiah and for Rosie. She prayed earnestly for her seven silent companions. And then, without making any kind of conscious decision to do so, she found herself praying for Connor. She could hear the fan running in the kitchen and she wondered what his story might be.

When Connor reappeared in the hall, smelling of freshly smoked weed, the expression on his face was part-weary, part-muddled, part-anxious, part-something impenetrable. He was stoned, of course, but there was more to it than that.

'Your name is Lee, right?' Grace had remembered it from his opening speech all those hours before.

'Yeah ... Lee Connor.' His words came slowly. As if he didn't understand why Grace was talking to him but was unable to think of a reason not to reply.

'Tell me your story, Lee Connor,' she said. There was genuine compassion in her voice.

'What do you mean?'

'Tell me about you.'

'Like what?'

'Anything you like. Why not start by telling me about your mum?'

Lee

At the mention of his mother, Connor's expression changed. His eyes flashed. He opened his mouth, but no words came out. He started pacing rapidly back and forth. His first instinct was to scream at her. How dare she ask about his mother? Back and forth, back and forth. How dare she, a *black* woman, ask about *his* mother? But the scream wouldn't come. It stuck somewhere inside him and faded to a whimper. Back and forth, back and forth. He hated Grace. He was absolutely convinced he hated her – and everyone like her. Fucking immigrants. They were all the same. Parasites. Cockroaches. *Fuck*.

When he had entered the hall several hours earlier, he had been absolutely certain of his beliefs – a set of views about society that had been reinforced repeatedly by his reading and research. By the voice of Nicholas Farmer and every other voice he listened to. Every time he switched on his computer, there was a fresh slew of evidence in support of his worldview. And he was convinced of it all. At least, he had thought he was. But in place of all that certainty, there was now growing confusion. What was it about this fucking black woman? She was supposed to be the embodiment of all he despised. But she had somehow got right under his white skin. He had seen her terror and he had seen her courage. At the start of the night, he had felt nothing but contempt for her, but, as the hours had passed, he had begun to feel a grudging sense of respect for her. And now he knew the name of her dead son.

Back and forth, back and forth. Rage and blame, bewilderment and fear.

Grace

Grace was alarmed by his response. Any lingering sense of peace had deserted her. The atmosphere in the room had changed completely and her immediate instinct was to try to make it right.

'I'm so sorry,' she implored. 'I hope I didn't say the wrong thing.'

Lee

He was just about to respond when his mobile rang in his pocket. It startled him.

'Who's this?' he asked.

'Mr Connor, it's Alex,' said the voice at the other end of the line.

'How the fuck did you get this number?' Minutes earlier, listening to Grace speak about Reuben, Connor had begun to experience a kind of vulnerability. Then came the question about his mother and the surge of anger and confusion that it triggered. Now the fucking police and their uninvited call.

'You've been using your phone to post on Twitter,' was all that Alex offered him by way of explanation.

'So why are you calling me? You'd better have something important to tell me.' His tone was aggressive and confrontational.

'Our last call didn't end too well and I wanted to say that I'm sorry about that. I was hoping we could start again.'

'Enough bullshit!' It was only a few seconds into their conversation but Connor had already had enough. 'Have you called to tell me about the release of Nicholas Farmer?'

'No, I haven't . . .' Alex began, but Connor refused to let him continue.

'Then I don't want to fucking speak to you . . . Don't even think about calling me again unless it's to tell me that Nicholas Farmer is being released.'

He let out a howl of frustration and indignation as he terminated yet another phone call.

'For fuck's sake!' he yelled at no one in particular.

Alex

Alex was surprised by his own reaction as the line went dead. He didn't spiral down suddenly as he half expected to. Instead, he felt strangely calm about the situation. The call had been so brief and his own words so simple and straightforward that he had no need to second-guess himself this time. He knew he hadn't said or done anything wrong, realisations that eased his conscience significantly.

It helped that he was now aware of the video feed, that he knew his colleagues were watching it and that there would be an emergency plan for a full armed entry should any of the hostages appear to be in imminent danger. And, for the first time that evening, he began to acknowledge the possibility that the outcome of the siege might not depend solely on him.

As if by way of confirmation, a line of three dark green armoured vehicles pulled up outside and a dozen or more heavily armed, balaclava-wearing, black-overalled soldiers, accompanied by a pair of Belgian Malinois service dogs, jumped out and ran up the hill in the direction of the hall.

Grace

Connor was all over the place. One moment silent and brooding, the next agitated and muttering to himself. The latest burst of rage had dissipated, but he remained a tinderbox of unpredictability. Grace watched him closely and anxiously, wondering whether there was something, anything, she should say. Of all things, the fact that she was by then absolutely desperate to go to the loo made her mind up for her.

'Lee?' Her voice was barely louder than a whisper.

He didn't immediately react.

'Lee?' A little louder this time.

He looked at her, but he didn't say anything.

'I need to go to the toilet.'

He seemed baffled by the banality of her statement.

'Please?'

And, once again, he found that he couldn't help himself. He sighed in frustration and picked up one of the knives that was lying on the carpet. He walked over to her and cut her cable ties. A gruff 'hurry up' was the best he could manage.

He watched her as she rubbed her ankles and wrists, as she stood up gingerly and as she walked slowly towards the front of the hall. He wedged the door to the Ladies' open with his foot, but he didn't follow her inside. His right hand rested on the handle of the Baikal, which was tucked into the front of his trousers.

Grace felt an overwhelming sense of physical relief. She sat in silence for a moment, trying to find a way to process the events of the last few minutes, never mind the last few hours. Lee Connor terrified her, but he also broke her heart. He was a ball of anger. But he was also a ball of pain. And there was doubtless a connection between those two things.

'Hurry up,' he grumbled at her.

She stood up slowly and realised that all the others would need to go to the toilet as well. She also remembered Alan's heart medication. She had been watching him, on and off, for any obvious signs of distress and hadn't seen any. But that didn't mean he wasn't due another round of pills.

She emerged from her cubicle and washed her hands, then she leaned forwards and drank at length, direct from the cold tap. Connor made no attempt to stop her. Her thirst satisfied, she looked round at him.

'Thank you,' she said. She hesitated again, before adding, 'If it's not too much trouble, would it be possible for the others to do the same?'

He didn't reply. Instead, he gestured to her to go back into the hall.

She sat back down in her chair as he fetched another set of cable ties.

'Please?' she asked quietly.

And, to her complete surprise, he appeared to acquiesce. He looked as though he was sleepwalking as he turned and

201

walked across the room. He approached Alan's chair first and, despite her immense reluctance to say or do anything that might provoke any sort of negative response, Grace decided that she had to say something.

'Lee?' she called across to him.

When he turned round, she found that she was unable to read the expression on his face. But her instincts told her that she was safe to continue.

'Alan – the man you're standing next to – has a serious heart condition. He has some pills in his pocket that he might need to take. Would it be all right for him to do that?'

Connor didn't say anything. His response was to crouch down next to Alan and cut his ankles free. Then he stood up and did the same with his wrists. The older man winced in pain as he attempted to stand up. He tried to steady himself by leaning on the back of his chair. Grace felt a pang of concern. Seeming to sense this, Alan looked in her direction and offered a slight nod. *Thank you*, he appeared to be saying. *I'm OK*, he seemed to add with his eyes. It took the best part of a minute for him to find his balance and for some of the feeling to return to his joints. Grace watched him take his medication out of his pocket as he began to shuffle towards the foyer.

Five minutes later, having re-secured Alan in his chair and placed a fresh strip of tape over his mouth, Connor turned to the remaining prisoners. One at a time, he escorted them to the toilets. Jean, followed by Mariam. Then it was the turn of the two children, Ittack walking awkwardly and uncomfortably in his half-dried trousers. Then Helen and, finally, Jack.

Grace eyed Jack nervously as he stood up. Throughout the course of the night, he had remained the most visibly distressed of all of them and she was afraid that he might try something stupid again. But Connor, armed with the Baikal, kept him constantly within arm's reach and a cowed Jack was faced with no other option but to comply.

None of the hostages spoke at any point during the entire exercise. None of them dared.

Their ordeal was far from over.

00.48 hrs

Alex

The latest developments in the hall were reported back, via Pip, to the team in the cell. The siege was deep into its sixth hour.

'What now?' asked Alex, enormously relieved to be feeling less haunted, but no less concerned for the hostages.

'As I see it,' Pip responded, 'we really only have two options. Either we get back on the phone or we watch and wait.' No one seemed to disagree, so she carried on talking. 'Were it not for the live pictures, I don't think we would have any option but to try him again. But we can see that the hostages are safe for the moment and he's made it pretty clear that he only wants to hear from us if we have news about the release of Farmer. So, for now at least, my instinct is to wait.'

She looked round at her team, her raised eyebrows an invitation to question or challenge her views. None of them did.

'In which case,' Pip continued, 'you've got about fifteen minutes' thinking time while I go to the next command team briefing.' She looked down and checked her watch. 'As soon as I'm back, I want to hear your ideas about where we go once the waiting is over. And don't limit your thinking – provided it's legal, nothing is off the table.'

She disappeared out of the room, followed by the firearms

officer, who explained that he was going to check in with members of his own team.

Alex took advantage of the brief hiatus to walk through to the kitchen and ask, if it wasn't too much trouble, for another pot of tea.

Lee

'Thank you,' said Grace.

'Thank you for what?' Connor looked at her.

'For letting everyone use the toilet,' she replied. 'That was kind of you.'

He looked at her, baffled. Kind? There was nothing kind about him, he knew that. And why on earth was she, his prisoner, thanking him, her captor, for anything – a man who had violently assaulted her friend and who had repeatedly terrified them all? It made no sense whatsoever to him.

Unable to offer anything by way of reply, he wandered instead to the back of the hall and checked the fire doors.

Alex

Pip reappeared in the cell.

'I'm hoping that, in the next hour or so, we're going to be joined by a DI from SO15 – one of their leading experts on right-wing extremism; someone who might be able to help us with our negotiating strategy,' she said. 'In the meantime, what have you got for me? I want something from everyone.'

Rich went first. 'Option one is to pick up where we left off: to keep challenging his beliefs; to keep trying to undermine his ideological foundations. It's a high-risk strategy – particularly with someone who appears to be so unpredictable – but it also seems to me to be the one most likely to succeed. We're dealing with someone who's stated that he's prepared to die for his cause, which doesn't leave us with a great deal of room for manoeuvre. What can you offer by way of an incentive to a person who believes he has nothing to lose?' It was a rhetorical question. 'The answer is "not very much". Far better therefore to question the very thing he seems prepared to sacrifice every-thing for. If we can challenge Connor's perspective fundament-ally enough, perhaps we can start to change his mind.'

Pip nodded and looked round the room. 'Angie?'

'Friends and family,' she began. 'Find someone who knows him and use them as a Third-Party Intermediary – a TPI. Get them involved in the negotiation, speaking directly to him if necessary. It might be that the sound of a voice he recognises will make a difference.' But, having pitched her initial idea, she was swift to acknowledge its potential limitations. 'The only problem is that I'm not sure who we would use. It sounds as though his relationship with his dad might have broken down and we currently have no idea whether he has any other relatives. We don't even know who his friends are – if he has any, that is.'

Pip nodded again, offering an unspoken acknowledgement that the idea was at least deserving of consideration. 'Any other thoughts?'

'Nicholas Farmer,' Angie said. 'Use him as the TPI.' Then she hesitated, unsure whether it might just be an idea too far.

'Keep going,' encouraged Pip, 'I'm listening.'

'The way I see it, Farmer might indirectly have been the one who persuaded Connor to release Rosie. That was the question Alex asked, wasn't it? What would Nicholas Farmer say? Farmer knew nothing about it of course, but that's not the point. He is the only person I can think of who might be able to exert any significant influence on our man. There's a sense in which Connor seems to be doing all of this for him. For all his talk of a cause, it's Farmer he seems particularly fixated with. What would happen if we got Farmer on the phone, or even if we got him here in person, and persuaded him to make a direct appeal for the release of the hostages?'

Grace

Grace continued to watch Connor. His behaviour was undoubtedly becoming more erratic. He went from pacing the room, to sitting down and staring at his phone, to kicking out at his kitbag, to checking the front door, to chuntering to himself, to staring at Grace. His facial expressions were constantly changing too, from pensive, to irritated, to frustrated, to anxious, to angry, to puzzled, to blank, to lost. He fiddled with his cigarette lighter.

Grace summoned all her courage again.

'Why don't you let the children go?' she asked him. She had been thinking about the question for several minutes. Connor had re-taped the mouths of all the other hostages, but she remained free to speak. At some subconscious level, perhaps he was waiting for her to say something, even willing her to.

'What?' he replied, distractedly, as though he was struggling to focus.

'Why don't you let the children go?' she repeated. 'Rahel and Ittack? They don't belong here.' She waited for him to explode.

But he didn't. Instead, he seemed to retreat back into himself. He remained silent for several long seconds.

'Why the fuck should I let them go?' He was trying to sound assertive, but his voice actually sounded rather frail. Once again, Grace sensed that it might be safe for her to continue.

'Because they are just children. Two completely innocent children. Because they have already lived through greater horrors than you or I could ever imagine. Because they have done absolutely nothing to harm you. Because your fight is not with them, or with Mariam for that matter.'

'But they *are* immigrants,' he responded in a surly voice. 'Dirty fucking immigrants. All of this is their fault.'

'All of what is their fault?'

'The whole fucking mess that this country is in. It's all their fault.' He jabbed his finger towards the three refugees.

Grace looked closely at him. His head was down and she wasn't able to catch his eye.

'Is it my fault too?' she asked him.

Alex

In the cell, the team had been debating the potential merits of Angie's last suggestion. Pip had the floor.

'Our first problem is that we have no idea whether Farmer would be willing to do it. But I actually have a bigger concern than that. Imagine we use him and imagine it works. Imagine that bastard emerging from all of this with any kind of credit. It doesn't bear thinking about.'

'But what if it's the only way of getting all the hostages out alive?' challenged Alex. 'Distasteful though it might be – and I'm with you all the way when it comes to Farmer – what if we actually end up with no credible or viable alternative? You said nothing was off the table.'

Before anyone could respond, Alex's phone rang.

'It's him!' Alex said, grabbing for the handset. In a flurry of fingers, he connected the call and switched on the loudspeaker. The dictaphone had been running continually throughout. 'Hello?'

'I'm letting the children go,' said Connor without ceremony. 'They will be at the front door in ten minutes.'

He hung up before the incredulous Alex had any chance to respond.

Pip was the first to react. She got straight onto her own phone. 'The kids are being released,' she said urgently. Alex assumed she was speaking to the Incident Commander. 'We've got ten minutes to get ready.' The rest of the negotiating team could just about make out an unfamiliar male voice at the other end of the line, but they were unable to hear what he was saying. 'I've no idea!' said Pip impatiently, responding to what was evidently an unnecessary question. 'We've only got ten minutes,' she insisted.

01.03 hrs

Lee

Connor had withdrawn into himself. He had made his decision and he wasn't going to change his mind, but, for the second time that night, it felt as though he was beginning to lose his grip on what was happening. Events once more seemed to be slipping like sand through his fingers.

He found himself engaged in a repeat of the frantic psychological wrestling match he'd endured after his earlier decision to release the priest. Would letting the children go help the cause or was he making another terrible mistake? Was he showing weakness or was he actually displaying strength? Nobody had forced him to release any of his prisoners – they were decisions taken of his own free will. And they had proven that he wasn't some kind of fanatic, that he was a man with righteousness on his side. What would the anonymous chatroom voices be saying? Would Nicholas Farmer be pleased with him? The swirl of questions plagued him: was he in control, or was he losing control?

He tried to steady his mind by telling himself that he was still holding plenty of cards. The hall was secure. He was unharmed. He had more than enough supplies to see him through the night and into the next day – and that was without needing to check the contents of the fridge and the kitchen cupboards. Most importantly of all, even after the kids were gone, he would still have six hostages. He was still in a very strong position to bargain for the release of Farmer. Perhaps even stronger. *Quid pro quo.* He was doing things for them; now they would have to do things for him. They would have to let Nicholas Farmer go.

He checked his phone and saw that his second Twitter account had been suspended. That particular discovery didn't bother him at all – there were plenty more where that one had come from. He closed the Twitter app and, for the first time since his arrival at the hall, looked at the BBC News website. What he saw there both surprised and delighted him. In rapid succession, he checked Sky, CNN, Reuters and even the *New York Times*. And it was the same with all of them.

His lips curled into a sort of smile. In the weeks and days leading up to the attack, he had anticipated making the news – indeed, that had been an important part of the plan – but he had never considered that it might happen on this scale. He was staring at his picture and his name on the front page of the *New York Times*. The sudden realisation sent the roller-coaster that had been rattling through his brain lurching suddenly upwards. He experienced a sense of elation, exultation even, that he had never felt before. He was front page news around the world. The fucking *New York Times*!

Every righteous supporter of the cause would know who he was. Nicholas Farmer would know his name.

His energy and confidence renewed somewhat, he picked up two empty chairs and carried them briskly to the foyer at the front of the hall. He set them down a few feet back from the front doors. He then collected two more chairs from the hall and returned to the foyer with them. Over the course of the next few minutes, he repeated the exercise multiple times until there were five tall – above head height – stacks of chairs lined up next to one another in the form of a makeshift barricade. That task completed, he picked up a bag of cable ties and one of the kitchen knives and approached Rahel's chair. She cowered back from him and let out a muffled cry. Mariam immediately started fighting another hopeless battle with her bonds. It was all she could do.

Ignoring Rahel's distress, Connor cut her wrists and ankles free and pulled her roughly to her feet. She was scared and exhausted. Her legs wobbled and she almost fell. Connor pulled her across the carpet, past Grace, and stood her in front of Ittack. 'Stay there,' he ordered her. She didn't understand the words, but she understood the instruction.

He cut Ittack free and then stood him up alongside his sister. Tucking the knife into the back of his trousers, he took a fresh cable tie out and secured Ittack's right wrist to Rahel's left. He then did the same with their ankles, affording them the incongruous look of a team entered in a three-legged race. The two children looked at one another in fear and confusion. Why was he doing this to them? Mariam was desperate with worry, rocking backwards and forwards in her chair. Grace was the only one of the four who knew what was happening – and why – and she was praying that he wasn't going to change his mind.

Connor pushed the children ahead of him, but their first attempt at movement ended before a proper step had been taken, with the two of them in a tangled heap on the floor. Connor pulled them impatiently back to their feet and, a couple of clumsy three-legged paces later, stopped them in front of Grace. Without saying anything, he cut her free, tucked the knife back in his trousers, then pulled out the Baikal and pointed it at her. He gestured at her to stand up. She complied, not daring to speak for fear of unsettling him or his intentions.

With his left hand, he shoved Grace ahead of him. With the

gun in his right, he pointed to the children to walk towards the front of the hall.

'Don't do anything stupid now,' he muttered.

Grace

Somewhere over to her left, Grace picked up a suggestion of movement. Connor didn't appear to have seen anything, but Grace was certain of it. She snatched a quick glance across the hall and, to her astonishment, saw that Jack had somehow managed to get one of his hands free. She had been right to be concerned about him. Her eyes widened and she stifled a gasp. What on earth did he think he was doing? Connor must have made a mistake. He must have left one of the cable ties loose after Jack had returned from the toilet.

Jack caught Grace's eye, but he paid her no heed, turning his attention instead to his other hand, still secured to the back of his chair. Whatever he thought he was doing, she wanted desperately to tell him to stop, to tell him that he was in danger of jeopardising the release of the children. But, in reality, all she could do was remain silent and look straight ahead. Her only consolation was the realisation that Connor didn't seem to have noticed a thing. His whole attention was taken up with the children and what he had in mind for them.

Alex

Outside the hall, everything was moving at pace. The team of armed officers and medics who had earlier helped Rosie away from the hall had reassembled for an urgent briefing. In the absence of any live contact between Connor and the negotiating cell, the decision had rapidly been taken to rely on exactly the same extraction plan as before.

With no direct part to play in the hoped-for release, Pip ushered the team out to the front of the house. Alex kept his phone in his hand, just in case.

As they emerged into the night air, an ambulance pulled up a few yards away from them. Pip slipped her arm through Alex's as they all stared up the hill and into the darkness.

Grace

Grace could hear Mariam crying. It wasn't difficult to understand why. Mariam's chair was positioned facing the front of the hall, so she could at least see what was happening, but the pain of sudden separation from her children must have been almost too much for her to bear. That, and the abject fear of the complete unknown. She had no way of understanding what was happening, and the terror of the moment must surely have carried echoes of horrors she had experienced in the previous two years. She and her children had managed to escape their devastated homeland and had only just begun the long, slow process of trying to rebuild their shattered lives. This was the one place in the world where they were supposed to be completely safe. How could this be happening to them?

Grace was jolted out of her thoughts by the jab of the gun in the small of her back. She reached forwards and placed a gentle hand on the shoulders of each of the children, attempting to offer some kind of reassurance. 'It's OK,' she said to them. Both of them were crying. 'It's OK,' she repeated. The little group reached the barricade of chairs and Connor issued his instructions.

'Exactly as before,' he announced. He seemed to be in a semi-delirious state and there was a tremor in his voice. Grace could hear it clearly. 'When I tell you to, I want you to unlock the door, open it and let the children out. The moment they're gone, I want you to close and lock it again. Understand?'

Grace nodded.

'I will be standing right behind you. Do anything stupid and I will shoot you in the head.'

Grace heard him, but actually felt less afraid than the last time she had been in the same position. The prospect of imminent freedom for the children demanded her absolute focus and attention. Just at that precise moment, it was the only thing that really mattered to her; so much so, that she had temporarily forgotten about Jack.

'Stand and face the wall.' Connor jabbed at Grace with the Baikal. She complied. Satisfied that she presented no threat, he switched his attention to the two terrified, tearful children and cut their wrists and ankles free. Turning back to Grace, who hadn't moved, he spun her back around and pointed the gun directly at her forehead. 'Get ready,' he said, his eyes flicking restlessly between Grace, the children and the door.

Alex

Outside, the waiting was agony. There was nothing Alex or his colleagues could do. Part of him wanted desperately to run up the hill and see what was happening, to see whether there was anything he might be able to assist with. The rest of the team no doubt felt something similar. But they all knew their place. They knew they might need to re-establish contact at any moment. They knew they needed to remain close to the cell. Alex checked and rechecked his phone every few seconds, grateful that Pip was alongside him, her arm still linked through his.

Immediately in front of the hall, all eyes were set on the building, watching for any sign of movement, listening for the slightest sound. If it all went wrong, they had their last resort plan of storming the building, knowing full well that they would be risking their lives and the lives of all the hostages in doing so. They hoped sincerely that it would never come to that.

On the far side of the street, two floors up, crouched alongside his partner, one of the snipers stared through his gunsight and reread the sign above the door.

Refugees Welcome

Lee

Connor was right on the edge. The intense *New York Times* high he had been experiencing was fading fast, replaced by a fresh surge of paranoia, worming its way back into the centre of his thoughts. He was on the verge of losing touch with reality. He was imagining the sound of explosions, of shattering glass, of gunfire. He could hear screaming voices. The one thing that hadn't crossed his ever-more haunted mind was the possibility that one of the other hostages might be attempting to escape.

Grace

As soon as Connor had turned Grace round, she had been able to see over his shoulder, back into the main hall. And her gaze had settled instantly on Jack. He had managed to free both his hands and he was bent forwards in his seat, working furiously on his right ankle. Grace squinted and refocused her gaze. In his left hand, Jack was holding a bunch of keys that had some sort of small multitool attached to it. The miniature folding blade he was using would have been of no use as a weapon, but it seemed perfectly adequate for the purposes of cutting through the cable ties. Grace guessed it had been in his pocket all along, that Connor had missed it when he was gathering up the mobile phones several hours earlier. She supposed that it hadn't occurred to Connor to search the attendees at a prayer meeting for anything sharp.

Having freed his right ankle, Jack switched his attention swiftly to his left. He was almost free.

Grace couldn't begin to imagine what he was planning to do next. Whatever it was that he had in mind, the likely consequences of his actions terrified her: for Jack himself, for the rest of the hostages, for the children in particular. She was certain that the situation was going to turn out badly. How could it not? Connor still hadn't noticed what was happening, but it wasn't going to stay that way for much longer.

Jack lifted his head to look across at Helen, and Grace caught sight of the wild look that was back in his eyes. She felt a fresh surge of panic as she realised he was acting on nothing more than terrified instinct and that, in all likelihood, he didn't actually have any kind of plan at all. At least, not one that stood the slightest chance of succeeding. She knew that there were only two ways in and out of the building and, when she'd gone through to the kitchen to fetch the first-aid kit earlier on, she'd seen the bike lock and chain wrapped round the bars of the rear fire doors. She knew there was no way for him to escape.

She stared at him intently, her eyes boring into him, willing him to stop what he was doing. At the same time, she noticed Helen, looking back over her shoulder, doing something similar. She was shaking her head furiously at him. But either he hadn't seen her or he hadn't understood what she was trying to communicate. He managed to release his remaining ankle and lurched out of his chair towards his girlfriend. And, as he did so, he stumbled and fell.

Connor jerked round in response to the jangling sound of the keys hitting the floor.

'What the fuck . . . !' he screamed.

Jack froze in terror. Grace grabbed the two children and pulled them in tight to her body. They buried their faces in her clothing.

'Don't fucking move!' Connor yelled back at Grace as he sprinted through the double doors and hurled himself at the still-rooted Jack.

Alex

Pip's phone rang. She connected the call and listened intently. Alex, Rich and Angie all looked at her, picking up the immediate change in her expression and body language.

'Everyone inside, now!' There was no mistaking the urgency in her raised voice. The three other members of the negotiating team scrambled after her as she raced back into the house.

'What's happening?' asked Alex as they reached the living room.

Standing next to the coffee table, Pip raised the palm of her hand in an instruction to the rest of them to be quiet. She was trying to absorb what she was being told.

'Connor is struggling with one of the hostages,' she reported anxiously. 'Stand by . . . it looks like the armed teams are going in.'

Alex held his breath and waited for the inevitable sound of flash bangs and automatic fire.

01.17 hrs

Alex

'Wait . . .' Pip had her hand raised again. 'Wait,' she repeated, at no one in particular.

'What the fuck is going on?' Rich looked and sounded every bit as troubled as Alex.

'The armed teams are being held.' Pip hurried her words as she tried to keep pace with what she was being told at the other end of the line. 'It looks like things are calming down in there.' She placed a hand over her phone's microphone. 'He was about to release the kids when one of the other hostages tried to escape.' She paused her commentary to listen to more of what was being said. 'There was a scuffle involving Connor and . . . we think it was the younger man, Jack.' Another pause. 'The teams were literally seconds away from putting the doors and windows in when Connor got Jack into a chair . . . Apparently, Jack's now tied up again.'

'Anyone hurt?' Angie asked.

'Not that I'm being told,' Pip replied, before turning and speaking directly to Alex: 'You need to be ready to put a call in to Connor the moment I tell you to.'

Lee

'What the fuck did you think you were doing?'

Connor was nose-to-nose with the now-seated Jack, screaming at him. The events of the previous few moments had rattled
Connor to the core. He had gone from feeling agitated about
the release of the children to being panicked by Jack's escape
attempt, and he was furiously trying to reassert his control of
the situation.

For his part, Jack was tangle-haired and terrified, straining
backwards so hard that he was in danger of tipping his chair
over. His top was untucked from his jeans and torn around the
collar. There was a trickle of blood coming from his nose, but
he had no other visible injuries. Helen couldn't look at him.
Her chin was buried in her chest and her eyes were tight shut.

Connor had rugby-tackled him halfway across the room.
After the briefest of wrestling matches and a single, sharp
punch to the ribs, Jack had once more realised that he was no
physical match for his captor. Connor had dragged him back to
his chair and, this time, had made no mistake with the tightness
of the ties.

'What the fuck were you thinking?' shouted Connor again
as he took a step back from his prisoner.

'Please . . .' Jack pleaded as he began to unravel completely.
The veins on either side of his forehead were bulging. Lines of
sweat and snot were streaked across his face.

'Shut the fuck up!' demanded Connor, raising an arm in
threat. He hadn't actually wanted an answer to his question.

'Please . . .' mumbled Jack, too far gone to care. He began to
sob uncontrollably. 'I don't want to be here,' he howled, almost
childlike. 'Please let me go . . .'

Connor responded with a backhanded slap that caught Jack flush on the cheek.

'I swear, if you don't fucking shut up, I am going to do you some serious harm.' Connor's voice was a mix of menace and alarm. None of this was part of any plan he'd rehearsed and his frightened aggression collided directly with Jack's distress.

Grace

Grace had been watching it all play out, her fears for Jack mingling with her determination to protect Ittack and Rahel. 'Jack! Please be quiet!' she shouted frantically from the front of the hall, the children still huddled under her arms.

Connor had temporarily forgotten about them and swivelled round sharply in response to the sound of Grace's voice.

'You three, get back in here,' he yelled at them, picking the gun up from the carpet and pointing it at them.

Grace obeyed and eased the children quietly and gently back into the room. 'It's OK,' she repeated to them again and again.

'Sit down, all of you.'

Connor pointed in the direction of the three chairs they had earlier vacated. Mariam's shoulders sagged in a mixture of despair and relief. At least she was close to her children again. Connor's eyes followed them across the room, but he remained where he was, standing next to the still-sobbing Jack, whose upper body was heaving in time with his laboured breathing.

For the first time that night, it appeared to Grace that Connor didn't have the slightest idea what to do next. If anything, it made him even more dangerous.

Alex

'Get ready to put that call in.' Pip still had her own phone pressed to her ear as she spoke to Alex. The armed teams had returned to their standby positions. 'All now seems quiet in the hall. Grace and the children are back in the main room – having been out by the front door. Connor is standing in the middle of them all, not moving... Just give it a moment or two.'

Alex looked at Rich, who gave him a nod of fresh support. Alex checked his phone and the digital recorder. Both still had plenty of battery life. He gathered his thoughts and tried to steady himself.

'OK, you're on,' Pip said to him.

Alex was just reaching for his phone when Rich grabbed hold of his arm. 'Hold on,' he cautioned.

Alex looked at him, confused.

'What?'

'Don't forget – you need to avoid mentioning any of the details Pip's been giving us. He still doesn't know about the video feed and we want it to stay that way.'

'Good shout,' said Pip.

Alex was grateful for the intervention. He had forgotten, and was almost certain that, were it not for Rich's reminder, he would likely have said something to betray the fact that they had eyes in the hall.

Pip allowed him a few moments to settle himself again.

'Ready?' she asked.

'Ready,' he affirmed.

Grace

Grace and the rest of the hostages could hear it clearly, but Connor seemed oblivious to it. Eventually, the phone stopped ringing in his pocket. He hadn't said a word or moved from where he was standing for the past two or three minutes. His thoughts appeared to Grace to be somewhere else entirely. She continued to hug the children, feeling enormously grateful that she was free to do so. Connor had so far made no effort to tie them up again. She exchanged repeated glances with Mariam, attempting to share whatever non-verbal reassurance she could with her. *I promise I will look after your children,* was what she was trying to say.

When Connor eventually spoke, it was to Jack, with a repetition of his earlier question.

'What the fuck were you thinking?'

But he was no longer shouting. In fact, he sounded more baffled than angry. Grace noticed a faraway look in his eyes that she hadn't seen before. Jack's face was blank.

Connor changed tack. 'And what the fuck are you doing with a black girl?' Again, his enquiry seemed motivated more by confusion than any immediate desire for confrontation. Jack succeeded only in looking bewildered. Connor was pointing at Helen. 'Is she your girlfriend?' This time, Jack managed to nod. 'So why are you with her? A pure white boy with a fucking black girl?' This last remark was accompanied by a look of complete incomprehension on Connor's part.

'Because I love her,' Jack managed to whisper. But Grace could tell that Connor had stopped listening. Even as he had asked the question, he had begun walking in a slow, distracted circle round the hall.

Lee

Connor's head was a mess. His phone rang for the third time, but he barely heard it. He tried to remind himself of the plan. He tried to focus on the cause. He tried to think about Nicholas Farmer. But nothing would sit still in his head. His thoughts were like a classful of restless and agitated pre-schoolers, all jockeying for attention, while he was the novice classroom assistant in danger of losing control of them all.

There were too many people in the hall. Too many hostages.

That was the only thought that seemed to settle in his mind with any degree of clarity or permanence. He told himself that one of his prisoners had been able to make an escape attempt because he was trying to control too many people, because his attention had been spread too thinly, because he wasn't concentrating hard enough. If he didn't do something, someone else was going to try to get away. So he needed to do something about the numbers. He stopped walking and stared at the two children.

'Get them out of here,' he barked at Grace.

Uncertain of his exact intentions, she didn't immediately move. This annoyed Connor. After all, his instruction had been perfectly clear.

'Get the fucking children out of the building,' he said, with no little menace.

This time, Grace responded. She nudged the children to their feet and began to usher them back towards the front of the hall.

Alex

'Movement in the hall!' Pip was back on her phone, addressing the rest of the team.

After the third attempt to get through to Connor, Alex had put his phone to one side. The knowledge that others were watching the live pictures meant that he felt safe to do so. For the last few minutes, his mind had almost been in neutral. After the relentless drive of the previous few hours, it had come as something of a relief. But as soon as Pip spoke, he was back on edge.

'Grace and the children are moving back towards the front of the building. Connor is behind them, holding the gun.'

Grace

Grace could feel the children's bodies quivering beneath her gentle grip. She had seen the anguished look on Mariam's face as her children were moved away from her again. A mother's grief. She had watched Jack's ordeal, powerless to intervene, other than to plead with him to be silent. She had seen Helen's hunched and horrified reaction to it all. She wondered about Alan and Jean, who had remained resolutely silent throughout it all. How were they holding up? How was Alan's heart? And Connor seemed to her to be more unpredictable than at any other point since his first arrival in the hall. As they reached the piles of chairs in the foyer, she tried to pray, but was unable to muster the words.

'Get them out of here now!' yelled Connor. He sounded on the edge of hysteria.

Grace was startled by his tone and the immediacy of his instruction. She felt the children jump too. She held them tighter still, while simultaneously urging them to the front of the line of chairs and towards the door. She reached for the lock. Keeping her hand steady, she was able to turn it at the first attempt. As the door cracked open, she felt the sudden burst of cool air. 'It's OK,' she repeated to the children.

She opened the door a little wider and this time was able to see the female armed officer, who had lowered her face covering, likely in order to reveal a human face for the children to see.

'Hello, Grace,' she smiled. She extended her right hand towards Ittack and Rahel, who were holding tightly to Grace and to one another. 'It's OK,' said the officer gently, unwittingly picking up Grace's refrain.

The children were terrified by the prospect of leaving the hall. The thought of leaving their mother behind was too much to bear and the sight of so many heavily armed police officers was as unsettling to them as it was reassuring to Grace. But they were equally terrified by the prospect of staying. They stood for a moment on the edge of the high board, summoning the courage to jump.

This time, Grace gave no thought to her own chances of escape. Connor was too close to her; he would surely shoot her before she had gone more than three paces. And, in any case, she wasn't prepared to leave the other hostages behind. So she untangled the children from her embrace and eased them gently out into the night. Then she closed the door and locked it. Trapped again.

Alex

On the second floor of the house across the road, one of the snipers had maintained a steady commentary on everything he could see. He and his colleague had been unable to get a clear line of sight on Connor, who had been using Grace as a shield. The marksman had described the appearance of the children in the doorway. He had informed those listening of the moment when they took their first steps towards safety. He had observed and reported as they were hurried away from the front of the building and out of his view. At the same time, the lone surveillance camera had been relaying the reverse of the same scene from inside the hall.

The two children were wrapped quickly in foil blankets, to guard against the shock as much as the cold. Then they were hurried down the hill.

Back out at the front of the house, Alex was the first to see them coming. 'There they are,' he pointed, as a wave of relief swept over him. As a parent himself, it was the plight of the children that had been weighing most heavily on him. He embraced Pip. 'I can't see that it was anything we said or did that got them out,' he remarked, 'but, bloody hell, it's good to see them.'

'It really is,' Pip agreed, exchanging handshakes and hugs with the other members of the team and watching as the fire-arms officers helped the children up the steps and into the back of the ambulance.

'Who's that?' asked Rich as an unfamiliar woman dressed in civilian clothes climbed into the ambulance with them.

'I'm not sure,' Pip responded, 'but I'm guessing she's a Syrian interpreter.'

The ambulance disappeared from view and any sense of relief and gratitude felt by Alex proved to be short-lived. 'Three down, six to go,' he remarked, as the weight began to settle on his shoulders once more.

01.26 hrs

Grace

'We're all going to die in here.'

Grace looked at Connor in alarm. She was back in her chair, hands and feet tied, and she had been watching and waiting to see what he did next.

'What do you mean?' she said, because she couldn't think of anything better to say.

Connor didn't answer her. Instead, he walked back through to the kitchen, apparently intending to roll another joint. Grace suspected that he was trying to calm himself down, but it occurred to her that, actually, it was only going to increase his growing sense of paranoia.

Grace heard the extractor fan switch on. In her mind, she left him alone and turned her thoughts instead to the two children and to the sense of relief she felt now that they were both safely out. Thinking about them once again set her thinking about Isaiah. Where was he? What was he doing? What was he thinking? He must be worried sick. She hoped he had someone with him, perhaps a neighbour or someone from the congregation. Maybe he'd gone round to the flat his friend Chris shared with his parents and was being looked after by them. She didn't care where he was, so long as he was safe.

She looked at Mariam and the two of them made fresh eye

contact. Mariam had run out of tears and her head dropped after a few moments. Grace looked round the room at the other four, each alone with their own thoughts and fears. Jack had lapsed into twitchy silence. His nose had stopped bleeding. The others offered no visible signs of their respective conditions.

She was still staring at Alan, wondering when he might next need to take his medication, when Connor reappeared from the kitchen sooner than she had expected, a stubbed-out, half-smoked reefer held between the index and second fingers of his left hand. There was a faraway look in his eyes.

Lee

Connor's mind was lurching, one moment preoccupied with the inevitability of death, the next with a renewed determination to see things through to the end. He looked at his six hostages, he thought of the worldwide headlines, and he tried to picture the moment when Nicholas Farmer would be released from jail. He was a man with a cause. It was his responsibility, his duty, to secure the existence of his people and a future for white children. He was the Home Front Liberator and he had come to set them free.

Grace

'Now they're out of the building, they can get the fuck out of this country,' Connor growled.

Grace assumed that he must be talking about the children. And, for whatever reason, he seemed to be trying to pick an argument with her. He was certainly expecting her to respond.

'But where would they go?' she asked him. Despite his language and mood, Connor seemed to present less of a physical threat to her than at any previous point in the night. He appeared, to Grace at least, to be more concerned with what was in his head than what was in the hall. And that made him a little less terrifying than before. It also allowed her to retain some semblance of steadiness.

'Back to wherever they fucking came from.' He was definitely trying to start a row.

Grace chose to stick to the simple facts.

'But they can't go back to where they came from. That place no longer exists. Their entire country is in ruins.'

'I don't care where they go,' he growled, 'so long as it's not here.'

'But why? They haven't done you any harm.'

'Yes they fucking have,' he grumbled, without elaborating.

'So tell me,' Grace insisted, 'what is the specific harm that Ittack and Rahel have done to you?'

Connor couldn't answer that question, so he ignored it.

'They're fucking immigrants. They're leeches. Cockroaches. They don't belong here.'

'But they're just children.'

'Who are taking money and attention and resources away from white working-class children and who, soon enough, will grow up to become adults and make things even worse than they are already.'

'But what you're saying just isn't true,' Grace insisted. 'Where are you getting your facts from?'

'From experience. From history. From research. From the internet, which, by the way, is the only source of real truth out there.'

'What do you mean?' He was ranting again and she was finding it hard to follow him.

'Are you really as stupid as that fucking police negotiator? Don't you watch the fucking news?'

'What news are you talking about?'

'All of it,' he said, as if that were a sufficient answer.

'I'm sorry, Lee,' she said gently, 'but I genuinely don't know what news you're talking about.'

He looked at her in frustration. 'Well, why don't we begin with the endless stories about those boats full of fucking immigrants floating across the Mediterranean and the English Channel?'

'What about them?'

'What about them?' His voice was rising again. 'What about the fact that those boats are carrying genocidal Muslims who want to turn Britain and the rest of Europe into some kind of caliphate.'

'A caliphate?' Grace wasn't sure what the word meant.

'A fucking Muslim state. They want to turn Europe into Eurabia. They want to end our way of life.'

'Is that really what you think?' she asked.

'Of course that's what I fucking think.' It had been a long time since it had last occurred to him that there might be an alternative explanation.

'But the people in those boats – with large numbers of women and children among them – are risking their lives to make those crossings.'

'So what? They're a bunch of fucking fanatics. That's what fanatics do. The women and children are just there to provide cover for the men.'

Grace studied his face, trying once more to work him out, trying to find some way of challenging the madness of his arguments without pushing him over the edge. 'Well, set to one side for a moment the fact that they're trying to get into this country. Have you ever thought about what it is they might be trying to get away from?'

'What are you on about?' He was fractious and argumentative.

'I've watched some of those news stories you're talking about. I've seen documentaries too. Did you know that a number of those boats never actually make it? They're overloaded and ill-equipped. They sink and the people in them drown. The refugees know the risks, of course. They know their chances of survival are limited at best. So think about it: what possible set of circumstances could be so indescribably terrible that they are prepared to abandon all they know and risk all they have, including their own lives and the lives of their children, in order to escape?'

When Connor didn't immediately respond, Grace kept going. 'These people are desperate. They are fleeing from the terrors of war: from the loss of their homes and livelihoods, from the murder of their loved ones, from the unthinkable realities of torture and starvation and disease. They are trying to get away from a reality that I can't even begin to imagine.'

Connor hesitated. He was struggling to come up with an adequate response to what Grace was saying, so he tried to shut the subject down.

'I know what I believe. I know the truth. And there's nothing you can say or do that's going to change that.'

'Do you know that Ittack and Rahel haven't seen their dad for more than a year?' she asked.

'So what? I haven't seen mine for much longer than that.'

'But that's your choice, Lee. Ittack and Rahel haven't been given a choice. They don't even know whether he's alive or dead. Mariam has no idea what's happened to her husband. Can you imagine how that feels?'

'I couldn't care less.' He was sullen and sulky. Grace knew that she needed to tread incredibly carefully. But she also knew that she had to try to get through to him.

'There's nothing a mother wouldn't do for her children,' she said.

01.45 hrs

Alex

The atmosphere in the cell was subdued. Pip had disappeared off to the latest command team meeting and there was a distinct lull in the room while they waited for her return. They were all tired and the fact that there had been a pause in the negotiation, albeit a temporary one, only intensified the feelings of exhaustion.

'Do you think he'll let the rest of them go?' Alex asked Rich.

'I hope so,' said Rich, sounding genuinely optimistic. Though he had never dealt first-hand with a negotiation like this one, he had, in the course of his day job at the Yard, looked at the outcomes of a significant number of other hostage situations, not just in Britain, but around the world – the ones that had ended badly, as well as those that had ended well. He had listened to the stories of survivors and had studied the behaviour of their captors. 'The fact that he's released any of them has to be good news for all of them,' he observed. 'It indicates a willingness on his part, not just to consider the possibility of letting people go, but to see it through. If we'd got to this point and they were all still in there, I'd be feeling a whole lot less optimistic. As it is, I'm genuinely hopeful. Three down, six to go,' he said, reiterating much more positively the phrase that Alex had used earlier on.

Grace

'Do you hate me?' Grace asked Connor.

Connor didn't reply.

'Do you hate me?' she asked again.

'I don't know you,' he responded.

'But you don't know the rest of the people you're describing as terrorists and invaders.'

'Maybe. But I know what they're like.'

'How do you know?' Without necessarily realising it, she was starting to peel away the inadequate layers of his arguments and he was struggling to respond.

'I told you,' he grumbled. 'From research. From the internet. From the overwhelming evidence that's there for all to see.'

'What about my parents?' she asked him, changing tack slightly.

'What about them?'

'My parents came here from the Caribbean in the early 1950s. They were immigrants. I'm the daughter of immigrants. They sailed halfway across the world at the invitation of the government of this country. My mum was a nurse and my dad became a bus driver.'

'So what?'

'They came here because this country needed them in the aftermath of the Second World War. And they spent the rest of their lives here: Mum looking after terminally ill cancer patients and Dad doing his best to make sure that everyone got to work on time. This is where I was born. This is my home. I can't *go back* to where I came from because I came from here.'

'Maybe you're the one fucking exception,' he said, trying

and failing to find any sort of adequate response. By now, it was Grace who appeared to hold the advantage in the conversation.

'How so?' she said. 'I'm the same as Rahel and Ittack. I'm the same as Mariam.' Grace nodded towards the silent figure sitting across the hall from her. 'The only difference is that I haven't escaped the destruction of war to get here.'

'At least you were fucking born here,' was the best he could manage.

'But does that really make any kind of difference?' she replied. 'At the end of the day, we all live on the same planet. We all come from the same place.'

Alex

Pip reappeared at the door.

'What news?' Rich asked.

'Well, the command team have asked me to pass on a "thank you" for all your efforts so far,' she replied, 'and they want us to know that there will be no decision on Farmer until the morning.'

'What does that mean?' asked Rich, helping himself to another biscuit from the now half-empty tin.

'They didn't say. Maybe it's their way of buying some more time. Let's be honest – none of us actually thinks anyone is seriously going to consider the release of a convicted terrorist, particularly one with Farmer's profile. But no one is saying that out loud just yet – at least, not to me.'

'What's happening out there?' asked Alex, changing the subject and nodding towards the window.

'The SAS have deployed alongside the SFOs,' she replied. 'And they're ready to take the building at a moment's notice.'

'And?' prompted Alex.

'And they're watching and waiting, just like the rest of us. Contain and negotiate – that's still the plan. The only way they will go in is if any of the hostages are in immediate danger.'

'And?' repeated Alex, willing her to say more.

'And they want us to get him back on the line, to keep him talking. I suspect they want him distracted while they deploy more kit.'

'Such as?' enquired Angie.

'They didn't say,' Pip replied, 'but I imagine it will be building-entry kit. That, and more technical surveillance equipment.' She paused before continuing, 'It's actually surprisingly calm out there at the moment. There are literally hundreds of police officers and soldiers within a few hundred yards of where we're sitting, but they're all playing the long game. As we are. The only people who aren't calm are the media. It's still an absolute feeding frenzy as far as they're concerned.'

'So let's get him back on the line,' said Rich, taking the initiative.

The team gathered round and took a few minutes to discuss their options. When they were ready, Alex turned back to his phone. He dialled the number and held his breath.

Lee

Connor responded with irritation when his phone rang again.

'What?' he snapped.

'Mr Connor, it's Alex,' responded the now-familiar voice at the other end of the line. 'I've got an update for you.'

'About fucking time,' he replied, standing up a little straighter.

'First, though, I want to thank you for letting the children go.'

'Get on with it,' said Connor impatiently.

'I've got an update on Nicholas Farmer for you.'

'Go on,' said Connor, more interested now.

'To be honest, it's not much of an update,' said Alex, 'but I did promise to let you know as soon as I heard anything.'

'Just get on with it,' said Connor, his shoulders sagging and his interest already waning.

'I've been told to let you know that there will be no decision about Nicholas Farmer until the morning.' Alex paused. 'For at least the next six or seven hours.'

'What the fuck?' Connor spluttered. 'Why the hell not?' He lurched quickly from exasperation to anger and back again.

'They haven't told me why. All they've told me is that there will be a delay. And, as I said, I promised to let you know if I heard anything at all.' Alex didn't sound as though he was willing to speculate beyond that point.

'Then what on earth is the point of this fucking conversation?'

'I wanted to keep the channels of communication open,' Alex said, before adding, 'Can I ask how everyone is doing in there?'

'No.'

'How's Grace?' Alex persisted.

Connor partially relented. 'Fine.'

'What about Mariam?'

'Are you going to go through every fucking name? They're all fine.'

'But you'll understand why I'm wanting to check. They must be terrified. And they must be exhausted.'

'I told you, they're all fucking fine.'

The negotiator switched focus from hostages to hostage-taker. 'How about you, Mr Connor? How are you doing?'

'Why the hell would you care?'

'Because I care about everyone in there,' Alex insisted, 'including you.' And, for a fraction of a second, it occurred to Connor that he might actually mean it. 'Are you hungry? Can we get you something to eat?'

'What the fuck?'

'Can we get you something to eat or drink?'

'What? And lct you fucking poison me?' His voice rose an octave. 'Do you think I'm some kind of total amateur?' Now he was agitated and angry again. 'Do you not think I came prepared for all this?'

'We wouldn't dream of trying to poison you,' said Alex, clearly startled by the suggestion. 'What on earth makes you think we'd do something like that?'

'Because you're the fucking police. Because you're just an-other part of the anti-white machine. Because you want me dead.' Much of the emotion had drained back out of Connor's voice. His sense of paranoia was escalating again.

'I don't want you dead, Mr Connor.' Alex's response was immediate and emphatic. 'I absolutely don't. In fact, it's the very last thing I want. Every single life in that building matters to me. Every single one, including yours.'

Connor didn't respond.

'Are you still there, Mr Connor?'

Connor grunted.

'I just wanted to check how you were doing,' said Alex, 'that's all.' He tried to switch focus back to the hostages again. 'What about Grace and Mariam and the others? They must be hungry and thirsty too.'

'This conversation is a waste of fucking time,' Connor

snapped. 'If there's going to be no decision about Nicholas Farmer until the morning, I suggest you don't bother calling me back until then.'

He hung up yet again.

Alex

Alex was frustrated that he hadn't managed to keep Connor on the line for longer; genuinely taken aback by the bizarre suggestion about poisoning and troubled by the mention of death; irritated that he hadn't been able to buy any more time for the teams out on the ground; anxious about what it all might mean for the six hostages still left inside.

As ever, Pip was there for him. 'Everyone is knackered, including him,' she said, gesturing towards the phone. She checked her watch. 'Look, it's two in the morning and I suspect we're not going to get him back on the phone for a while. I suggest we all take a breather.'

'I could do with some caffeine,' said Rich.

'Me too,' agreed Angie.

As the two of them headed off to the kitchen in search of coffee, Pip turned to Alex. 'What about you? Can I get you something to drink?'

'I'm all right, thanks,' he replied wearily.

'Why don't you take advantage of the lull and try to grab some rest?' she asked him.

'Rest? Now?' Pip's suggestion was just about the last thing Alex had been expecting. He was exhausted, but there was no way he would be able to rest while there were still hostages in the hall.

'It might do you some good,' she said.

'I'm fine,' he replied.

Pip walked slowly across the room and stopped in front of him. She placed her hands gently on either side of his face and turned it slightly, so that he was looking straight at her. 'Are you sure?' she asked him.

'Honestly, I'm fine,' he insisted.

'That's good,' she responded, all the while studying his expression, 'because I'm going to need you to be at your best the next time we get him on the phone.'

'I know,' he replied. 'And I promise you I will be.'

'All right then,' she said as she lowered her hands from his face. 'Are you sure I can't get you a coffee or something?' she asked as she turned towards the door.

'I'm sure,' he said.

His eyes followed her out of the room and, once she had disappeared down the corridor, he wandered over to the bay window. He stared out into the night and allowed his thoughts to wander. Almost immediately, they took him back to East London. Back to the one that didn't end well.

02.18 hrs

Lee

Inside the hall, Connor jerked suddenly upright. He had been sitting on the floor with his back to the wall and, despite his long-established nocturnal routines, he had begun to nod off. The repeated adrenaline surges and the relentless uncertainties and anxieties of the past few hours were taking their toll.

He stood up and started walking round the room in an attempt to force some energy back into his body. Grace watched him as he walked.

'What are you looking at?' demanded Connor in a gruff voice as he noticed her staring at him.

Grace

Once again, Grace was brave; far braver than him. She had already decided that, given the right opportunity, she was going to try to keep him talking. She considered that she had very little to lose by doing so, and potentially something to gain. As long as he was involved in a conversation with her, and provided she was careful not to provoke him with anything she said, she reasoned that he might be less likely to cause further harm to her or any of the other hostages. But that wasn't her only motivation. There was a measure of idealism mixed in with her remarkably clear-headed pragmatism. Because she was also thinking about the boys in her primary school.

'I'm trying to understand why you're doing what you're doing,' she said. 'I'm trying to understand who you are.'

Connor responded with a look of weary frustration. 'Haven't you listened to a single thing I've said?' he asked her. 'Are you telling me that you want me to go over it all again?'

'No, I'm not,' she replied. 'I understand what you've said to me and I disagree with pretty much every word of it.' Her tone was much less confrontational than the words themselves. 'But I still don't understand why you're doing what you're doing.'

'I'm trying to free an innocent man.' Connor sounded unexpectedly defensive.

'But he's not innocent, is he?'

Connor either didn't hear her challenge or he chose to ignore it. 'And I'm trying to stand up for our way of life,' he continued, without defining who 'our' referred to. 'I'm trying to make our voices heard. They ban our marches. They ban our demonstrations. They ban our fucking organisations. What alternative is there to this?' he said, gesturing round the room.

'I suppose there are some things we're never going to agree about,' Grace said quietly, 'so why don't we talk about something else? Why don't you tell me your story?'

Lee

Connor supposed that he ought to have been irritable and impatient with her. That would have made sense. He ought to have been raising his voice and stamping his feet, delivering another of his supremacist speeches. But the energy and the inclination to do any of those things had deserted him. He found that he was strangely fascinated by her. He'd never met anyone remotely like her before. And it had been a long, long time since he'd been involved in any kind of genuine, face-to-face conversation with another human being.

'What do you want to know?' he asked before he could stop himself.

'I want you to tell me about your family.' She had obviously made a conscious decision not to mention his mother specifically.

'I don't have a family – at least not in the sense you mean it,' he said. 'Home Front is my family.' As he spoke, he leaned against the wall and slid back down into a seated position. He crossed his legs and, initially, said no more. But she had flicked some kind of switch inside him, something he hadn't even known was there, and he realised that he was going to talk; that he was going to tell her everything.

She allowed him silence and space. And, when he was good and ready, he began to talk. He started not quite at the beginning, but at the end of the beginning.

'My mother died when I was thirteen years old,' he said. 'She was killed in a car crash.'

'Good grief! I'm so sorry.' Grace's response was a spontaneous and entirely genuine expression of empathy and sympathy. Connor barely heard her.

'She didn't much like driving when it got dark,' he continued, 'but I'd gone to a friend's house after school, and so she came to pick me up. If I'd just gone home as normal, it would never have happened...' His face was etched with pain and regret. He was remembering the journey. Remembering the conversation. He was even remembering the song – 'Stuck in a Moment' by U2 – that was playing on the car radio at the time. '...The van that hit us had just gone through a red light, doing more than forty miles an hour. We were halfway across the junction and she took the full force of the impact. She was killed instantly.' He stopped talking, lost in his recollection. It was the first time he'd spoken to anyone about it in almost ten years.

Grace

Grace realised that she'd been holding her breath. Connor looked broken. Thirteen years old again.

'I don't know what to say,' she said.

'What can you say? It's done.'

'What was her name?'

'Her name was Nancy,' he replied.

'I really don't know what to say. Except that I am truly, deeply sorry.'

'It's done,' he repeated.

'Were you hurt?'

'Concussion. A broken arm. Stitches. They had to cut both of us out of the car. I was lying in a hospital bed wondering where she was when they told me.'

'Who told you?' asked Grace.

'A police officer.'

'What about your dad? Where was he?' she asked.

At first, Connor said nothing. He simply rested the back of his head against the wall and stared into space. 'My father is dead to me,' he said eventually. He seemed to insist on referring to his dad as his 'father'. It was an exact repetition of the phrase he had used earlier in the night, but said this time more in sadness than rage.

'What do you mean?' Grace reckoned that Connor wanted to say more.

'My father was a horrible man,' he began. 'Horrible to my mother and horrible to me.' He stopped again.

'Go on,' Grace prompted. For a moment, she had almost forgotten where she was and who he was and what he'd done. For a moment, she felt only compassion and concern for a boy who was hurting.

Lee

'I don't think he ever actually hit her – at least, I never saw him hit her – but he made her life utterly miserable. He made *our* lives utterly miserable. He was a controlling bastard.'

In his mind's eye, Connor tumbled back in time. He saw himself walking along the first-floor corridor of his childhood home, past his parents' open bedroom door. He heard his father's angry, raised voice. He saw his mother, sitting on the end of their bed, eyes red, cheeks flushed. He called out to her and she appeared startled. She stood up quickly, adjusted her dress and forced a smile. 'Oh hello, darling,' she had said as she tried to maintain the pretence that nothing was wrong, 'I thought you were downstairs reading'.

The memory was a deeply unsettling one and it required a significant effort on Connor's part to keep talking to Grace. 'She had no life of her own – only the one he allowed her. He wouldn't let her go out on her own. When they did go out together, he chose her outfits and she wasn't allowed to speak to any other men. He was furiously jealous, and she was forced to live with the consequences of it. We both were. He wouldn't let her get a job or even have her own bank account. He gave her a little red notebook and made her keep records and receipts of any money she spent. Then he inspected it at the end of every week. Like I say, he was a bastard.'

'So how did he react when your mum was killed?' Grace asked.

Connor shrugged and didn't answer the question. He didn't tell her that his mother's death had actually broken his father's heart. Nor did he offer the observation that this was a thoroughly unexpected thing to have happened to a man who had never once indicated that he had a heart capable of breaking. And he kept to himself his father's swift descent into alcoholism and the rapid realisation that he was utterly incapable of coping with – much less caring for – his son.

Grace

Realising that Connor was reluctant to talk about his father, Grace tried a different question. 'What about you?' she asked him. 'What happened to you?'

'I was sent away to boarding school. When the holidays came round, I mostly stayed with friends. My father was a wealthy man – he still is – and he paid for my education and for everything else, but that was just about the full extent of his involvement in my life. I still get the money paid into my account every month, but I haven't seen or spoken to him since I was eighteen.' He sounded utterly lost and entirely alone.

'I really am sorry,' said Grace as she examined his face once again. The mystery of Lee James Connor was beginning to make a tiny bit more sense to her. 'I'm sorry for everything that's happened to you.'

Connor remained silent.

'What about the driver of the van?' asked Grace, trying to engage him back in the conversation. 'The one involved in the crash? What happened to him?'

Connor looked up and stared directly at her.

'Him?' he said, his face flushing with colour and his voice turning bitter. 'He barely had a scratch on him. Isn't that always the way? The innocent die while the guilty walk away unharmed. He'd been drinking – he was more than three times over the limit, they said. They told me that he didn't have a driving licence or any insurance. I found out much later that they deported him at the end of his jail sentence.'

'Deported? Why?'

'Because he was a fucking illegal immigrant.'

02.33 hrs

Alex

Pip walked back into the sitting room to find Alex still staring out at the street, apparently lost in thought. Unknown to her, he had spent the past fifteen minutes back in Romford. The glass in the bay window had been a kind of cinema screen to him, on which he had watched every last detail being played out. The children. Their mother. The firearms officers. The falling, dying man. As always, it had been as real to him as the day it had actually happened. His brow was furrowed and his body was tense.

Pip wandered over and stood beside him. She sensed his unease and guessed the reasons for it. When he didn't immediately react to her presence alongside him, she leaned her weight gently against him.

'A penny for them,' she said softly as she glanced sideways at him.

He turned to look at her and, as his eyes focused on her face, Romford vanished from his imagination and the fierce, nagging tightness in his body started to ease. He held her gaze for a silent moment and, as he did so, he experienced the strangest and most unexpected of feelings, in the midst of what had already been the strangest and most demanding of nights. But there was no time to dwell on it.

'Oh, you know,' he said to her, 'I was just taking a few moments to get my thoughts together for whatever comes next.'

Pip could feel him relaxing, which helped to ease her concerns.

'Any news?' he asked her.

'Nothing much,' she replied. 'There's been no change in the hall and all's quiet outside. But there's someone from SO15 on their way over to brief us.'

'OK,' he responded. 'I just need to take a quick comfort break before they get here.'

He headed to the downstairs loo to relieve himself and splash some water on his face. When he got back to the living room, Rich and Angie had reappeared. Before he could say anything to either of them, there was a firm knock at the front door. Pip went to answer it and reappeared at the entrance to the room, accompanied by a man in his late thirties, wearing a dark green fleece and what looked like a brand-new pair of jeans.

'This is Detective Inspector Andrew Day from SO15,' said Pip. 'Here to tell us a little bit more about our man.'

'And it really is only a little bit,' said the DI apologetically, as he began a round of handshakes, 'because I'm afraid there isn't a huge amount to tell.'

'Every little bit helps,' said Rich. 'Let's hear what you've got.' He gestured to one of the armchairs, inviting DI Day to take a seat. Angie grabbed a fresh marker pen and walked over to the flipchart page that had Connor's name at the top, ready to record anything of note. The rest of the team sat down with the DI, who opened the hardback A4 notebook he was carrying and flicked through it until he found the page he was looking for.

'You already know the basics,' the detective began. 'Lee James Connor, twenty-two years of age, born in Edmonton, North London; previous for drugs possession and supply, but not for anything else.' He paused to study his notes. 'There are one or two family details here that you might not be aware of yet. He's an only child. His mother, Nancy, was killed in a car crash when he was thirteen years old.'

This was news to the negotiation team. They knew Connor's mother was dead – he had told them that much – but they had remained unaware of the circumstances in which she had died.

'And it would appear that he doesn't get on with his dad,' said Alex.

'Correct,' said the DI. 'We'd have had more information about that earlier in the night were it not for the fact that we've only managed to track the father down within the last forty-five minutes.'

'How come?' asked Rich.

'We had an address in Hertfordshire, but no phone number for him. When we first went round to the house, there was no one home. We left a couple of officers in a car outside and he finally got home some time after one this morning. He and his wife had been out for a late dinner with friends.'

'His wife?' queried Pip.

'His second wife,' DI Day clarified. 'He remarried three years after Nancy was killed. My colleagues are still talking to him, but, suffice to say, he was completely devastated when they told him what his son was doing.'

'What else can you tell us about him?' enquired Alex.

'No startling headlines. He's a fairly wealthy man, who hasn't seen or spoken to his son in more than four years. He told us that Connor got increasingly into drugs in his late teens and early twenties — a snippet of information that doesn't exactly come as a surprise. Halfway through his second year at Nottingham University, he was arrested for Possession with Intent to Supply. It looks as though he was keeping his fellow students stocked up with cannabis, as well as smoking an increasing amount of the stuff himself. He was convicted at court and somehow managed to get away with a suspended jail sentence and community service.' The DI turned over to a new page in his book. 'At some point after that — no one is sure exactly when, but at least eighteen months ago — he dropped out of university and vanished off the radar.'

'Nothing at all since then?' asked Rich, sounding slightly sceptical.

'Aside from his online life, nothing that either SO15 or the security services have been able to find so far. We're trying to track down any of his contemporaries from university, but nothing yet.'

'What about money?' It was Angie again. 'What does he do to get by?'

'His dad still puts fifteen hundred pounds a month in his bank account,' said DI Day, double-checking the figure in his book. 'They might not have any kind of relationship, but it looks as though he's still happy to take his old man's money. He's been claiming benefits as well, so he's definitely not short of resources. His only recent cashpoint use is at a bank about half a mile away from where he's been living. He doesn't own a credit card and he doesn't appear to have any debt.'

'Oyster card usage?'

'We've checked with Transport for London and he doesn't have one registered in his name. The investigation team are going to have to rely on CCTV if they're to have any chance of tracking his recent movements.'

'What about his laptop and phone?' asked Angie. 'Anything from those?'

'Nothing new from the laptop yet. He's been accessing a series of encrypted chatrooms, but the technicians haven't been able to get into them yet. What I can tell you is that the results of almost all his open web searches from the last few weeks lead to a succession of white supremacist sites hosting all sorts of extremist content. As far as his mobile is concerned, almost nothing. He doesn't really seem to make phone calls.'

'What?' said Rich, disbelievingly.

'We've got all his call records from his service provider and there's practically nothing on them.' The DI offered Rich a sheet of paper to look at for himself. 'There are no numbers he calls regularly and none that appear to belong to private individuals. There's the odd taxi firm and takeaway, but not much more than that.'

'Lee Connor must have friends somewhere,' said Rich.

'None that we've been able to find so far,' replied the DI.

Grace

'So is that why we're here?' asked Grace gently.

'Is what why we're here?' Connor had got up, wandered over to his bag and picked up a can of energy drink. He was sitting down again with his back against the wall and he opened it as he replied to her. His eyes darted round the room, checking that everything was as it should be.

'The fact that the man who killed your mum was an illegal immigrant. Is that why we're here?'

'What do you mean?' Connor knew exactly what she meant, but he was trying to form a response to her question.

'Do you hate illegal immigrants because of what happened to your mum?' she asked.

'That would be a convenient little theory, wouldn't it,' he said with a sneer, drawing his knees up to his chest. 'Poor little middle-class boy loses his mother and takes his rage out on the world.' He took a sip from his can of drink and stared down at the carpet, avoiding her gaze.

'I would understand if that was the reason,' said Grace. 'I might not agree with you, but I would understand.'

'Well, it isn't the reason.' He was a mixture of obstinacy and defensiveness. 'The opinions I hold about immigrants are based on science and facts, nothing else. And I certainly don't need some fucking pseudo-psychoanalytical justification for what I'm doing. The reasons must be obvious to anyone with half a brain. It's time to send these parasites back to where they came from. It's time to send them home.'

'But this is my home,' said Grace.

'I don't mean you,' he said, without any trace of irony.

Grace recognised that there was a risk of the conversation going round in ever-decreasing circles and she definitely didn't want to aggravate or infuriate him. She could tell that he was still volatile – simultaneously combustible and fragile. His argument was nonsensical – there was no logical reason to make an exception of her, and nothing else he was saying made much sense to her either – but she wasn't about to point that out to him. She knew Mariam was no different from her – they were just two mothers, trying to cope with all that life had thrown their way, doing the best they could for their children. And they shared virtually all of their DNA. She decided to change the subject.

'Tell me some more about your mum,' she said, adopting a

much quieter tone. 'It sounds as though you loved her very much.'

'What's the point? She's gone.' His face clouded as he frowned.

'Because remembering matters,' said Grace, 'and because I think she must have been a remarkable person.'

'She was,' Connor responded, an even more distant look on his face.

'So tell me about her.'

Initially, he didn't respond. His eyes flicked round the room again. He seemed to be having difficulty concentrating. He rested his chin on his knees and, for the time being, seemed to forget that Grace was even there. After a while, she repeated her question and he stirred.

'She was beautiful. She was kind. She somehow managed to survive the worst my father could do to her. And she never once complained – at least she never complained in front of me. I mattered to her more than anything in the world and there's nothing she wouldn't have done for me.'

'That's exactly how I feel about my son,' said Grace.

'Isaiah?'

'How do you know his name?' Grace felt a jolt of pure panic.

'Because your phone kept buzzing with text messages from someone called Isaiah. At least, it did until I smashed it.' Connor almost sounded apologetic.

Grace gasped. She thought of Isaiah sending all those messages and getting no reply. She thought of him calling her number and finding it cut off. Her chest started hurting.

Lee

Connor didn't notice Grace's reaction to his mention of Isaiah's name. He was far too preoccupied with himself, with the sense that the ground beneath his feet was beginning to give way and that there was nothing he was going to be able to do to prevent it from happening.

Alex

DI Day was nearing the end of his briefing.

'Can you tell us a bit more about what he was looking at on the internet?' asked Alex.

The DI nodded and looked back down at his notes.

'The full extent of his dark web activities will take longer to unravel, but his search and viewing histories on the open web follow a depressingly familiar path. From what we've uncovered so far, his journey into right-wing extremism would appear to be a recent and rapid one. Up until about a year ago, the stuff he was looking at wasn't much different from any other young man of his age – mostly porn and gaming sites and very little else besides. But then things started to change.' He glanced up and saw that he had everyone's full attention.

'The internet is a rabbit hole for people like Connor,' he continued. 'Take his YouTube viewing history as an example. We've already started to analyse the content he's been downloading during the past year and it starts innocently enough – with a succession of what look to be not much more than basic, fairly amateurish, self-help videos. But, having watched one or two, he started watching hours of them. And I mean *hours*

– frequently twelve or thirteen hours at a time – one film after another after another.

'Sites like YouTube operate by feeding you a relentless diet of what they think you want. Their business model is based on maximising your viewing time and, consequently, their advertising revenue. Put simply, they want you to keep staring at your screen for as long as possible – and the most effective way to do that is by taking advantage of what the experts refer to as "the filter bubble".'

Nobody interrupted him with a question, so the DI continued.

'The internet runs on algorithms: artificial intelligence systems that analyse what you're watching and then supply you with a stream of suggestions about other, similar, content in the hope of catching your eye. The effect of all this is to create a kind of self-reinforcing reality, devoid of any kind of balance or any form of counterargument. You only get to see what the algorithm thinks you want to see and what starts out as a series of relatively harmless videos can lead very quickly onto content that is much more concerning.

'That's certainly what seems to have happened to Connor. After not much more than a week or so of the self-help videos, he started turning his attention to content that was edgier. To begin with, it was little more than the online equivalent of those old radio shock-jocks – provocateurs who delight in starting polarising arguments about emotive or controversial subjects. But, with every week that passed, the stuff he was viewing became steadily more extreme. For the past six months, all he seems to have been watching is material posted by neo-Nazis, white supremacists and alt-right extremists. He's viewed hundreds and hundreds of hours of it.

'When you hear the term "Preachers of Hate" being used, it

most often seems to be in relation to those who teach a distorted form – or forms – of Islam. But there are at least as many hate preachers on the far right, and they are every bit as dangerous. The internet is their pulpit and many of the biggest technology companies in the world have been complicit in spreading their message. Even the most cursory review of what Lee Connor has been watching in the last few months reveals a mountain of deeply alarming material.'

'Such as?' prompted Alex.

'Violent films showing clips from 1930s Germany, calling for an armed global uprising against Muslims and Jews and people from other minority communities.'

'But what the hell is that stuff even doing on the internet in the first place?' asked Angie, voicing the thoughts of everyone else in the room. 'Why aren't the big tech companies doing more about it?'

DI Day shrugged his shoulders and rubbed the tip of his thumb against the tips of his fingers. 'The power of the buck?' he offered. 'It always seems to come down to money in the end; to old-fashioned greed, pure and simple. If you were trying to be a little bit more charitable – and I'm not sure I want to be – you might say that the tech companies didn't see it coming; that they couldn't have foreseen the monster it would turn into. And now they can no longer control it. There are millions of hours of content being created and posted on the internet every single day and there's no way they can hope to keep track of it all. The consequence is that people like Lee Connor can become radicalised in the darkness of their own bedrooms without ever having actual face-to-face contact with another human being.'

'So he's gone from weed-smoking college dropout to hostage-taking armed terrorist in little more than a year? And all it took was a laptop and a broadband connection?' said Rich, voicing his thoughts as questions.

'That sounds about right,' said the DI.

Grace

Inside the hall, Grace was still recovering from the shock of hearing Connor use Isaiah's name, and from the haunting thought that her son had received no reply to his messages. What on earth must her boy be thinking?

'What did Isaiah's text messages say?'

She couldn't help asking the question out loud. She desperately wanted and needed to know the answer. But Connor's mind was somewhere else entirely and he didn't even hear her speak.

Alex

DI Day was standing up and getting ready to leave. 'The only other thing that might be helpful,' he ventured, 'is some of the early learning to emerge from the counter-radicalisation programmes we've been developing and running.'

'Go on,' Alex encouraged him.

'There's undoubtedly some potential benefit in offering a direct challenge to the extremist beliefs that people hold – not least in presenting a compelling counter-narrative to the one delivered by the hate preachers – but there's also a pressing need to identify and address some of the basic human factors that render people vulnerable to radicalisation in the first place.'

'Such as?' asked Pip.

'Such as the impact of childhood or adolescent trauma,' the DI replied. 'Or something as basic as loneliness: the fracturing of relationships and the loss of proper human connection. People are not supposed to be on their own.'

'Are you seriously saying that we should be feeling some sort of sympathy for people like Lee Connor?' asked Rich, struggling to mask his incredulity.

'No, I'm not,' said DI Day matter-of-factly. 'I'm simply suggesting that a better understanding of what got him into this situation might help us to identify a way to get him out of it.' He paused before offering a final observation.

'The worst thing in the world is to be nothing to nobody,' he said.

03.04 hrs

Alex

After the departure of the DI, and in light of the information and advice he had given them, the team turned their attention back to the negotiation and, in particular, to the question of how best to approach Connor when they next spoke to him.

'Have we had anything come through from the Yard in terms of offender profiling?' asked Alex.

'I haven't seen anything yet,' Pip replied, 'but I'll chase it up at the next command team briefing.'

'Is he mad, bad or sad?' asked Angie. 'That's the question I want the experts to answer for me.'

'Or some combination of all three?' suggested Alex.

'You've got more experience than the rest of us,' said Pip, looking at Rich as she spoke. 'Which do you think he is?'

'I tend to agree with Alex,' Rich replied. 'Invariably, it's a combination of factors, though you know how the media tend to play these things. If a suspect is black or brown and claiming Islam as his religion, the press have no hesitation in calling him a terrorist. None of them would leave the rest of us in any doubt that he was "bad". But, whenever the attacker happens to be a white man, the default reaction seems to be to label him as a "lone nutter" rather than as anything more sinister. It happens almost every time.'

'Does Connor have any history of mental illness?' asked Angie.

'None that we know of,' replied Pip. 'Certainly none that's been mentioned in any official record I've seen.'

'What about cannabis-induced psychosis? That has to be a possibility,' said Angie.

'Again, nothing diagnosed,' said Pip, 'but I agree that it has to be on the cards.'

'Remind me of the specific symptoms,' said Alex.

Pip picked up her phone and started typing. 'Let me make sure I get the details right,' she said. The first thing she read aloud was a direct quote from the main NHS website: 'People who use high-strength cannabis daily are five times more likely to have a first episode of psychosis.' She paused as she scanned quickly through a couple of other websites. 'Symptoms include agitation, isolation, paranoia, suspicion and dissociation.'

'Dissociation?' queried Angie.

'Losing touch with reality,' Pip replied. 'A general loss of connection with the real world.'

'It all sounds very much like our man,' said Alex.

Lee

Inside the church hall, Connor had once more sought sanctuary in the kitchen. The extractor fan was back on. Grace and the rest of the hostages were silent in their chairs. He was smoking another joint in the hope that it would offer him respite from the fire that was crackling in his brain. But, if anything, it was making him worse. His mind was being overrun by a cacophony of colliding and frequently contradictory voices and thoughts.

He had been trying to replay the chronology of the night's

events in search of errors or flaws in his execution of the plan. But he was struggling to remember all the details. And he had begun to confuse the actual events of the past few hours with his recollections of the dry run two weeks earlier, and with the visualisations he'd been rehearsing for weeks, in which everything had gone exactly according to plan. Even as he was trying to work out what was real and what was not, he was a boy again, being cut out of a car wreck, being told that his mother was gone, packing for a new school term, hiding from his father, smoking his first reefer.

Then there was the black woman. Where did she fit in? What *was* her name? He started to hear her voice – *I am so sorry for your loss* – but, in his frayed imagination, the sound of her talking to him morphed into the sound of Nicholas Farmer delivering one of those speeches that Connor had listened to so often that he knew it word for word. Suddenly, it was as though Farmer was in the room. Perhaps he actually was in the room. Maybe the police had listened to his demands and let him go and, perhaps, having been released, Farmer had come straight to him. Farmer was going to be pleased with him. Proud of him.

Connor spun round, only to discover that there was no one there. His mind was stalling. He thought he heard more noises on the roof. He thought he heard noises outside the window. He thought he heard voices beyond the locked fire doors. Whispering, conspiratorial voices. Voices and more voices.

Alex

The familiar ringtone on Alex's mobile interrupted the conversation in the cell.

'It's him!' shouted Alex as he grabbed his phone, set it down on the coffee table next to the dictaphone and connected the call. Before he could say anything of substance, Connor was shouting at him.

'I want to talk to Nicholas Farmer right now.' His voice sounded panicky, but his demand was unequivocal.

'You want to do what?' Alex was stalling, looking to Rich for inspiration.

Rich made another rapid circular movement with his right hand. Keep him talking.

'I want to talk to Nicholas Farmer – and I want to do it right now,' Connor said, less loudly but with more menace.

'But he isn't here.' Alex was still struggling to get his thoughts together.

'I know he isn't fucking there, that's why I'm asking to speak to him. On the telephone. Now.'

Alex was trying to compose himself. 'Well, I can certainly pass your request on, but, as you know—'

Connor interrupted him, back at full volume. 'Stop fucking delaying me,' he yelled. Alex leaned back from the coffee table. He looked at Rich, who was likewise momentarily stunned. 'Stop fucking delaying me,' Connor repeated, in a sort of hiss this time.

'I'm not delaying you.' Alex was still on the defensive. 'I promise you that's not what I'm trying to do, but I can't just produce Nicholas Farmer out of thin air. What I can do is—'

Once again, Connor interrupted him, this time in a startlingly matter-of-fact voice.

'You're never going to release him, are you?'

'What do you mean?'

'I mean that Nicholas Farmer isn't coming out of prison. Not now, not tonight. Not at any point in the foreseeable future.'

'Who told you that?'

266

'No one has told me that. No one needs to. You've been stringing me along all night. You're too afraid to tell me the truth. Too fucking afraid of what I might do.'

'But I have told you the truth,' said Alex, trying to regain a foothold in the conversation. 'Every word I've spoken to you tonight has been true. I told you the police wouldn't attempt to come into the hall and we haven't . . .' He was checking off the list of PPAs on the living-room wall. 'I told you I'd listen to you and I have. I told you I'd pass on your requests to the people in charge, and that's exactly what I've done.'

'I don't believe you.'

'But all of it is true.'

'I don't believe you and I don't trust you.' Connor was sounding increasingly agitated.

'But what have I said or done tonight that would cause you not to believe or trust me?' Alex didn't like the direction the conversation was going in. 'I promise you that everything I've told you is one hundred per cent true. And, as far as I am aware, no decision has been taken about what happens to Nicholas Farmer. You have my word.'

'How can I believe you when I can't even fucking see you?'

'What do you mean?'

'How can I possibly know whether or not you're telling me the truth if I can't look you in the eye?'

'You have my word,' Alex insisted, uncertain of what else he could say.

'Where are you?' Connor demanded. It was another question from left field, another one that Alex had failed to anticipate. He looked at Rich, who, in turn, looked blank.

'What do you mean, where am I?'

'I mean where are you physically standing or sitting at this exact moment in time?'

'I'm not far away.'

'Oh, for fuck's sake, just tell me where you are.' Connor wasn't going to be put off and he was growing more and more impatient.

'I'm in a building down the hill from where you are.' Alex realised there was no point prevaricating any further.

'In which case, you've got fifteen minutes. At the end of those fifteen minutes, I want to see you standing out at the front of this building. And if you're not there in time, someone in here is going to get hurt. I'm sick of talking to you on the fucking phone. I want to see the whites of your eyes.'

With that, Lee James Connor hung up for the last time.

03.20 hrs

Alex

Alex stared at his phone. Then at Rich. Then at Pip. He stood up.

'What the hell are we going to do now?' asked Angie.

'We're going to walk up that hill,' Alex responded as he picked up his mobile and put it in his pocket. 'We're going to stand in front of that church hall and we're going to talk to him face-to-face.' Alex was still processing his thoughts as he was speaking, but he was in no doubt about what was now required.

A fresh surge of adrenaline, triggered by the end of the call and the obvious change in circumstances, had taken the edge off the anxiety he would otherwise have been feeling. He reached into his rucksack and pulled out an additional fleece. Then he started moving towards the living-room door.

'Hang on!' said Rich, raising his voice and grabbing Alex by the arm. 'Not so fast. We need to think this through.'

Alex pulled his arm away in annoyance and was about to swear at his colleague when Pip intervened.

'Rich is right,' she said.

'Well, we need to think it through fast,' said Alex bluntly. He was already putting the extra fleece on. 'We don't have the luxury of time.'

'We've got fifteen minutes,' said Pip calmly. 'I need to speak to the rest of the command team. I'll be back in five, by which time I want you to be able to give me every possible reason for and against doing what Connor is asking.' She looked at Alex in acknowledgement of his evident frustration. 'We can't move without the firearms teams,' she insisted, 'and they can't move until I've briefed their boss.' She hurried towards the front of the house and, once outside, she started running.

Grace

Inside the hall, Grace watched as Connor began reinforcing the barricade in the foyer with additional piles of chairs. She had been able to hear everything he had said on the phone but, as before, none of the responses from whoever was on the other end of the line. And she had absolutely no idea how they were going to respond to his latest demand.

Every now and then, Connor stopped and leaned his head to one side, apparently listening for sounds that she couldn't hear. And between each trip to the front of the hall with a fresh pile of chairs, he made an obsessive circuit of the building, checking all the windows and doors, before crouching on the floor and going through his remaining stock of equipment and supplies.

Alex

'All right, quickly, give me five reasons why this is a bad idea,' said Rich, the urgency clear in his voice.

'We're putting ourselves in harm's way,' said Angie, 'and

we'll be putting the armed officers in harm's way too. We're also placing additional demands on them, just at the moment when they need to be giving their full attention to their own plans.'

'We've no need to get a visual on him,' said Alex, joining the conversation reluctantly. His mind was already on the front of the hall and the next stage of the negotiation. They had less than fifteen minutes and he wanted to start heading up the hill. 'We already have the video feed,' he added by way of clarification.

'That's three. What else?' demanded Rich.

'We have no idea what his intentions are,' said Alex impatiently. 'He might simply be looking for an audience for whatever he has in mind to do next. And we might not want to provide him with that audience.'

'What do you mean?' asked Angie.

'Perhaps he's planning to escalate things,' replied Alex. 'Perhaps he's grown tired of what he perceives to be a lack of progress on his primary demand – the release of Nicholas Farmer – and maybe he's planning to up the ante, with us as his audience.'

'Maybe we're looking at another suicide by cop,' said Rich with a grimace. As he said it, he caught the change in expression on Alex's face and immediately wished that he'd kept the thought to himself. He quickly changed the subject. 'How about five reasons why this might actually be a good idea,' he said.

Alex didn't hear him the first time he said it. It was as though there was some invisible force drawing him back to that other time and place. Angie stared at him.

'Come on,' Rich exhorted them, 'five reasons why we should do what Connor is asking us to do.'

'It might actually help move the negotiation forward,' suggested Angie.

'Tell me more,' said Rich, encouraging her.

'Well, it feels as though we've got a bit stuck on the phone. We've bought time, but it doesn't feel as though we've made a huge amount of forward progress since the children were released.'

'And I think we'd all agree that the release of the children had very little to do with us,' said Alex, struggling to rejoin the conversation.

'OK, the opportunity to move the negotiation forward is our first reason,' said Rich, ignoring Alex's remark. 'I need another four.'

'It's another positive police action isn't it – a PPA?' suggested Angie. 'He's asked us to do something and we'll be able to say that we've done it.' Rich nodded.

'It will allow us to read his non-verbals in real time,' said Alex, forcing his fears to the back of his mind. 'It will give us a much better feel for where he's at and even what he's thinking. Face-to-face is always better in any kind of communication.'

Rich was still nodding. 'Nothing will ever be completely safe, but I have every confidence in the ability of our armed colleagues to look after us while we're out in the open.'

'And, from a purely practical perspective,' Alex added, 'if he's talking to us through an open door, that ought to make it a little easier to get into the building in a hurry, should the need arise.'

The three of them appeared to be moving towards some kind of consensus.

Lee

Connor hadn't said a word out loud since ending the last phone call. Not to Grace, not even to himself. But the voices in his head were becoming relentless. Different voices, saying different things; some he recognised, some he didn't; some he agreed with, some that frightened him; the voices of the living and the voices of the dead; the voices of strangers, all talking over one another.

He wandered slowly in the direction of Jack's chair and came to a stop just behind him. He was still unsure of what he should do next. Jack couldn't see him without turning his head – something he was far too afraid to do – but he could certainly feel him. A haunting sense of terrible dread reached over his shoulders from behind him. It wrapped itself around his chest and began to tighten its grip. Connor took hold of the back of his chair and jerked it backwards. Jack responded with a muffled howl of terror. Connor dragged him into the centre of the room and set him down close to Grace.

He stood back and stared at the scene. Then he changed his mind. He grabbed Jack's chair again and pulled him all the way to the foyer at the front of the building. He left him next to the makeshift barricade and turned his attentions to the rest of the group. One by one, he manoeuvred them into the foyer and lined them up next to one another. He walked from one end of the line of hostages to the other, surveying the arrangement from every possible angle. Finally satisfied, he stalked off to the kitchen to smoke his final joint.

Alex

Pip was out of breath as she reappeared at the gate. The rest of the team were already out at the front of the house, waiting for her.

'The command team are prepared to give their approval, provided we can reassure them that it's in the best interests of the negotiation,' she said, between gulps of air. 'So what have you got for me?'

Rich provided her with a rapid summary of their conversation and she was quick to agree.

'Those were my instincts too,' she said, 'and more or less exactly what I went through with the command team. On the basis of my advice, they've given us the green light.'

'Why didn't you just tell us that straight away?' asked Angie.

'Because I wanted to hear your views first. You might well have come up with something I'd missed and you might have held it back, even subconsciously, if I'd told you the decision had already been made.'

They all understood that they and their colleagues were taking massive, life-and-death decisions, in fractions of seconds, on the basis of imperfect information and without the benefit of the kind of twenty-twenty hindsight that observers and critics alike would no doubt be relying on in the days ahead. They recognised they were doing the best they could with what they had.

A marked armed response vehicle pulled up in front of the house. 'Having said all that, I anticipated what you might come up with and I asked them to bring us some kit,' said Pip by way of an explanation for the arrival of the BMW.

A uniformed officer, with a yellow Taser attached to the front of his bulletproof vest and a Glock strapped to his right thigh, jumped out of the front passenger seat and ran round to open the boot.

'Right,' said Pip, 'this is how I think we should play it.' She set out her thoughts and ideas and listened to suggestions from the team. They reached rapid agreement, understanding that they were running out of time.

03.33 hrs

Alex

Alex lifted the ballistic body armour over his head and secured the Velcro fittings on either side of his ribcage. He took the helmet that was handed to him, put it on and adjusted the chin-strap. Rich was standing a few feet away, mirroring his actions. One of the PCs from the firearms team was speaking to them.

'The officers on the armed teams will not interfere with the negotiation in any way, but they will respond to any immediate threat to life. We've got a loudhailer should you need it, though you may find you're fine without. We'll just have to wait and see. Any questions?'

Neither Alex nor Rich had anything to ask. Pip stepped forward.

'Angie and I will be out there with you, but behind cover on the other side of the road. We'll be close enough to hear you, but not to speak to you, so this next bit is going to depend very much on the two of you. No flipcharts. No Post-it notes. Just you and your wits.' She paused to look at them both in turn. 'You've got this,' she said to them.

Alex was acutely conscious of the repeated ebb and flow of anxiety and adrenaline. As long as the emotional tide was on the way in, as long as the supply of adrenaline was greater than the sum of his anxieties, he felt all right, actually as good as he could have done in the circumstances. The problem was that he had no way of knowing when the tide – or the currents – might change. For the moment, his head was set. He understood what was required of him and the proud professional in him actually welcomed the responsibility. Far better to be in the heart of it all, with the capacity to influence what happened next, than to be on the sidelines, powerless to intervene.

'Ready?' said Pip, eyeing him carefully once more.

'Ready,' he affirmed, and they began to walk up the hill, his mind locked in on what was about to come. Rich strode alongside him in silence.

Lee

The hostages were lined up in the foyer, in closer proximity to one another than they had been for several hours. As fate would have it, Alan and Jean were sitting next to one another, Jack and Helen too. While Connor was elsewhere in the building, the two couples were able to make and maintain eye contact with one another and each of them took some small fragment of comfort from this. Jack and Helen were actually close enough together to be able to reach out and make physical contact, fingertip to fingertip. Jack wanted to tell her that he loved her, but the gaffer tape made that impossible. All four of them had faces that were stained with tears and strained with exhaustion. Mariam and Grace sat silently at either end of the line, thinking more about their children than about themselves. Close to where Grace was sitting, Connor had left a space at one end of the barricade, just wide enough for one person to pass through on their way to the door.

In the kitchen, the inside of Connor's head was becoming

more and more like the inside of a pinball machine: all flashing lights and clanging noise and frantic speed and jerking movement. Chaos, anxiety and paranoia were crowding in on him. He took another desperate drag on his spliff. *I am the Home Front Liberator,* he insisted once more to himself, *and I have come to set my people free.*

Alex

Rich and Alex arrived outside the hall. They stopped for a moment on the pavement, on the opposite side of the road to the building, in almost exactly the spot where Connor had been standing more than eight hours earlier. They read the sign: *Refugees Welcome.* And they surveyed their wider surroundings. The fire brigade had been able to set up two sets of powerful arc lamps and both the street and the building were now bathed in bright light. Immediately in front of them, just outside the gate leading up to the hall doors, two armoured Land Rovers had been parked on the street, facing one another in a 'V' formation. Half a dozen black-clad firearms officers crouched behind each vehicle, guns levelled in the direction of the building. Though they couldn't see them, Alex and Rich knew that there were scores of their armed colleagues surrounding the building, together with members of the SAS, watching and waiting, ready to move in an instant. The air was quiet and still; there was no wind, no birdsong, no planes flying overhead and no traffic noise. The street had never been as silent.

A fully kitted officer with sergeant's stripes on the shoulders of her overalls stepped away from the Land Rover on the left and hurried across to meet Alex and Rich. She extended her hand in greeting and, as soon as the rapid introductions were

over, explained the plan to them. They were to position themselves by the front passenger door of the Land Rover on the
right. Rich, as Number Two, would be covered completely by
the vehicle. Alex would have his head exposed for as long as he
was speaking. She acknowledged the obvious risks involved in
the set-up and described in detail what he was to do if Connor
presented an immediate threat to him, or to anyone else for
that matter. Alex could feel his heart beating in his chest. The
sergeant beckoned to a second officer, who jogged over and
handed Alex a loudhailer.

'Any questions?' she asked them.

'Can you just give us a moment?' said Rich to her, indicating
that he wanted to be left alone with Alex.

She gave them their space.

Rich placed a hand on each of Alex's shoulders and squared
him up, so that they were facing one another.

'Are you ready?' he asked.

Alex nodded. He was.

'You are, genuinely, one of the very best negotiators I have
ever worked with,' Rich said. 'There is no one else I would
rather have in this position. And I will be right here next to
you, every step of the way. Take your time and, if I've got
anything helpful to add, I'll whisper it to you.'

Alex nodded again, having only half heard what Rich was
saying. Like an Olympic sprinter in the last moments before
the start of a race, seeing only the track immediately in front
of them, his field of vision was narrowing to just the bonnet
of the Land Rover, the gate, the path and the front door of the
hall. Everything else was disappearing into the periphery. He
was about as ready as he was ever going to be.

He tightened his grip on the loudhailer and started across
the road, with Rich following immediately behind him.

Lee

Connor checked the rear fire doors for what must have been the thirtieth time that night. They were still locked and secure. He put his ear to the doors and listened for any sound outside. Hearing none, he walked through the hall, the wreckage of broken chairs scattered everywhere, and stopped beside his kitbag. He took a handful of trail mix from a fresh packet and opened a second can of energy drink. He ate and drank sitting on an unbroken chair, his right foot tapping constantly on the floor, his eyes making restless circuits of the room.

For a few brief moments, his thoughts eased a little and he found that he was able to regain some small measure of his previous coherence. What had he achieved? What would he do next? They were never going to release Farmer, were they? But maybe they would at least get him on the phone from prison and let the two of them speak to one another. Nicholas Farmer would know what to do.

Connor tried to remind himself that, in the meantime, the world was still watching. In that regard at least, he thought it possible that he might even be winning. The truth was out there now; no more fake news. People would be talking about the cause, forced to acknowledge the stark realities of the immigrant problem. And they would be talking about him. And that meant he was *some*body. It meant that he was significant, that he was important. He would be a hero to some out there, just as so many other freedom fighters were heroes to him. Someday soon, there might even be pictures of him pinned on the bedroom walls of people he had never met.

His brief reverie was interrupted by the sound of a voice

coming from outside, apparently amplified through some sort of loudspeaker.

'Mr Connor, it's Alex. I'm outside the front of the building, just as you asked. I'm ready to listen when you're ready to talk.'

Connor looked at his watch. He hadn't been certain that they would comply with his request, but they were pretty much on time. He put the last of his handful of nuts and dried fruit into his mouth and took a final swig from his can of drink. As he did so, uncertainty, anxiety and fear resumed their dominant occupation of his mind. He bent down and picked up one of the cans of lighter fuel. He studied it for a moment before tucking it into one of his pockets, double-checking that he also had the lighter with him. Then he picked up both knives and tucked them into the back of his trousers. Finally, he grabbed the gun in his right hand and walked towards the front of the hall.

03.47 hrs

Lee

Connor walked into the foyer, an agitated expression on his face. Sensing him coming, Alan and Jean looked quickly away from one another and back down at the floor. Jack and Helen did the same, losing their precious fingertipped connection as they did so. All felt a renewed surge of aching fear.

Connor tucked the Baikal into the front of his belt and began a crude check of his barricade. He grabbed hold of the stack of chairs at one end of the foyer and gave them a firm shake. He proceeded to do the same with each stack, walking between them and his prisoners as he did so. He eventually came to a stop next to Grace.

'You're coming with me,' he said without further explanation. He pulled out one of his knives, bent down and cut her free from her chair. Once she was standing upright, he grabbed an unused cable tie that he'd discarded on the floor earlier in the night and retied her hands behind her back. Then he drew the gun and pressed it against the back of her head, urging her through the gap between chairs and wall and towards the front door. The narrow passageway widened as it reached the entrance, leaving just enough space for the doors to open fully.

Alex

Alex listened to the sound of the lock turning and watched as the right-hand door swung slowly inwards. Every sinew and fibre in his body tensed. A moment or two later, a face appeared in the open doorway and it caught him unawares. He had assumed that he would be looking at a white man, but he was staring instead at a black woman. Her head was down and her shoulders were sagging. There was a gun being held to the back of her neck.

'Grace!' Alex called out, before he could stop himself. He immediately felt Rich pulling him backwards as he stepped further beyond his cover than he ought to have done. Grace glanced up a fraction, but said nothing.

'Don't fucking speak to her,' a voice shouted out. 'You only speak to me.'

Alex saw the shape of a man, evidently Connor, move out from behind the cover of the door and take up a position immediately behind his prisoner. He watched as Connor placed his left arm around Grace's throat and, with his right hand, held the barrel of a handgun against the side of her head. The smallest part of his face was just visible over Grace's right shoulder. Probably not enough for a clean shot.

Alex caught his breath.

Lee

As he looked up and out towards the street, Connor was surprised by the brightness of the lights. In a swift, involuntary movement, he drew the gun away from Grace's head and used his right hand to shield his eyes. It took several seconds for them to adjust.

'Where's the man I've been talking to?' he called out.

'I'm here, Mr Connor,' a voice called back, this time without the aid of the loudhailer. 'It's me – Alex.'

'I can't fucking see you,' Connor shouted back irritably. 'Show yourself.'

He could now make out the shape of the two vehicles and the silhouettes of a number of different people, but he had no idea which of them the police negotiator was.

'Over here, by the Land Rover on your left.'

Connor followed the sound of the voice and was able to see the mostly hidden figure of a person with their arm raised.

'I still can't see you – you're going to have to come closer.' Connor wasn't prepared to trust the voice alone. He wanted to see the negotiator's face. He wanted to be able to look directly at him when the questions started.

'I'm not allowed to come any closer,' the voice replied. 'I've been told I have to stay where I am.'

'What's the fucking point of that?' Connor could feel his blood rising. 'I told you that I wanted to look you in the eye. Otherwise, what is the fucking point of you being here? You might as well have stayed on the fucking phone.'

Alex

Though unsettled by Connor's outburst, Alex sensed the glimmer of an opportunity.

'I'm not allowed to come any closer,' he said, 'because you're holding a gun.' There was no opportunity for him to check what he was about to say with any of his colleagues, so he just went with it. 'Perhaps if you were to put your gun down, my colleagues might allow me to come a little closer.'

'Fuck off!' came the instant reply. 'Do you really think I'm some kind of fucking idiot? The moment I put my gun down, you lot are all going to pile straight in through the door.'

'We won't,' Alex insisted immediately. 'I promise you no one is coming in through that door. I made that same promise to you earlier in the night and we have kept it ever since. You're still in control here, Mr Connor, and none of us is going to do anything that might risk the safety of anyone in that building.'

Connor didn't reply. Instead, he made a display of pressing the gun even more firmly against the side of his hostage's head. Grace was a powerless pawn in it all, cast once more into the valley of the shadow.

'Please put the gun down, Mr Connor,' pleaded Alex, alarmed by what he was seeing. 'You have my word that nobody is coming through that door.' Connor responded by lowering the gun no more than a millimetre or two, but it was enough to give Alex a sliver of hope. 'Quid pro quo. If you put the gun down, I will see if I can persuade my colleagues to let me come a little closer.'

'Can you see the piles of chairs behind me?' demanded Connor.

'Yes, I can,' confirmed Alex. 'What about them?'

'There are five hostages tied up immediately behind them. If you shoot at me, you are shooting at them. If I die, they die.'

This information was already known to the armed officers who had their guns trained on the front of the building, and to the assault teams mustered in the gardens to the rear of the building. It had been relayed to them by those monitoring the live video feed. But it was news to Alex, who now understood that opening fire on the front of the building would almost certainly have catastrophic consequences.

'Nobody wants to shoot at you,' responded Alex urgently. 'I don't want anyone in there to get hurt. And that includes you.' Connor lowered the gun another fraction. 'Quid pro quo, Mr Connor.'

Alex realised that he was putting his armed colleagues in a difficult position – that he was suggesting a course of action they might not be happy with. It was for that reason he had chosen his words so carefully, leaving himself a small amount of room for manoeuvre in committing only to an attempt to persuade them to allow him closer. The fact was that, at that precise moment in time, it seemed to represent the best opportunity of realistic progress – of saving lives – and, consequently, Alex was determined to pursue it. Silently, Rich was in agreement with him.

'So if I put the gun down, you will move forwards to where I can see you?' Connor asked suspiciously.

'If you put the gun down, I will ask for permission to do that, yes,' Alex replied.

'And if you don't get fucking permission? What then?'

'Why don't we cross that bridge if we get to it,' Alex suggested. When Connor didn't respond, Alex reverted straight back to the most pressing question. 'Now would you be willing to put the gun down?'

Lee

Connor weighed his options as best as his muddled mind would let him. He was determined to ask about speaking to Nicholas Farmer, but he had allowed himself to become completely fixated with the notion that he had to be looking directly at the negotiator when he did so. Nothing else would do; he wanted to see the whites of the police officer's eyes. He had convinced himself that this would be the only way to know whether they were telling him the truth. And now it appeared to him that the only way any of this was going to happen was if he complied with the request to put the gun down. But would that be giving in? Or would it be the police who were giving in by agreeing to move forwards? Pinball thoughts. Actually, hadn't they given in already by coming to the front of the hall in the first place? He desperately wanted to believe that he was still in charge of what was happening.

He lowered the gun a little further. It was now level with Grace's shoulder, pointing at her neck. His mind continued to whirr. Surely they wouldn't shoot at him, not with Grace standing in front of him; not with the rest of the hostages lined up behind the stacks of chairs. He made up his mind, and immediately changed it again. Yes, he would put the gun down; no, he wouldn't.

Grace

All of this was happening in milliseconds, but to Grace, it felt like forever. She wasn't sure how much more of it she could take. She wanted to call out to the police, but she didn't dare. She wanted to sink to her knees and sob, but she refused to allow that to happen. She wanted desperately for it all to be over. More than anything, she wanted to hold Isaiah in her arms and never let him go.

At last, Connor seemed to make up his mind. Or, at least, he acted before he could change it again. He squatted down and laid the Baikal on the carpet next to her feet.

Alex

'Thank you, Mr Connor,' Alex called out, as the heavy tension in his neck and shoulders eased a fraction. 'That was the right thing to do.' But any sense of relief he might have felt lasted no more than a handful of seconds. He watched as Connor reached into his trouser pocket and pulled out an object he couldn't immediately identify.

Lee

Connor's fast-fracturing mind was grasping for anything that might allow him to retain control of what happened next. He might have given up his gun – for the time being at least – but he was damned if he was going to give up his position of strength. On instinct, he had let go of Grace for a moment, reached into his pocket, pulled out the can of lighter fuel and twisted off the cap.

'What are you doing?' It was the anxious, raised voice of the police negotiator. Connor ignored him.

Grabbing the back of Grace's collar with his left hand and holding the lighter fuel in his right, Connor turned round and began spraying the contents of the can over the barricade of chairs.

'What are you doing?' The voice of the negotiator was even more urgent this time. 'What's that in your hand?'

'Insurance,' he growled.

'What do you mean, insurance?' asked a clearly alarmed Alex.

'Putting down my gun doesn't mean I'm putting down my

guard. This is a bit of additional insurance,' he said, as he shook the last drops of fluid over the chairs.

'What's in the can?' Alex asked, fearing the answer.

'What do you think?' Connor replied, tossing the can in the direction of the street. 'If anyone even thinks about trying to come in through these doors, everything is going to go up in flames.' He pulled his lighter out of his pocket and waved it in defiance at the police lines.

'No, Mr Connor!' shouted Alex. 'Please don't do that!'

Connor put the lighter back into his pocket. 'Well I won't need to if you stick to your fucking promises about not coming in.'

'You have my word,' the negotiator replied. 'I promise you we're not coming in.'

Alex

Alex could feel Rich's hand resting on his shoulder. It was a simple gesture of reassurance and Alex was grateful for it. He had no time to dwell on the new threat of the lighter fuel; he was simply relieved that the Zippo was back in Connor's pocket.

'You have my word,' he repeated. 'Now, please can you give me a moment or two with my colleagues – so we can work out how to do this next bit safely.'

'You've got ninety seconds before I pick the gun up again,' Connor shouted as he stepped back into the shadows of the foyer.

The sergeant from the firearms team rushed across from the other Land Rover and crouched down next to Alex and Rich. The three of them were joined by Pip, who had sprinted across the road. They had not much more than a minute.

'We need to make this happen – and fast,' urged Alex before anyone else could speak. They had no time to refer anything up the full chain of command. This was their call.

'We can use the wall on either side of the gate as cover,' said the sergeant, nodding her head towards the hall. The wall was about four feet high and, whilst it didn't offer as much protection as the Land Rovers, it offered some.

'And you're sure that you're happy to do that?' asked Pip.

'I don't see that we have much choice,' the sergeant responded. 'It isn't perfect, but we can make it work.'

'If you can make it work, then we will too,' said Pip.

The sergeant turned away from them and towards her armed colleagues. She began speaking into her radio.

Pip looked at Alex.

'Are you good?'

He offered only a quick nod by way of response. This was no time for small talk and his mind was already set on what needed doing. They had less than fifty seconds.

'Here's the plan,' said the sergeant, moving back across to them. She gestured towards a number of her team. 'These guys will give you the cover you need. They will take up a position along the wall to the right of the gate as you look at it. They will place a line of ballistic shields along the top of the wall and you can then move into position behind them. Clear?' She looked at Alex for confirmation that he understood and, having received it, issued her last instruction. 'If he picks up the gun – or even looks like he is going to pick up the gun – I want you flat on the ground, crawling back behind the Land Rover.'

Alex nodded again. He actually felt unusually calm and his mind was once again clear of everything, save the task immediately in front of him. They were almost out of time.

'I'm coming forwards,' shouted Alex, not wanting to

antagonise Connor by missing his deadline. 'You are going to see a group of armed officers moving up to the wall. I will be right behind them.'

His voice rang out in the silence of the street. Initially, there was no response.

'Can you hear me, Mr Connor?'

'Just get on with it,' came the jumpy, belligerent reply.

Alex looked across at the firearms sergeant and saw that she was already directing her team to move into position. Crouching low, they emerged from the cover of their vehicle and hurried to the wall. Once their shields were in place, the sergeant grabbed Alex by the shoulder.

'Go!' she said.

He followed the exact path taken by the armed team and stood up slowly, next to the tallest of them. As ever, Rich was right beside him.

Lee

At first, all that Connor could see was a line of shields and, behind them, a line of ballistic helmets. No faces. No voices. Just shapes. And it unnerved him to a far greater degree than he had anticipated. How the fuck had it come to this? He counted at least twenty police officers. He knew that there would be scores more beyond his view – more coppers and more hardware than he could possibly count. He fought the instinct to reach for the Baikal, for whatever small insurance it might give him. In the distance, he heard the sound of a helicopter. And he felt afraid.

'Mr Connor, can you hear me? It's Alex.'

He could hear him all right.

'Show yourself,' he shouted.

He saw one of the figures in front of him raise an arm.

'Over here,' came the recognisable voice of the negotiator, 'with my arm in the air.'

Connor could see him much more clearly now, standing about fifteen feet away. He was behind a line of officers who were wearing goggles and pointing guns. The fact that the negotiator didn't have goggles on made it much easier to pick him out from the line-up. It also made it easier to see his face. And, just about, the whites of his eyes.

'Has Nicholas Farmer been released yet?' Connor already knew the answer to his question, but he asked it all the same.

'No, he hasn't,' Alex replied. 'As I mentioned to you on the phone before, I've been told that no decision on that is going to be taken before the morning at the earliest.'

'You're never going to release him, are you?'

'What do you mean?'

'Exactly what I'm saying. You're just stringing me along. You're never going to release him.' Connor was getting stirred up again.

'What gives you that idea?'

'It's fucking obvious, isn't it. All you've done tonight is delay things.'

'To be fair, that isn't all we've done,' said Alex, protesting perhaps a little bit too much. 'I've been listening to you. I've been trying to understand what you want. I've kept my promise that nobody would attempt to come into the building. And I've been doing my best to respond to the things you've been asking me. That's why I'm standing here now.'

Connor wasn't going to allow him any ground.

'I want to speak to Nicholas Farmer. If not in person, then

on the telephone. And I want to do it now.' There was a note of determined finality in his voice.

The negotiator appeared to hesitate before responding. Connor watched as a man standing alongside him, also not wearing goggles, leaned over and seemed to whisper something in the negotiator's ear.

'Who the fuck is that?' demanded Connor.

'Who do you mean?' came the concerned reply.

'The bastard standing next to you, whispering to you.' Connor sounded as paranoid as he felt, instantly suspicious of the unknown figure. 'Who is he and what's he saying to you?'

'His name is Richard,' said Alex, 'he's a police negotiator like me and he's been next to me all night.'

'So what the fuck is he whispering to you?' shouted Connor, his voice rising an octave. When Alex didn't answer instantaneously, Connor's paranoia overtook him. 'What did he just say to you?' he screamed. As he did so, he tightened his grip around Grace's throat. It was an involuntary act, an external manifestation of the sudden escalation of internal tension. And she immediately began to struggle for breath.

'Mr Connor!' Alex shouted in an alarmed voice. 'Grace is choking!'

03.59 hrs

Grace

Connor finally came to his senses and relaxed the muscles in his arm. Grace gasped, gulping air into her lungs. Her knees buckled and she wept fresh tears. She could see the police officers – they were almost within touching distance – but they couldn't get to her, nor she to them. She was trapped and she was utterly terrified.

Alex

'Grace, are you OK?' Alex called out.

He had been shaken deeply by the sight of her struggling for breath. He felt powerless and yet wholly responsible for the desperate situation she was in. He tried to calm her terrorist captor by offering an explanation for the whispering that had apparently so disturbed him.

'Richard was just offering to pass on your request to speak to Nicholas Farmer,' he said.

Taking his cue, Rich disappeared for a few moments, doubtless to speak with Pip.

'That's him going now,' Alex continued. 'He's going to pass on your request to the people in charge.'

'I told you that I wanted to speak to Nicholas Farmer *now*,' Connor growled.

'That isn't going to be possible,' Alex said as calmly as he could manage. 'You know that's not my decision to make.'

'You really are completely fucking useless!' Connor complained. 'It's a total waste of time talking to you.' He started to shift his weight. For a moment, it appeared to everyone watching that he was going to disappear back inside the building, taking Grace with him.

'Wait!' yelled Alex, scarcely able to conceal the desperation in his voice. Connor paused where he was and looked warily in Alex's direction. Standing there on his own, without Rich by his side, struggling to remember the detail of the various negotiating options he and the team had been discussing earlier on, Alex went with the first thought that came into his head. 'While we're waiting for a response from the people in charge, can I ask you a question?'

'About what?' Connor replied in exasperation.

'About your cause?'

It worked. Whatever Connor might have been intending to do – and he may well not have been certain himself – the renewed reference to his 'cause' seemed to register with him. He didn't go back inside. He stayed where he was, still holding Grace in front of him. Alex breathed a sigh of relief and his mind clicked into a fresh gear.

'Go on then,' Connor said.

'I've been doing some thinking,' Alex began, 'about your cause and all that it means to you.' He slowed the pace of his words, allowing his thoughts to catch up.

'Go on,' said Connor suspiciously.

'I've been thinking about how much you've already achieved

tonight,' Alex continued, 'and I'm wondering whether it's enough.'

'What the fuck are you talking about?' Connor snapped in reply.

'This has obviously been a remarkably well-planned operation,' ventured Alex, adopting a kind of quasi-military language he hoped might appeal to Connor. It was certainly in keeping with the clothes Connor was wearing.

The riled-up expression on the hostage-taker's face eased a little and he tilted his head to one side. He was listening. Recognising that he had his attention, Alex tried to seize the moment.

'Everything you've done has been remarkably well planned – and remarkably well carried out,' he said. 'Just look at everything you've managed to accomplish.' The idea of paying Connor any kind of compliment sat uncomfortably with Alex, but he was trying to find an approach that stood a chance of working.

'Go on,' said Connor, seeming to embrace the flattery.

'First, you planned and prepared for tonight without any law enforcement or intelligence agency picking up on what you were doing. That very rarely happens.' Connor was nodding. Beginning to puff up. Alex kept going. 'Second, you appear to have done all of this on your own. Am I right?' While keeping the conversation going, Alex was also trying to confirm the suspicions of SO15. Connor nodded, happy for his audience to know that it was all his own work. 'Third, you've made it successfully across London with all your kit.' Alex was unaware of Connor's earlier encounter with the PC in Morden. Connor was listening with increasing intensity. 'Fourth, you succeeded in taking nine hostages. Fifth, you gave a speech that has been viewed tens of thousands of times on the internet and you have published your manifesto for all the world to see.' Connor actually responded to this last observation with a smirk and by further relaxing his grip round Grace's throat. Alex felt a gentle tap on the small of his back – an unspoken encouragement from Rich, who had just reappeared, an exhortation to keep going. 'Sixth – and this seems to me to be the most important thing of all – you have demonstrated your humanity by letting Rosie go, by letting Rahel and Ittack go. And no one else has been hurt in the process.'

'I told you I wasn't a monster,' said Connor, with a mixture of defiance and pride.

'I've never said that you were. I might disagree with what you're doing, but I don't doubt the strength of your belief in your cause.' The last statement might have been a risky one for Alex to make, were it not for the fact that Connor seemed to be lost in the glow of perceived affirmation.

'I am the Home Front Liberator,' he declared with a dramatic sweep of his right arm, 'and I have come to set my people free.'

Alex wasn't going to be distracted or deterred by Connor's theatrics. It finally felt as though he might actually be getting somewhere.

'Like I said, Mr Connor,' he continued, 'it seems to me that you have already achieved a remarkable amount. That's why I asked you whether you thought it was enough.'

In an instant, Connor's tone of voice and body language changed again. Like the flick of a switch, the suggestion of a smile vanished, his eyes flashed and his face tensed. He planted his right foot aggressively forwards and adopted something resembling a fighting stance.

'It will be enough when Nicholas Farmer is free.'

The sudden change of mood was troubling. Just as Alex had been sensing a possible breakthrough, it appeared that all bets were off again. Connor was once again liable to explode at any moment. Like a hand grenade with a loose pin. The fact remained that nothing about him was remotely predictable; that none of the normal rules of human interaction or behaviour seemed to apply. One minute he appeared to be fine – relatively speaking at least – and the next he would be teetering on the edge again. It was emotionally and psychologically exhausting for Alex to deal with. The only small consolation was that Connor's hold on Grace was now round her shoulders, rather than her neck.

Alex felt another nudge in his back from Rich. *Don't give up now. Keep going.*

'As I've tried to explain, Mr Connor, any decisions about Nicholas Farmer – whether he's released, whether he's allowed to speak to you – aren't down to me. They're way above my pay grade.'

'So you keep telling me,' Connor replied with contempt.

'So what will you do if Nicholas Farmer isn't released tomorrow?' The question was out of his mouth before Alex could check himself. If he had given it even a moment's thought, he wouldn't have dared ask it for fear of the inevitable reply. But pure instinct had taken over.

'Are you now telling me that he isn't going to be released tomorrow?' Connor snarled. It was as much a challenge as a question.

'I genuinely don't know the answer to that,' said Alex in a hurry. 'I promise you that's the truth. But I'm asking you a "what if" question. What if he isn't released tomorrow?' Alex was fully committed now.

'Then I will do what I promised to do. I will kill all the remaining hostages. Every single one of them.' His voice rose to a renewed crescendo. 'Is that what you fucking want?'

04.12 hrs

Alex

'Of course that isn't what I want.' Alex actually felt – and sounded – unexpectedly calm as he said this, in contrast with Rich who was thinking that his colleague might just have made a terrible mistake. 'But I don't believe it's what you want either, Lee.' It was the first time all night that he had used Connor's first name. 'I don't think you actually want anyone to die here tonight.'

Lee

Connor stared at the police negotiator. He could see his face clearly under the glare of the lights, gritted with determination and creased with concern. And, somewhere in the deepest recesses of his mind, it occurred to Connor that he didn't look like an enemy should. He found this thought utterly disorientating. Here was a complete stranger suggesting something he hadn't considered. He'd been insisting precisely the opposite all night, both out loud and to himself. He'd been saying the same for weeks in the lead-up to tonight.

He was prepared to kill for his cause.

He was prepared to die for his cause.

He was certain of it. Wasn't he?

The man standing a handful of yards away was now suggesting otherwise and there was a strength and a conviction in his voice that carried his words beyond Connor's defences. Connor felt a fresh wave of confusion and uncertainty, swiftly followed by a renewed surge of crippling anxiety. Inaudible thoughts collided with one another in his brain: whether to kill and be killed; whether to live and let live; above all, how to stay true to the cause. But, wait, what was the cause? In that moment, he wasn't certain he could even remember. It felt as though the ground beneath him was giving way again and he reached desperately for something – anything – to hold onto.

'Didn't you see what I did to the priest?' he stammered. *I hurt her, I could have killed her*, was what he was trying to say. *I've already proven to you how serious I am.*

'I did see,' Alex replied. 'I watched the film and I looked at the photos and I found them incredibly upsetting.'

Upsetting? What an unusual, unexpected thing for a police officer to say.

'But here's the thing,' Alex continued. 'You let her go and now she's safe in hospital getting all the medical help she needs. You didn't kill her.'

'I could have killed her if I'd wanted to,' said Connor sounding once again like a sullen child caught in the wrong. Inwardly, he was reeling.

'But the point is you didn't,' Alex maintained. 'You didn't kill her. You did the right thing and you let her go. Then you did the right thing a second time and you let the children go.' He stopped speaking for a moment and seemed to be weighing up whether or not to go further. 'You haven't hurt Grace or any of the others.' He paused again. 'Now I am asking you to do the right thing one more time and let them go too. I think you've achieved enough, Mr Connor.'

Connor forgot about keeping hold of Grace and clasped his hands to either side of his head. He let out a gut-deep howl of despair.

Grace

There was now nothing physically to stop Grace running into the arms of the watching police officers. Connor was still holding his head, now moaning to himself. The gun was on the floor, out of his immediate reach. All she needed to do was throw herself forwards, as fast as her exhausted, unsteady legs could carry her and, in moments, she would be safe. The arsenal of weaponry ranged on the front of the hall would make certain of that.

But she didn't move. She couldn't.

In part, she felt a weight of responsibility for her fellow hostages. Their lives were precious to her. But there was more to it than that. Somehow, Connor's life was precious to her as well. In spite of everything – in spite of all he'd subjected her to, in spite of the damage he had done to Rosie, in spite of the terror he'd inflicted on all of them – she realised that she cared about what happened to him. As they'd been standing together on the steps of the hall, she'd felt every twitch and movement in his body. And she'd sensed every twitch and movement in his mind. She had been feeling desperately afraid – at times, her fears had threatened to overwhelm her completely – but she realised that he was desperately afraid too. Was it some sort of maternal instinct? Was it a reflection of her compassionate, empathetic nature? Or was it just overwhelming exhaustion, combined with a basic sense of humanity that was holding her there?

Whatever it was, she made no attempt to move.

Alex

Alex stared at Connor, then at Grace, and then swiftly back at Connor.

When Connor had first released his hold on her, Alex had willed Grace to make a break for it. The fact that she had stayed where she was had initially made no sense to him. He had to stop himself from shouting out at her to run. What was keeping her there? Perhaps she was too afraid to move – frozen to the spot. Maybe she had some unseen injury or was too physically shattered to cover even the short distance in front of her. Or was it that she knew something he didn't – something about the other hostages? And as soon as he thought about them – about Mariam and Jean and Alan and Jack and Helen – he realised that, whether it was by choice or not, she had done the right thing. There were still six lives to be saved – seven when he included Connor. It wasn't just about her.

Connor appeared to be lost in his own distress, so Alex fixed his attention on Grace.

'How are you doing, Grace?' he asked, so softly and gently that his voice only just carried to her.

'I've had better nights,' she replied quietly, her lips quivering as she bravely attempted a smile. Connor seemed to ignore her, if indeed he had even heard her.

'I bet you have,' Alex murmured. 'You're being incredibly brave.'

'I'm trying to be,' she replied, her eyes filling with tears. 'How's Isaiah?'

'Isaiah's your son, isn't he?'

She nodded.

'He's OK. He's completely safe. He's being looked after by the family of one of his school friends. There's an officer with them as we speak.'

Grace nodded slowly, a combination of weariness and relief etched on her face. 'Does he know what's happening?' she asked.

'I'm not sure if he knows all the details, but he knows where you are. And he knows that we're doing everything we can to get you safely back home to him.'

'Thank you,' she said.

'You absolutely don't need to thank me, Grace,' said Alex. 'I'm the one who should be thanking you – for looking after Rosie, for helping to get the children out, for being so unbelievably strong.'

'I don't feel strong,' Grace replied. 'And, anyway, I don't think that I've had any choice.' She stared in silence for a moment before continuing. 'How is Rosie?' she asked.

'She's going to be all right,' said Alex. 'She's got all sorts of bumps and bruises, but she's going to make a full recovery.'

'That's good to know,' said Grace, almost absent-mindedly now. Her thoughts were filling with images of her friend and her son. She was overcome with a deep sense of longing to see Isaiah: to fold him up in her arms, to tell him that she loved him, to let him know that she was all right – that everything was all right.

Grace

Connor let out another loud groan and wrung his hands in anguish. His upper body collapsed as the air seemed to escape from him. Grace looked at him in alarm.

'Go,' he said to her, failing to make eye contact. It was the voice of a drowning man.

His instruction made no sense to her. She half turned and looked more closely at his ashen face. He appeared utterly defeated.

'Go,' he repeated, gesturing towards the path and the gate that lay at the end of it. He even gave her a slight push in the back.

Alex

Alex found that he could scarcely breathe. It was likely the same for every single police officer looking on. Grace escaping could cause all sorts of problems, primarily for the other five hostages, but Grace being told to go by her captor was another thing entirely. Was that really what was happening? It certainly appeared so. And Alex realised that he had never wanted anything to happen more in his entire professional life. All she had to do was step out into the open into the arms of the dozen or more police officers who were waiting to receive her.

'I can't,' she said.

Grace's voice was quiet but resolute. Connor looked at her in complete and utter bewilderment. He tried to speak, but the words wouldn't form in his mouth.

'I can't leave,' she said. 'Not without the others.'

04.18 hrs

Lee

'Your choice,' Connor muttered to Grace. Taking her by the right arm, he turned her round and pushed her ahead of him back into the hall. The Baikal pistol remained where it lay, on the carpet by the doors.

Alex

As they disappeared from view, Alex had to fight the urge to go after them. He wanted to shout out, but was still finding it difficult to process what had just happened. As soon as he had heard Connor telling her to go, Alex's imagination had started to race ahead of him. He had seen Grace walking down the path. He had watched the gate open and the protective shield of armed officers forming all around her. He had pictured himself back behind one of the Land Rovers, arms open wide, as she walked slowly towards him. He had sensed the elation and the relief.

Agonisingly, all of it had been too soon. He sank to his haunches, before rocking back unsteadily into a seated position on the pavement. He might have fallen over completely had Rich not caught hold of him.

'Shit!' was all that Alex could manage to say.

Grace

Connor shuffled forwards and nudged Grace round to the rear of the chair barricade. He reached round to the back of his trousers and pulled out one of the knives. He turned it over in his hands, before throwing it into the main hall. It landed on the floor a few feet away from his kitbag. He said nothing.

Leaving Grace standing where she was, he drew the second knife out and approached Mariam's chair. He bent down slowly and cut the cable ties holding her ankles in place. Straightening up a little, he freed her wrists as well. Then, with a tired jerk of his head, he gestured to her to make her way over to Grace. Mariam hesitated, unsure of what was happening and frightened as hell. But Grace understood.

'Mariam, come,' she whispered, beckoning urgently to her. Mariam was still confused, but she managed to stand up and, with laboured steps and aching limbs, made her way along the line of chairs, carefully peeling the strip of gaffer tape away from her mouth as she did so. Grace pulled her into an embrace unlike any that either of them had ever experienced before. Agony and anguish and heartbreak and hope.

Connor wandered over and slumped down onto the chair that Grace had earlier vacated. He leaned forward with his head in his hands.

'Go,' he said. 'Just fucking go.' He let out another deep groan.

Grace relaxed her hold on Mariam and found that she needed to ease Mariam's grip on her. Mariam still didn't fully understand what was happening and she was reluctant to let go. Grace managed to turn her gently round and she guided her past the chairs and towards the front doors.

Alex

'Bloody hell!' exclaimed Rich, grabbing at Alex and attempting to pull him back to his feet. 'Look!' The tone in his voice cut through the sense of despair that had been threatening to engulf Alex. He struggled to his feet and stared disbelievingly. His heart surged.

Mariam had appeared in the doorway, shielding her gaze against the brightness of the arc lights. Grace was just behind her, edging her forwards.

'It's OK,' Alex heard Grace say, 'you can go now.'

Mariam stepped out into the open and onto the path. She looked over her shoulder at Grace, who was nodding her encouragement. *You can go now.* The realisation finally hit her and, falteringly, Mariam started to run.

There was a flurry of movement among the waiting officers. One of them shoved the gate open. A group of them raced forwards and surrounded her, weapons trained on the front doors, before hurrying her away to safety. A police medic produced a foil blanket from somewhere and Mariam disappeared into it.

'Bloody hell,' Rich repeated, struggling to believe what had just happened.

Alex, having followed Mariam with his gaze until he was sure she was safe, turned back round to speak to Grace.

But she wasn't there. Once again, she had disappeared from view.

Grace

Connor was rocking backwards and forwards in his chair, moaning quietly. Something had finally dislocated in his damaged mind, leaving him barely able to form a single coherent thought. Grace studied him and wondered whether it was safe to speak. She decided to take the risk.

'Lee,' she said as calmly as she could manage, 'would it be all right to let the others go now?'

He kept rocking, oblivious to her question. The remaining knife fell from his hand and onto the floor. The four hostages were looking at Grace imploringly. They had seen Mariam leave. They presumed she was now safe. They were desperate to follow. Grace held up her hands, palms facing them. She was caught in a dangerous dilemma. Should she just go ahead and release them, assuming his consent? What if she was wrong? What if he erupted again? Rescue for all of them was so close, and yet still so far away. And, if she were to release them, how would she do it? Should she use the knife he had thrown into the hall?

What about the knife by his feet?

Alex

'What the hell is Grace doing?' Rich asked.

'It can only be one of two things,' replied Alex. 'Either Connor is coercing her or she's gone back in there of her own accord.'

'Why the hell would she have done that?' began Rich. 'Why didn't she get out of there when she had the chance?'

308

'I have a feeling she's trying to get the rest of the hostages out,' said Alex, attempting to process his thoughts out loud.

Rich looked across at his colleague. 'In which case, she's either the bravest person I've ever met or she's taken complete leave of her senses.'

'She's brave all right,' said Alex.

There was no sound coming from the hall; no immediate evidence of further movement. A minute or so had elapsed since Mariam had been led away. 'So what do you suggest we do now?' Rich asked.

'We wait,' said Alex, without sounding entirely convinced that it was the right thing to do. 'They still have the video feed into the hall,' he remembered suddenly, his voice brightening a fraction. 'We'd soon know if anything was going seriously wrong in there.'

Grace

'Connor?' said Grace again, trying to get through to him.

He half raised his head, but didn't answer her.

'Would it be all right to let Alan and Jean and Jack and Helen go too?' she ventured.

His shoulders heaved and sank again. He made the slightest of gestures with his left hand. Grace wasn't certain of its meaning, but decided she had to take a chance. She was so consumed with the idea of getting everyone out that she had almost forgotten to feel afraid. All the same, she didn't risk approaching him. Instead, she walked into the main hall and picked up the knife that was lying on the carpet.

Returning quickly to the foyer and observing no change in Connor's demeanour, she began the task of cutting the next of the hostages free. Jean was first. As the older lady reached up to pull the tape away from her mouth, Grace put her finger to her lips, urging her to remain silent. Jean tried to massage some life into her wrists and ankles as Grace knelt down next to Alan. His heart had held out. Once she had cut his cable ties, she faced a delicate decision. Should she carry on and release the other two, or should she get Alan and Jean out first? She decided to leave Jack and Helen for the moment. One step at a time. Steady now.

She offered what unspoken reassurance she could to the younger couple, as she encouraged Alan and Jean to stand up. She looked across at Connor and tried again to read his body language. Seeing and sensing no obvious response from him, she ushered Alan and Jean towards the space between the chairs and the wall. Then she pushed them towards the door.

Alex

'Look!' Alex exclaimed. 'Here come two more of them...' Though he had begun to suspect what Grace might be doing, it was still more than he had dared hope for. Alan was the first to appear, his left arm reaching behind him, searching for the hand of his wife. As they both stepped out of the building, he put his arm round her and the huddled couple hurried as best they could towards the gate. Within moments they were behind the police lines. Seeing that they were safe, Grace turned round and walked back inside.

Lee

'Thank you, Lee,' Grace murmured as she reappeared in the foyer. 'Thank you for letting Alan and Jean go.'

Connor's whole body shuddered. He stared straight ahead of him. His expression was baffled and broken. His mind was in free fall.

'Why are you still here?' he asked falteringly, struggling even to form the words of his question.

'Because Jack and Helen are still here,' Grace replied, gesturing in the direction of the young couple, still bound and gagged and fear-filled on the far side of the foyer.

Connor appeared to have forgotten all about them. He glanced silently and uncomprehendingly at them.

'I can't leave until they do,' insisted Grace. She was watching Connor as she spoke. All the boldness and bravado had gone from him. All the anger and aggression too. He appeared simultaneously to have aged and to have regressed into some sort of primitive, childlike state. But there was still a knife lying on the floor beside his feet. She knew that she still needed to be incredibly careful.

Alex

Out in the street at the front of the hall, Alex saw Angie hurrying over to Alan and Jean, no doubt with a series of urgent questions she wanted to ask: about the condition of the remaining hostages, about Connor's demeanour and behaviour, about any other insight or detail they might be able to offer that could be of use in the next stage of the negotiation. Alex was

311

staggered by the speed at which the situation had changed and his emotions and thoughts were struggling to keep pace with reality. He had experienced a moment of pure elation when he had seen Mariam and then Alan and Jean coming out of the hall, but he knew that there was still so much hanging in the balance.

There were still three people trapped inside the building, four including Connor.

Four lives still to save.

04.27 hrs

Grace

'I think it might be time to get Jack and Helen out of here,' said Grace, choosing her words carefully and watching Connor closely as she started to move slowly towards his two remaining prisoners. Jack was straining forwards in his chair, beside himself in his desperation to get out of there. Helen looked completely shattered, drained of every last ounce of her strength. 'And, when they're out,' Grace continued, 'you can leave as well.'

'I'm not leaving,' slurred Connor.

'What do you mean?' asked Grace, as she sidestepped her way cautiously behind his chair, watching him all the time.

Lee

'I'm not leaving here,' he insisted. 'It's over. I'm finished,' he added, his despair complete. Though he remained unable to generate a single thought of his own, the ugly voices of accusation were starting to multiply in his mind. And they were all talking over one another in a race to condemn him. 'You're a failure; a fraud; a fool,' they jeered. 'You're a coward,' hissed the ugliest voice of all, 'a complete fucking coward. You're not like those brave men in the pictures you pinned to your wall; men who had the courage of their convictions, men who saw it through to the end. You're nothing like them. Nicholas Farmer is still in prison and no one is going to remember your name.' The cacophony of voices assailed him, hounding him into the depths.

Grace

'I don't understand,' said Grace. She had reached Helen's chair and was ready to start cutting her free. But she remained concerned about Connor. There was certainly no mistaking the hopelessness in his voice. She looked across at him.

'Can't you see it's all over?' he moaned. 'Can't you see that it all ends here?' As he said this, he reached down and picked up the knife that was lying by his feet. It was the very last thing Grace had expected him to do. Every fibre and muscle in her body snapped taut. He was sitting between her and the others and the only way out of the hall.

Alex

Alex was staring at the front of the building, willing the last three hostages to appear in the doorway. There was no sound coming from inside and his imagination was once again running away with him. He was a little boat in a raging sea, one minute lifted high on hope, the next plunging downwards into renewed anxiety and fear.

'Hang in there,' said Rich, sensing his friend's unease. 'We're almost there. Six down, just three to go.'

'Four,' Alex corrected him. 'We need to get Connor out of there as well.'

Grace

Connor was fixed in his chair. He made no attempt to move towards Grace and the others. He made no threats. In fact, he made no sound of any kind. Instead, he gripped the knife tightly in his right hand and pressed the point of the blade onto the palm of his left. He drew it slowly back and forth, initially without breaking the surface of the skin. Then he repeated the motion, this time pressing harder. Back and forth the blade moved, as his skin began to redden. Back and forth it went, and the first, faint line of blood appeared. Back and forth.

Grace was horrified. 'Lee, please stop!' she cried out. But he paid her no heed. Back and forth the blade went, in a growing criss-cross of scarlet lines. 'Lee, what are you doing?' she shouted in distress. But still he didn't respond. She wanted to look away, but found that she couldn't. She didn't dare approach him. 'Please stop hurting yourself, Lee!' she pleaded. She wasn't ready to give up on him.

He held the knife still for a moment. He stared at her, his eyes empty of light. Then he lifted up his hand and showed her his palm. It was a grim, bloody mess – a visceral metaphor for the state of his mind. Trickles of blood ran down his wrist and onto his sleeve.

Alex

Pip had moved forwards and was now standing between Alex and Rich. All of them had heard Grace's raised voice through the building's open front doors and Alex was visibly unsettled by what she had said. A concerned Pip was at least able to offer him some comfort. She was back on the phone to one of the command team and was once more able to relay the details of what could be seen on the video feed.

'Grace is all right,' she said, hoping to set Alex's mind at ease. 'They can't see exactly what Connor is doing – his back is to the camera – but he's sitting down and seems to be very preoccupied with something immediately in front of him. He's some distance away from the three hostages and hasn't moved from there for several minutes. It looks as though Grace is trying to reason with him.'

Alex was about to respond, when they heard her again.

'Look at me, Lee!' Her voice was clear in the pre-dawn air. She sounded unexpectedly steely. It was more of an instruction than a plea.

Lee

Connor held the knife still again. He looked at Grace and, this time, he managed to hold her gaze.

'Please stop hurting yourself,' she said to him. He looked down at his hand and back across at her. For a moment or two, the hailstorm in his head eased in its fury. Seeing that she had his attention, she continued speaking. 'Jack and Helen and I are going to leave in a moment,' she said, 'and I want you to leave with us.'

'I'm not leaving here.' He sounded desolate.

'Why?'

'Because I've reached the end.' His voice began to fade. 'Because I'm a failure and there is no longer any fucking point.'

'But that isn't true,' she insisted. She stared at him and felt only compassion.

He looked blankly at her. A lone tear fell onto his cheek.

'Think about the people who care about you,' she urged him.

'Nobody cares about me.' His words were scarcely audible. He wiped the back of his hand across his nose and face. 'Nobody fucking cares about what happens to me.'

'I do,' she said. 'I care.'

'What are you even talking about?' Connor whispered, tears now running in little rivulets down his cheeks.

'I care about what happens to you,' Grace said simply. 'I care about you, Lee Connor.'

'How could you possibly care about me,' Connor replied, 'after everything I've done to you – to all of you?'

'That's a good question,' she replied, making no effort to diminish the horror of his crimes. 'And I'm not sure I can fully explain why. All I know is that I do.'

'But ... why ... ? Why the fuck don't you hate me?' His words were disjointed. He was by now practically blind with confusion and distress.

'What good would that do – hating you?' Grace replied. 'Hating never helped anyone.'

'Because I deserve to be hated.'

'No, you don't.'

'How can you say that?'

'Because I believe it.'

'I don't understand. I wanted you to hate me. I hated you . . .' But his voice began to trail away. He no longer knew what he thought or believed.

'It's hard to hate up close,' she said quietly. 'It's hard to hate a person once you start to get to know them, once you begin to hear their story. Because we've all got our stories, Lee. And we've all got our scars.'

He had no answer to that. He was all out of answers.

04.36 hrs

Grace

'You need to leave,' he said. Connor stood up, his left hand, still dripping with blood, hanging limply at his side. Grace sensed the shift in his mood.

'Don't do this,' she whispered to him.

'Don't do what?' he mumbled, looking away from her.

'Whatever it is that you're planning to do to yourself.' She could tell she was losing him.

'You need to leave,' he insisted, his voice growing louder.

To her right, Jack started to struggle frantically in his chair and that brought Grace to her senses. Connor might be slipping beyond her reach, but Jack and Helen certainly weren't.

'I want you to come with us,' she said in one last, forlorn attempt to reason with him, even as she crouched down next to Helen and started to cut her free. But Connor didn't respond. Grace released Helen's ankles first, followed by her wrists. 'Wait there just a moment,' Grace said, as Helen wobbled uncertainly in her seat, the strip of gaffer tape still covering her mouth. She turned her attentions to Jack, who managed to control his panicky movements for long enough for her to release him.

As she helped the two of them to their feet, Connor turned round and stumbled back into the main hall.

Alex

Pip grabbed Alex's arm. 'I think they're coming out.'

'Who is?' Alex couldn't hear the voice on the other end of her phone. He was entirely reliant on Pip for any updates.

'All of them.'

'All of them?'

It was too much to hope for.

'All of them, except Connor.'

Even as Pip was speaking, the three remaining hostages appeared in the doorway. Helen stepped out first, followed quickly by Jack. They were immediately enveloped by members of the firearms team, who hurried them straight out through the gate.

Grace hesitated for a moment on the steps. This time, Alex hadn't taken his eyes off her and he was the first to shout her name.

'Grace!' he shouted, as loud as he could.

She lurched forwards in response to his cry, into the waiting arms of another armed PC.

Forgetting for a moment about Connor, Alex ran round to the back of the armoured Land Rover and pushed his way through the crowd of officers until Grace was standing right in front of him. He pulled his ballistic helmet off, opened his arms wide and she fell into his embrace. Her clothes smelled strongly of lighter fuel. Somehow, Alex managed to hold his tumbling emotions in check, acutely conscious of the fact that he was surrounded by a large number of his more junior colleagues. Grace was faced with no such constraints and she wept uncontrollably.

'It's OK,' Alex whispered in her ear, 'I've got you. You're safe now.'

Lee

It was Connor who was now walking into the valley of the shadow of death.

Standing in the middle of the hall, he picked up a chair and, blocking out the searing pain in his damaged hand, he raised it above his head and smashed it repeatedly onto the floor. It broke into a dozen or more pieces. He did the same with a second chair, then a third, and a fourth.

Alex

Pip appeared from somewhere, holding a red ambulance blanket. She wrapped it carefully round Grace's shoulders. Alex could see that Grace was shaking.

'Where's Isaiah?' Grace asked, her voice cracking.

'He's on his way,' Pip replied. 'He's being driven here in a police car.'

A barely audible 'thank you' was as much as Grace could manage by way of a response.

'We need to get you away from the front of the hall,' Pip said to her. 'Do you think you might be able to walk a short distance?'

When Grace nodded in reply, Pip turned and beckoned to Angie, who had been waiting and watching from the other side of the road. Angie hurried over and took Grace gently by the arm. Moving very slowly, pausing every few steps, the two of them headed about thirty yards down the hill, to a waiting paramedic who had a large green kitbag slung over his shoulder. He and Angie lowered Grace into a sitting position on

321

the edge of the pavement. Then the paramedic crouched down in front of her, put his bag on the ground and asked quietly if she could tell him her name.

Alex turned away from them and looked at Pip. 'Bloody hell!' he said. 'I don't think I've ever been so relieved to see another human being in my entire life.' He could feel his chin trembling. His own tears were only just below the surface.

Pip grabbed both of his arms. 'You did it!' she said.

'Really?' he replied doubtfully. 'I don't know . . . It seems to me that Grace did most of it.' His legs buckled as the flow of adrenaline began to subside. Pip caught hold of him more firmly.

'Easy now,' she said, as she steered him across the road. She sat Alex down on the edge of the nearest garden wall and he waited for the shaking in his limbs to start to ease. Glancing at his watch, he realised that he had been awake and on the go for the best part of twenty-four hours. Pip sat down next to him. 'You more than played your part,' she said, resting a gentle hand on his back.

A minute or so later, Rich appeared from the direction of the cell, holding two steaming mugs of tea. 'Get this down you,' he said to Alex, as he handed him one of the cups. 'It's got at least five sugars in it,' he added with a grin.

Alex raised the cup gingerly to his mouth and took a careful sip. It tasted good. Rich handed the second cup to Pip and, as he did so, his face turned serious again.

'What are we going to do about Connor?' he asked.

04.47 hrs

Lee

Lee Connor was staggering around the church hall like a Friday-night drunk after closing time, breaking up chairs and scattering the broken pieces in every direction. The state of the room, much like the state of his left hand, offered a reasonable approximation of the state of his mind.

He had reached the very end.

Alex

'The firearms teams could go in after him,' suggested Pip, though she knew that wasn't going to happen. Not immediately anyway.

'Why take the risk?' responded Rich, giving voice to her thoughts. 'Not while we still have other options available to us.'

'We need to get back over there,' said Alex as he forced himself to stand up.

'You've done enough,' said Pip, pulling him back into a seated position. 'Rich can take it from here.' She looked at Rich, who nodded.

'Well, if he's going to take over the negotiating, he's going to need someone as his Number Two.' Alex was a mix of duty and defiance, of professionalism and pride. He was prepared to step down as Number One negotiator – for the first time since the siege had begun, the thought of doing so actually came as a relief to him – but he wasn't yet ready to step away completely. He recognised that he had little, if anything, left to give, but he was determined now to see it through to the end. 'I reckon I'm still good for that at least,' he said as he stood up a second time.

'There's no need for you—' Pip started to reply, but Alex interrupted her.

'What if Connor asks to talk to me? I'm the only one he's spoken to all night. What if he asks for me and I'm not there?'

'Hmm,' mused Pip. She glanced at Rich, who raised his eyebrows in acknowledgement. Alex had a point, and they both knew it. 'All right,' she said reluctantly, 'but let Rich take the lead.'

The three negotiators returned to a virtually unchanged scene at the front of the hall. Having recovered the Baikal pistol from the steps, the armed officers were back behind the cover of the Land Rovers, but, otherwise, everything was as it had been following the release of the last three hostages. The front doors were wide open and, as they got closer, they could hear the intermittent sounds of Connor's continuing trail of destruction.

'Any updates?' asked Pip, as they approached the sergeant from the armed team.

'Nothing of substance,' she replied. 'You can hear most of what's happening in there,' she indicated, nodding in the direction of the doors. 'From what I'm being told,' she continued, tapping her earpiece as she spoke, 'he's completely lost it. He's smashing the place up.'

Alex looked up at the sign above the door. *Refugees Welcome*.

'What do you have in mind?' the sergeant asked.

'Well, we need to find a way to get him out of there without anyone getting hurt, including him,' Pip replied. 'And that isn't going to be easy.'

As she said this, two of the stacks of chairs blocking the doorway toppled inwards, landing with a disconcerting crash on the foyer floor. Fleetingly, Connor stood in the space he had just created, before turning and dragging two of the chairs back into the main hall.

'Have you still got that loudhailer to hand?' said Rich, thinking on his feet. The sergeant shouted to one of her team and it was handed to Rich a few moments later.

'What are you thinking?' asked Pip.

'Nothing remotely clever,' said Rich. 'I just thought I'd try to catch his attention.'

'Fair enough,' said Pip. 'Go for it.'

Rich stepped forwards and took cover behind the right-hand Land Rover, with Alex by his side.

Lee

Inside the hall, Connor heard the amplified sound of the police negotiator's voice, but it barely registered with him. None of what the voice was saying made sense to him anyway. Nothing made sense anymore. He was struggling to remember where he was or how he had got there. Discordant thoughts and voices and images clashed repeatedly in his imagination: the black woman and Nicholas Farmer and the refugee child who wet his pants and a car crash and David Lane and the priest with the broken face and boatloads of desperate migrants crossing the Channel and the Fourteen Words.

He slammed another chair into the wall.

Grace

Further down the hill, Grace could hear Rich shouting through the loudhailer. And, as the paramedic continued to examine her, the only thing she could think about was what might now be happening inside the hall. The face of Lee James Connor filled her imagination.

Alex

'I think we may need to move forwards.' Rich was addressing Pip. 'He isn't showing any signs that he's going to respond to me shouting from out here.'

'How far forwards?' Pip asked him. 'Actually,' she added quickly, 'hold on before you answer that.' She beckoned the armed sergeant over to join their conversation. 'How far forwards?' she repeated.

'Maybe into the foyer itself,' began Rich. 'I don't think we're achieving anything out here and my concern is that the longer we leave it, the less chance we're going to have of getting through to him.'

'What about the risk to the firearms teams? And to you?'

'I don't think he's a risk to anyone but himself now,' said Rich.

'I agree,' said Alex.

'How can you be sure?' asked Pip.

'I can't be,' accepted Rich. 'None of us can be. But every indication suggests that the only person he's intending to hurt now is himself.'

'And we've recovered the gun,' added Alex.

'But he might have another one in there,' said Pip, playing devil's advocate, trying to ensure that they were considering every possible eventuality.

'He might,' conceded Alex, 'but it seems very unlikely.'

'What do you think?' asked Pip, turning to the sergeant.

'I'll need to check in with my boss,' she said, 'but tell me what you need and we'll find a way to make it work.'

'It all comes down to identifying what's going to give us the best chance of saving his life,' said Rich. 'And I think that means getting as close as we can.'

05.03 hrs

Alex

Rich and Alex stayed low behind the firearms team as they approached the front of the building. Weapons trained on Connor, the lead officers stepped through the main doors and advanced forwards cautiously, coming to a halt at the inner set of doors that opened out into the main hall. They set up a line of ballistic shields and one of the team turned to beckon the two negotiators forward. Rich and Alex responded straight away, taking up their pre-agreed positions, one on each side of the inner doorway.

Connor seemed oblivious to all of them, lost in his own disintegrating unreality. He picked up a Bible and looked blankly at the front cover. He turned it over in his hands before releasing his grip and letting it fall to the floor. It landed with a thud at his feet.

'What are you doing, Lee?' Rich called out.

Connor didn't react.

'Can you hear me, Lee?'

Connor said nothing. He picked up a broken chair leg that was lying on the carpet next to him and studied it for a moment, before turning and throwing it onto a pile of wooden fragments gathered in the middle of the room. As he did so, Alex and Rich both noticed the bloodied state of his hand.

'What have you done to your hand, Lee?' Rich called out,

raising his voice in an attempt to break whatever spell Connor was under.

This time, there was the slightest flicker of a response. Connor stopped what he was doing and stared intently at the palm of his left hand. For several seconds, it seemed that he might be trying, then failing, to make sense of what he was seeing. Without replying to the negotiator's question, he bent down and picked up another piece of splintered wood.

'What are you doing, Lee?' Rich called out, even more insistently.

Alex looked on as the unresponsive Connor began to walk in a slow circle around the hall. He picked up another Bible and, this time, tossed it aimlessly onto the woodpile. Then he did the same thing with two more copies. With his stooped, laboured movements, haunted features and hollow eyes, it occurred to Alex that Connor was starting to resemble the sort of character you might encounter in the pages of a particularly unsettling horror story. Like one of the undead, Alex thought, as another swell of dread swept over him. He could see no possible way in which this was going to end well.

'Lee!' Rich shouted at the top of his voice.

Connor stopped and looked at him.

'What are you doing?' said Rich, lowering his voice again.

'What does it look like I'm doing?' Connor replied, his voice blank. He was staring straight past Rich, his eyes apparently unable to focus properly. He seemed oblivious to the fact that it was Rich talking to him, not Alex.

'I'm honestly not sure,' said Rich, much more softly this time, 'but why don't you stop and come outside?'

'I'm not leaving,' Connor said, as he crouched down and picked up yet another piece of broken chair. He added it to the growing pile.

'Why not?'

'What do you fucking want with me?' said Connor, raising his voice and throwing his arms up in exasperation.

'I want you to stop what you're doing and I want you to come outside with me.' Rich's voice was measured and calm.

'Leave me alone.'

'I can't do that, Lee.'

'Oh, for fuck's sake!' shouted Connor. 'Can't you see that it's over – that we're done here?' His head was tilted back and he was yelling into space.

'I know it's over, Lee,' Rich said. 'That's why I want us both to leave.'

'It's time for *you* to fucking leave!' he bellowed. The force of his words bent him double, spittle flying as he folded.

Grace

Grace heard it. The sound of Connor's distress carried out of the hall and all the way down the hill to where she was still sitting. She pushed the hand of the paramedic to one side.

'I'm nearly done,' the paramedic said. 'Just give me another minute or two.'

Grace ignored what he was saying, got to her feet and started back up the hill.

Angie, who was standing just a few feet away, reacted immediately. 'Grace!' she called out, scrambling to catch up with her. 'Grace,' she repeated, 'what are you doing?'

Grace kept walking, her pace quickening. Angie caught up with her just as she reached the front of the hall. Grace came to a stop next to one of the Land Rovers and stared in through the front doors.

Alex

Inside, Rich was looking sideways at Alex, whose eyes were locked on Connor. He suspected that Alex was thinking about Romford. That was certainly what Rich was doing. Remembering it all: the rescue of the children, the eventual rescue of their mother, the final moments before the shots were fired, the suspect collapsing to the ground. Now, here they were again, standing behind a line of armed police officers, watching the grim scene playing out in front of them, seemingly powerless to affect whatever was going to happen next.

Connor turned his back to the door. He shuffled over to his kitbag and tipped the few remaining contents out onto the floor. He twisted the cap off a bottle of water and took a brief sip before casting it to one side. Alex watched as the water glugged out onto the carpet. Connor reached for the last two cans of lighter fuel.

'Lee!' Alex called out in alarm. He wasn't trying to take over from Rich; he was reacting instinctively to what he was seeing. 'Put those down!' he shouted.

But Connor was deaf to his words. He walked towards the mound of broken chairs and stepped into a small space that he had left in the middle of it. He removed the top from the first can and, turning in a gradual arc, began to squirt the contents all over the wood.

'No!' shouted Alex with even greater urgency. 'Please don't do that!'

Connor finished with the first can, cast it aside and twisted the cap off the second one. Alex stared in horror as Connor emptied the contents of it over his head and onto his clothes.

'Lee!' he yelled at the top of his lungs.

Grace

It was all too much for Grace. From where she was standing, she could see the line of armed police officers and she could see the two negotiators positioned on either side of the inner doorway. But she couldn't see Connor.

The moment she heard Alex call Connor's name, she lurched forwards, catching Angie unawares. And before anyone else could stop her, she was through the gate and running back towards the front of the hall, no thought in her head save an utterly irrational, incomprehensible urge to be back inside.

Alex

Alex heard the commotion behind him. He turned and was astonished to see Grace appearing at the doorway, two armed officers just behind her. She continued into the foyer and only stopped running when Alex caught her up in his arms.

Grace

'You can't be in here,' the police negotiator was saying to her. 'It's not safe.'

She was staring over his shoulder into the hall, resisting as he tried to ease her back towards the building entrance.

'We need to get you back outside,' he was saying.

But Grace paid no attention to him.

'Lee!' she shouted as loudly as she could manage.

He looked in an even worse state than the last time she had seen him.

'Lee!' she yelled again.

This time, he looked over in her direction.

'You don't have to do this,' she pleaded. Alex stopped trying to push her towards the doors and let her speak.

Connor opened his mouth as if to reply, but no sound came out. His head dropped.

'Lee, please look at me,' Grace insisted.

Finally, he spoke.

'It's too late,' he said.

'It's never too late,' she insisted.

He lifted his head for a moment, his face pale and drawn, his eyes struggling to focus, his arms limp by his sides.

'I'm sorry,' he mumbled, as he looked away again.

Grace watched in helpless desperation as he reached into his trouser pocket and pulled out the Zippo. He flicked the lid off the lighter and, with a firm brush of his thumb, ignited it. He paused to survey the wreckage all around him and sank to his knees.

Then he let out a piercing, primal scream.

Alex

Before Alex could say or do anything, he was grabbed firmly from behind and propelled backwards by a pair of armed officers. They didn't stop moving until they were outside the hall. The same thing was happening to Grace and Rich. Grace was protesting loudly, but, like the two negotiators, she had no hope of resisting what was happening to her.

Grace was escorted through the gate and back out onto the street. Rich stayed outside the front of the hall, staring in mortified disbelief at the scene unfolding inside. Alex could no longer bear to watch. He turned away, leaned against the wall of the building and covered his face with his hands.

Lee

Connor was kneeling on the carpet, arms stretched out to his sides, staring up into the unknown. He appeared to be listening for something – a sound or a voice that no one else could hear. The flame of the Zippo was flickering in his right hand.

He began mouthing silently to himself. And then he released his grip on the lighter. It fell as if in slow motion, end over end, towards the floor.

05.22 hrs

Lee

There was a sudden *whump* as the lighter hit the floor and the accelerant ignited. The fire began to dance on the broken chair fragments. A moment later, Connor's clothing was alight, flames rippling across his body and up towards his head. His hair caught fire and he toppled sideways into the gathering inferno, his hands clawing frantically at his face.

At the same moment, a sudden rush of water sprang from multiple points on the ceiling as the building's sprinkler system burst into life. Simultaneously, several members of the armed team raced forwards, those at the front holding firearms, those behind them holding fire extinguishers. Within moments, the centre of the room was covered in a mixture of water and foam. Somewhere in the middle of it all, Connor was wailing in agony.

'Help me!' came his strangled cry.

Alex

Pip moved Rich and Alex away from the front of the hall. Both men were in deep shock at what they had just seen. Grace was out in the road with Angie and in a similar state of distress.

'Don't move!'

'Keep your hands where I can see them!'

Alex could hear the shouts of the armed officers coming from inside the building.

Pip glanced back over her shoulder. The flames appeared to be out, but there was smoke billowing everywhere as water continued to cascade down from the ceiling of the hall.

As Angie led Grace back down the hill, the other three members of the negotiating team made their way slowly across the road, back to the same stretch of garden wall that Alex had been sitting on not much more than half an hour earlier. The whirlwind of activity continued to blow all around them, but they each stayed silent and still, trying to process all that had happened, not just in the preceding few moments, but in the previous nine hours. It was several minutes before any of them managed to speak.

'Fucking hell,' said Rich.

'Are you OK?' Pip asked.

'I'm shattered,' he replied.

'I'm not surprised,' she responded. 'What about you, Alex?'

'I haven't got a bloody clue,' he whispered.

Pip edged closer to him and put her arm round him. As she did so, she noticed the firearms sergeant hurrying across to them.

'He's alive!' the armed officer announced as she reached them. 'I thought you'd want to know.'

Despite his mental and physical state, Alex was straight up on his feet.

'Is he going to make it?' he asked.

'Looks that way,' said the sergeant. 'Difficult to be a hundred per cent certain of course, but we got to him quickly and the fire was out in seconds, helped in no small measure by the building's sprinkler system.'

'Thank you,' said Alex, struggling to hold himself together. 'For everything.'

'No problem,' said the sergeant as she started back towards her colleagues, 'it's what we're here for.'

Alex waited till she was out of earshot. 'I just didn't know how it was going to end, Pip,' he said, swallowing hard. In his mind, he was trying to untangle the scenes of the last half hour from his memories of Romford.

'Well, it seems to have ended all right,' she replied. 'Actually it's ended more than all right,' she said, 'you've done a bloody brilliant job.'

'Have I?'

'Yes, you have,' she said, almost laughing. 'You all have,' she added, making sure that she included Rich – who was sitting quietly on the other side of her – in what she was saying. 'All nine hostages out,' she continued. 'All nine lives saved. And it's looking like Connor is going to live to face the consequences of all that he's done here tonight.'

The three of them lapsed back into silence. Alex watched as a pair of paramedics were led by officers to the front of the hall and ushered inside. Eventually, Pip took her mobile out of her pocket, tapped on the screen a couple of times and lifted the phone to her ear. The call connected almost immediately. 'Where are you?' she asked. 'OK,' she said after a pause, 'we'll be with you in a couple of minutes.'

The three of them walked down the hill and arrived at the house that had been their base for so much of the night just as a marked police car was pulling up outside.

The uniformed driver wound down the window. 'Do you know where I can find Grace Wheatley?' he asked.

Pip peered into the vehicle. 'You must be Isaiah!' she said to the teenage boy sitting in the front passenger seat. She walked round and opened the door for him. He looked understandably frightened. 'I'm Pip,' she said to him.

'Isaiah!'

It was Grace, who had appeared at the front door of the house, her exhausted, tear-stained face suddenly alive with joy.

'Mum?' he yelled, pushing past Pip and throwing himself towards her. She hurried to the pavement and tumbled into the arms of her boy. The two of them stood there, weeping and hugging and never wanting to let one another go.

05.30 hrs

Grace

The little group was still standing out at the front of the house when an ambulance drove past them and disappeared up the hill.

'Looks like they're bringing him out,' said Alex.

'Lee?' asked Grace. The reunion with Isaiah had restored some of her strength and she was desperate to know what had happened to Connor.

'Yes,' Alex replied.

'Is he going to be all right?'

'We think so.' It was Rich speaking now and he seemed surprised by her concern.

'So what's going to happen to him?' Grace asked.

'They'll take him to hospital first,' said Pip.

'And then what?'

'When they've fixed him up – which might take a while, depending on how bad his injuries are – he'll be taken to the police station,' Pip replied. 'He'll be interviewed and charged and then he'll be remanded in custody to await his trial.'

'Will he go to prison for a long time?' Grace asked.

'Yes,' said Pip, 'for a very long time.'

'Will I be able to write to him while he's there?'

The three police officers stared at her in bewilderment.

'What?' said Rich, sounding completely baffled.

'Can I write to him while he's in prison?' repeated Grace, as if it was the most natural and normal thing in the world to be suggesting.

'Surely you can't be serious?' said Rich, still struggling to comprehend what she was saying.

'Of course I'm being serious,' she replied.

'But what about everything he's done here tonight?' Rich asked her. 'Surely you must hate him?'

'He said pretty much the same thing to me,' she sighed. 'So I'll tell you what I told him. Hating him wouldn't do the slightest bit of good. It certainly wouldn't do him any good, but the truth is that it wouldn't do me any good either.' She put her arm round Isaiah and pulled him in close. 'I don't want my son growing up in a world ruined by hate, where the only conceivable response to hatred is more of the same. Somehow, some of us are going to have to break that cycle.'

Rich shook his head in disbelief. It wasn't difficult to imagine what he thought of Lee James Connor.

'It's like Dr King used to say,' Grace continued, looking up at the sky as she tried to recall the words spoken by one of the giants of the American civil rights movement. 'If I remember it right, it goes something like this,' she said. '"Returning hate for hate only multiplies hate, adding even deeper darkness to a night already empty of stars. Darkness cannot drive out darkness. Only light can do that. Hatred cannot drive out hate. Only love can do that".'

Epilogue

Nine Months Later

Alex

Alex Lewis strolled into his office on his first day back at work after a much-needed week off. He'd been held up in meetings at Scotland Yard all morning and had only just arrived at Kentish Town. The first thing he noticed – it would have been hard not to – was the large pile of folders and dockets sitting on his desk, apparently awaiting his attention. *Some things never change,* he thought to himself. Jonesy had returned to his patrol team a few weeks earlier, his broken arm fully mended, and Alex had been trying to catch up with his paperwork ever since.

He took his jacket off, sat down and thumbed through a selection of the files sitting at the top of the pile. Finding nothing particularly urgent or interesting, he pushed them to one side and switched on his computer, dreading to think how many unopened emails he'd find when he logged into his account.

His boys were smiling at him from the photographs sitting alongside his keyboard. He grinned back at them. He'd spent his week's leave with the two of them, walking the Pembrokeshire Coast Path, and it had done them all the world of good. Five months earlier, following a series of painfully honest and long-overdue conversations, he and Kathy had taken the decision to separate. When it finally came to it, it had actually been a remarkably amicable parting of the ways. After more than twenty years together, many of them genuinely happy, they had both chosen to set aside any animosity in favour of quiet acceptance. Alex had been the one to move out of the family home, initially to a friend's spare room and then to a small flat of his own and, while it was undoubtedly taking time to get used to all the changes, he felt certain that, eventually, they were all going to be better for it. In the meantime, he was actually seeing more of his sons than at any other point in the previous two or three years. He was setting aside the time to see them, they were doing the same, and all three of them were making the very best of the situation. They were going to be all right.

The computer screen flickered into life in front of him and Alex typed in his password. The digital clock in the top right-hand corner told him it was just after 1 p.m. His counselling appointment was back in central London at 4 p.m., so he made the most of the time he had to review the latest crime and intelligence reports and to respond to as many messages as possible.

Just over two hours later, he was back at Kentish Town Underground Station, the latest edition of the *Big Issue* tucked under his arm, waiting for the southbound train. In the days following the siege, it was Pip who had first suggested the idea of therapy to him. She had been at his side throughout the lengthy post-incident debriefing process and she had known that he was struggling. Reluctantly, he had come to accept that she was right. The Romford flashbacks had continued intermittently, intertwined with faces and voices from Herne Hill that were even more recent and vivid. When he was on duty, he usually found plenty to distract him, but it had become harder to escape his thoughts once the working day came to an end. At night, it was sometimes impossible. In the past, he had always resisted the idea of counselling, viewing the need for it as a sign of personal weakness. But Pip had persuaded him otherwise, insisting to him that, in fact, the opposite was true. Putting up a hand and asking for help was a sign of strength. 'None of us is invincible,' she had said to him. 'We all have our limits.' Given all that he'd been through, she explained patiently, the most natural and healthy thing in the world was to need to talk it through with someone who understood trauma and its complex consequences.

Listening to Pip had been the right thing for Alex to do. He saw a specialist police psychiatrist who prescribed him medication to help with sleep and who referred him for psychotherapy. He also encouraged him to take a couple of weeks off work, an opportunity to rest both mind and body. And the remarkable thing – to Alex at least – was that no one seemed to judge him for any of it. The response from friends and colleagues alike had been incredibly supportive.

He'd been seeing his therapist regularly for the past eight months and it had done him no end of good. Among many things, it had allowed him the time and space he needed to make the right decisions about his marriage and home life. It had also given him an opportunity to properly consider his future as a negotiator. In the immediate aftermath of the siege, he had felt sure that his time in the role was done. If he wasn't going to take the decision to step down, he supposed that someone else might well take it for him. Not because he had done anything wrong, but because it had taken so much out of him. But, with the passing of time and with the support of his therapist and the encouragement of Pip, he had started to think differently. Though it might take him many months, he had begun to realise that he would almost certainly find his way back to it in the end. So much of his working life seemed to be dominated by meetings and computer screens, by paperwork and politics, by box-ticking and form-filling; by things that really didn't make much of a difference to anyone or anything. But hostage negotiation was different. It was about the real stories of real people. It was about matters of real life and death. There was still a world out there that needed saving.

As his train headed south, his thoughts turned to Grace. He had seen her on a number of occasions since the siege, both formally and informally, and they stayed in touch via phone calls and text messages in between times. It helped both of them to be able to talk to one another and they had formed a remarkable bond. He very much hoped that the two of them would always remain friends.

It was just after five when he emerged from his therapist's office, located in a terraced building just off Piccadilly. He was feeling peaceful. He stopped at a Marks & Spencer food store to buy a bottle of wine, before heading back down to the Underground. Forty minutes later, he was standing outside the front door of the ground-floor flat in Islington that was now his home. He turned the key in the lock.

'Anyone home?' he called out as he pushed the door open.

Pip appeared at the far end of the corridor, a broad smile on her face.

'How was counselling?' she asked him.

Grace

Isaiah was sitting at the kitchen table, hunched over his schoolbooks, when Grace got home from another day at work.

'Hi, Mum,' he called out as he heard the rustle of shopping bags being put down in the hall. 'How was your day?'

'Pretty good actually,' she replied as she appeared, bright-faced, in the doorway. 'I've just been given a pay rise!'

'Great! Does that mean I can get the new FIFA...' he began to ask, before stopping himself. 'Sorry,' he said with an apologetic grin, 'I ought to have said "well done" or "congratulations" or something like that before I actually started asking for stuff!'

She laughed at him. She would surprise him with the new computer game when her next pay came through. 'Will you be ready to eat supper at seven?' she asked him.

'Seven's good for me,' he replied.

'What are you reading?' she enquired as she walked over to where he was sitting. She peered over his shoulder at the textbook lying open on the table.

'History,' he replied, holding the cover up for her to look at. '*The Rise of Fascism in Pre-War Germany.*'

Their lives had settled back into some sort of routine. They had both been bewildered and even a little unsettled by all the attention that had come Grace's way in the days following the siege. Some of it had been unavoidable – interviews with the police, official statements to be given and that sort of thing – but the rest of it was baffling to them. The local Member of Parliament, whom she'd never met before, had asked to see her and wanted to have his picture taken with her; journalists from national newspapers wrote a series of articles about her (with 'Amazing Grace' as the pick of the headlines); strangers stopped her in the street and told her how brave she had been. There had even been talk of her getting nominated for some sort of award. Grace found it all rather overwhelming.

She preferred to concentrate on the simple things: the gentle rhythms of her job and life at home with Isaiah. When she did venture out for a reason other than work or to do the shopping, she sought out the company of people she knew and trusted. Her meet-ups and conversations with Alex meant an enormous amount to her and, like him, she was seeing a counsellor. The therapy was helping, but, again like Alex, she knew it was going to take time. Every other Saturday, she and Isaiah cooked lunch for Mariam and the children. Ittack's and Rahel's English was coming on well – better than Mariam's – and Ittack's favourite thing in the world was to play computer games with Isaiah.

Grace also met up regularly with Rosie, whose body had mended, but whose mind was taking longer to heal. Rosie had been given an extended sabbatical, prior to taking up a new role in a North London parish, and Grace understood the need to move on. Having rarely missed a Sunday in the past, she hadn't been back to church since the night it had all happened. It was less a crisis of faith and more a crisis of confidence. She just couldn't face the sight of the hall, much less the prospect of going inside it. There were too many memories and, even nine months later, they were still too raw.

But, in spite of that rawness, Grace often found herself thinking about Lee James Connor. About who he was and why he had done the things he had done. And, true to her word, she had written to him in prison. Three letters so far. There had been no response to the first two, but, the previous week, she had received a reply. His words had been awkward and brief, but they had included what seemed to Grace to be a genuine expression of remorse for his crimes. This had meant a great deal to her.

Though she made no attempt to conceal or deny the immense harm he had caused, she had found a way to separate the man from his actions. A few months back, she had watched a TV interview with an American lawyer who worked with inmates on Death Row. It wouldn't normally have been her kind of thing, but she had been captivated by the man and his story. The lawyer's name was Bryan Stevenson and one thing in particular that he said had stayed with her ever since. 'I have come to believe,' he had told the person interviewing him, 'that we are all more than the worst thing we have done.' She had thought a great deal about those words and, though some of the people she talked to disagreed with her, she had come to believe that they were true.

'I've got to get the early train in the morning,' Grace said to Isaiah, 'and I probably won't be back till late, so I'll cook enough tonight to last you tomorrow as well.'

'Thanks, Mum,' he said distractedly, his head buried back in his books.

Lee

Lee Connor stood up as soon as he heard the keys rattle in his cell door.

'Ready?' asked the prison officer as the heavy door swung open.

'Ready,' Connor replied, producing his prison ID card for inspection and following the officer out onto the fourth-floor landing.

Following the conclusion of the siege, he had spent three weeks in hospital, under armed arrest, and, apart from a couple of days spent in custody at Southwark Police Station, he had been held on remand ever since. His trial was still two months away and his lawyer hadn't wasted the court's time with an application for bail.

His hands, arms and face all bore marks and scars that would serve as a permanent reminder of his crimes. The worst of his injuries had been those to his left hand. Three operations had been needed to repair the damage he'd done with the knife, and he still struggled to hold a fork properly or to do up the buttons on his shirt.

Every day in prison was a struggle for him, but the earliest days had been the hardest of all. He had been a complete mess of a man when he had arrived there. He was suffering with severe anxiety and depression. He was subject to intermittent episodes of acute paranoia. The period of enforced abstinence in hospital had started to wean him off his dependence on skunk and he desperately wanted to stay clean; his tortured mind had settled on it as a form of penance for his sins. But he had found it almost impossible. With drugs readily available inside the prison walls, the easiest thing would have been to give in; to try to find a way – any way – to numb the pain.

It was the prison psychologist who had saved him. She had done so with kindness, patience and immense skill. She saw him three or four times a week in those early days, as she began with him the halting, incredibly delicate process of unravelling the desperate state he was in. She was the one he spoke to when he felt as though he couldn't carry on. She was the one who taught him that, though he couldn't change his past, he could at least try to understand it. If he was able to do that, she had explained, it would help him to make some different choices about his future. On his better days, he almost believed her.

He followed the prison officer down the stairs to the ground floor, feeling more optimistic than he had done for a long time. Today, for the first time since his arrival on the remand wing, he had a visitor. He followed the guard along a succession of corridors and through a series of heavy-duty doors. Eventually, they reached a holding area.

'Shoes off,' the guard instructed him. Connor did as he was told.

A second prison officer scanned him, back and front, with a digital wand.

'Show me the soles of your feet.'

Connor complied.

'Open your mouth.'

Connor was handed an orange bib, similar to those worn by footballers when they're training. He slipped it on over his head and was led out into a hall the size of a school gymnasium. Tables were arranged in rows and bolted to the floors, with a single chair fixed on one side and three seats on the other. Places were allocated in advance and Connor had been given table number seven. There was a raised CCTV podium in the middle of the room and, at the far end, a snack bar where visitors were allowed to buy food and drinks.

He felt suddenly nervous. He took his seat and waited anxiously as a number of other prisoners did the same. His fingers drummed on the table and his feet tapped on the floor. He fought a sudden urge to make a break for the door he'd just come in through. He tried to remember some of his old breathing exercises. He just about managed to hold himself together.

Once everyone had settled around him, the door closest to the snack bar was opened and visitors started to file in. Connor strained to look, still shifting restlessly in his seat.

His eyes filled with tears the moment she appeared.

It was Grace.

Acknowledgements

As a serving police officer and hostage negotiator, I spent countless hours listening to people and the stories they had to tell. I listened to criminals and their victims, to the lonely and the lost, to good people having bad days, and to those who had reached the very end of themselves. In retirement, I have spent much of my time reflecting on all that I heard and what it might mean.

The story of *The Siege* is one that I have been wanting to tell for a long time. The three main characters in the book – Grace, Alex and Lee – had been occupying a space somewhere in the back of my mind for several years before I actually started writing about them. I've no idea where they came from, or how they got there, but I'm glad they turned up. While they are very much a product of my imagination, their stories are as real as any I encountered during my twenty-five years on duty.

I read and watched and listened to all sorts of things that were helpful in pulling the story together. The following sources were particularly engaging and informative: *How to Argue with a Racist* by Dr Adam Rutherford (Weidenfeld & Nicolson, 2020); *How to be Right*, by James O'Brien (WH Allen, 2018); *The Great Replacement: The Violent Consequences of Mainstream Extremism* (Paper for the Institute for Strategic Dialogue, Davey

& Ebner, 2019); *Hate Inc.* (Article in the *Sunday Times Magazine*, 20/10/19); *Hunting the Neo-Nazis* (BBC Panorama programme, June 2020); *Rabbit Hole* (*New York Times* podcast series).

Beyond the general research, I owe a debt of gratitude to a whole host of people who offered me their particular help and support along the way.

My sincere thanks go to all those who read and commented on various drafts of the text, each of them adding something to the tale. To Eddie Hamilton, a man who knows a thing or two about storytelling, who pointed me in all the right directions and cheered me on every step of the way. To Phil Williams, highly respected former head of the Met's Hostage Unit, on whom the character of Pip is based. It was Phil who rang me up many years ago – back when we were both still serving – and asked me whether I was 'ready to save a life?'. To Andy Day and Iain Scott, who were so generous in sharing their professional expertise with me. To Janet Hills and Gamal Turawa, inspirational friends and former colleagues.

Thank you to Mike Luckett, who told me a little of his own story.

Thank you to John Carnochan, co-founder of the Glasgow Violence Reduction Unit and one of my real-life heroes, who gave me permission to use the quote at the start of the book.

Thank you to Laura Williams, who isn't just the best agent in the business. She's my friend too.

Thank you to the wonderful Jenny Lord at Weidenfeld & Nicolson, who edited my last book and knew exactly who to send this one to. Thank you to the equally wonderful Fran Pathak at Orion Fiction, who opened Jenny's email, who was prepared to take on an untried fiction writer, and who has been such an incredible source of encouragement ever since. From day one, working with her has been a complete pleasure.

Thank you to the wider Orion family who are, without exception, lovely: Sarah Benton, Lucy Brem, Cait Davies, Tom Noble, Leanne Oliver, Maggy Park, Paul Stark, Clare Wallis and, of course, the big boss, Katie Espiner.

Thank you also to the remarkable women and men who stand on the real thin blue line. I am so proud to have served alongside you for so much of my life. This book is dedicated to you.

Most of all, thank you to Bear, Jessie, Charlie & Emily: the four corners of my life. I love you.

Credits

John Sutherland and Orion Fiction would like to thank everyone at Orion who worked on the publication of *The Siege* in the UK.

Editorial
Francesca Pathak
Lucy Brem

Copyeditor
Clare Wallis

Proofreader
Jade Craddock

Audio
Paul Stark
Jake Alderson

Contracts
Anne Goddard
Humayra Ahmed
Ellie Bowker

Design
Debbie Holmes
Joanna Ridley
Nick May

Editorial Management
Charlie Panayiotou
Jane Hughes
Bartley Shaw
Tamara Morriss

Finance
Jasdip Nandra
Afeera Ahmed
Elizabeth Beaumont
Sue Baker

Marketing
Tom Noble

Publicity
Leanne Oliver

Production
Ruth Sharvell

Operations
Jo Jacobs
Sharon Willis

Sales
Jen Wilson
Esther Waters
Victoria Laws
Rachael Hum
Anna Egelstaff
Frances Doyle
Georgina Cutler

A searingly honest memoir of the uplifting highs and crushing lows of a life spent policing on the front line . . .

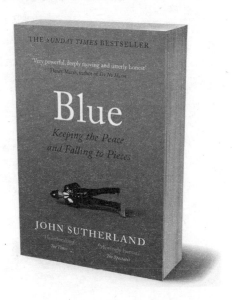

'Powerful'
Henry Marsh

'Heartbreaking'
The Times

'Brave and very honest'
Bear Grylls

An urgent look at the biggest challenges facing society through the unique lens of an experienced police officer and hostage negotiator . . .

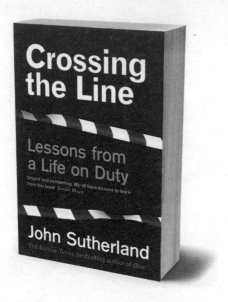

'Urgent and compelling'
SIMON MAYO

'I've never heard *the job* described better by anyone'
PETER JAMES

'An important book . . . should be read by the Home Secretary and every member of Parliament'
JEFFREY ARCHER